HARD LESSONS

Four erotic novellas

SOMMER MARSDEN

Published by Accent Press Ltd – 2011
ISBN 9781907761522

Cover design by Adam Walker

For the man. I love you. Forever and ever. Amen.

Acknowledgements

Thanks so much to all my readers, the ones who speak up and the lurkers alike. You rock and I heart you!

Contents

BLANK

Chapter One

THE TRICK REALLY IS to blank out the face in your mind. To go above and beyond the call of duty to erase the thought of your obsession. Drugs, booze, sex, running, sleeping, fighting. All of the above would help to lessen the pound of a memory on your brain like a fist. Every single one of them could fuck you over, too.

I touch the boy's face and close my eyes. My mind wants to supply Jason's face there. I push the thought aside; focus on the sensation of him sucking my middle finger into his hot wet mouth. I think of him as a boy because he, at nineteen, is a good decade younger than I am. If you consider life experience, probably two. His youth and beauty and innocence almost make me feel guilty for what I am about to do. Almost.

'Why won't you look at me?' Matthew says. His name is Matthew. Something Irish for the last name but it escapes me.

'I am looking at you.' I push my pointer finger past his lips and watch it sink into oblivion, trapped between two plump perfect lips the colour of early summer roses. 'See me looking at you?' I can hear the arousal in my voice and my cock is harder than it has been in a long time. That's mostly because this boy is so close to Jason physically. His voice has almost the same timbre. His cologne is even close. Something faint with a touch of sandalwood and leather and sunshine.

Matthew, he of the beautiful big green eyes, sucks my

finger harder and there is that invisible tug between finger and dick. It's as if my cock is on an unseen string that Matthew with the Irish last name can control with his wet, wet tongue. I press my shoulders back into the green sofa cushions and he kneels on the floor. His rug is the colour of tomato juice. He presses his lean, hard self between my thighs and leans into me. Kisses me. His tongue is like an electric spark when he touches it to mine. My hips rock up and my cock rubs his. This should stop.

'Will you look at me naked?' he asks, kissing over my jaw. His fingers are pushing my polo up just a bit, thumbs rubbing softly along my flanks. It almost tickles, but mostly it just makes me want to take him down. Flip him and fuck him because he is paying for Jason's sins today.

I want him because he could be a stand-in. I hate him because he could be a stand-in. Poor kid doesn't stand a chance.

'If you insist.' I try to keep my tone light but it rumbles out of me with a hint of anger. Matthew catches it and stops, big green eyes searching mine. I force a smile.

'You don't like me?'

'I do.'

'What's wrong?'

'Nothing.' I touch his face. I force my hand to be gentle. I stroke. 'Nothing at all.' Again, my mind supplies Jason's image. His face when he's laughing. His face when he's angry. His face when he's coming. My throat shrinks two sizes too small and I try to swallow.

Matthew nods, seeming satisfied. My eyes are watching him work my belt and my fly but my ears hear only the tick of the clock on the wall and the slam of my heart. When he bows his head and runs his tongue over me, takes me in his mouth, his profile is so strikingly familiar I feel insane. Have I finally gone and lost it?

'Do you like that, Kyle?' he asks, his mouth full of my cock.

4

I nod, my breathing rushing in and out like I might die. 'Yeah. Yeah, I do.'

'Show me.' He pushes my thighs hard to the sofa. Pinning me. He's not big but he sure as shit is strong. But my hips fly up all on their own, blindly seeking to sink deeper into his throat. His eyes tilt up to study me and he smiles around my shaft.

'Brat.' I laugh when I say it, but I mean it. If he keeps that up, I'm going to come. And I don't want to come yet. I want to stay trapped in this mind-fuck, this bittersweet remembering. The place where if I close my eyes it's Jason sucking me: Jason holding me down: Jason kissing me and wanting me inside him. And even when he's being an asshole, Jason loving me. My throat shrinks again and I just wonder in passing, a casual thought – can you die from a broken heart? It sure as fuck feels like it. Then the anger rushes in, red and wet and messy and I growl at the kid, 'Let's lose the pants, Matt. Let's see what you're packing.'

I don't care what he's packing. I want to fuck him and call it a day. My little plan has become too much and I want to run home and lick my wounds. But first, I'll give him what he's expecting.

He is everything that haunts my thoughts – long legs, wiry with muscle, a Celtic tattoo along his calf. A perfect ass, perfect cock, jutting to the left so that I had to turn my head a bit to catch up with it. His hands are big and they slide under my hair and across my scalp like a rush of warm air. I sigh, forcing my lips further down. Forcing my tongue to still and my lips to a perfect "O". I force myself to breathe and take in the scent of him. Force myself not to cry when he says my name and his voice sounds so much like one from my past.

This is entirely Hazel's fault. Entirely. I know that when I slide a condom on and work my fingers into him. I curse her when he touches my dick with only the tips of his fingers so I shiver. I hate her when I rock into him on that first perfect stroke and his long-lashed lids slide closed over his gemstone coloured eyes and he arches up under me, taut smooth belly fluttering with pleasure. The muscles rippling with his movement like a human wave. I watch him and then when I am about to come, I close my eyes. Because Matthew isn't Matthew any more. He's a ghost of emotions past.

Chapter Two

'JESUS, KYLE, YOU WEREN'T supposed to fuck him!' Hazel says. Oddly, her eyes are blue. She runs a hand through her long, crazy blonde hair. A ring snags in a wind-tossed tress and she struggles for a minute. A mermaid caught in a net of her own hair.

'Well, he sure was pretty, Hazel. What *was* I supposed to do with him?' My coffee tastes like motor oil and I'm hot. I'm so fucking hot that my jeans feel like a wool blanket and my hair is wet with sweat. It's only April. What the hell? I think of what it would have been like in my cramped cell and I figure it could be worse.

'You were supposed to get your feet wet again. I knew he looked too excited when I said you'd done some time. Dammit. I got you a jailhouse boy.'

I laugh. 'Well, damn you for getting me some ass. I did get my feet wet. And my dick wet, too.' I try to wink. I even try to laugh. All I manage is a tired chuckle. Anxiety crawls under my skin, restlessness clogs my chest. I need to do something – anything. There is a surge of need. A need to break something or someone, kick something, hit someone until they bleed. I close my eyes and let the feeling pass.

'Christ, Kyle. Getting over Jason isn't going to happen by boning some young, pretty boy. And getting past the whole jail thing isn't going to happen that way either. Are you going to your NA meetings?' She gathers that bundle of blonde curls into a topknot and secures it with a pencil from her purse. She is gorgeous. I love her. My very best friend in the world. The only one who came to visit when I got busted in that drug raid and ended up doing a year of time. I want to cry she's so gorgeous. Instead, I study my sneakers.

'What's there to get over? I did my time, I was released. Bada-bing, bada-boom. Case closed.'

Hazel rolls her eyes. 'Jesus Christ on a cracker, you are a hard head, aren't you? That is not case closed. That is simply what happened. You're completely over Jason? No more pain? Because that's what drove you to doing that shit in the first place. I mean, heroin, what the fuck were you thinking K?'

I shrug. The truth is I was thinking that if I were high out of my mind, I could not hurt. I could not miss Jason, or pick and obsess over his betrayal. I would not miss him and my heart, which he took with him when he moved 3,000 miles away to live with a man named Allen, who had been his shrink. I thought nothing other than to escape. And it had seemed an available way to do it. The sedating rush of warm euphoria and the lazing about with pretty thin things of indeterminate gender. The lack of worry over food or money or sex or love because everything was lost in a cotton-wrapped reality. It had been lovely. At first. And then it hadn't and I had gone to jail. Now I was out and my brain was running like a coked up hamster in a greased wheel.

'I was thinking nothing. Can we drop it? What's new with you? How is Zach?'

'Zach is trying to be a cowboy.'

I nearly choke on my coffee. 'Pardon?'

'Yes, that dumb fuck is trying to be a cowboy. He wants to go to Montana and … I don't know – do cowboy things. Some working ranch is hiring and his cousin went off and did it a few years back. It changed his life, says Zach. Made a man out of him. I don't know. To me it sounds like a bunch of bullshit. So, I told him, Zach, if you go off and be a cowboy we are done.'

'And?' I lean in and feel my sweat-soaked shirt pull off

8

my skin. It is a pleasant and disgusting feeling all at the same time.

'He fucked me blue and then told me he was leaving in two weeks. Come with him or stay here. Either way he was going to go rope some dogies.'

'He did not say dogies.'

'No. But he said the rest of it.' She finishes her Chai latte and tosses it toward a waiting trash can.

'And you said?' I prompt.

'I said, "I hope those cows look good in the thongs you bought me," and I tossed them all at him and kicked his dumb ass out.'

I laugh. 'He was turd, Hazel.'

'I know. But he was my turd.'

'How many slots to be a cowboy left?' I ask. I'm kidding – mostly. But when I ask her the question, that crawling, gaping-wound feeling in my gut stills for a moment.

'Just a few.' Her eyebrow goes up and her mouth flies wide. 'Why? Oh, no Kyle! You can't leave me too!'

'Just for a bit. Just to get my feet wet again. And my head on straight. I have visions.'

Hazel makes a gagging motion. 'Don't tell me!' She waves her hands and lowers her voice, imitating Zach. 'Of wide open skies and big fields of grass. Campfires and fish fries and beans before bed.'

I laugh. Feeling a real laugh come out of me is strange still. 'No. More like wide open men and big strapping men and cowboys before bed. Or in bed. Or all of the above.'

'Christ. You think with your pecker.' She takes my hand and we head toward her apartment.

'Is there any other way to think?'

'Probably not,' she says. 'Come on. I'll make you some dinner and give you the number to call. You shit.'

'I love you too, Hazel.'

Chapter Three

THERE HAD BEEN HUMILIATION in prison. And penance. I had
done my time to pay back the people I had hurt when I was
chasing away my loss with drugs: Hazel; my mom; my
brother Jack; my friends; the boss I stole from and then quit
on; the people who had to see my emaciated, dirty ass
hauled out of that abandoned house on the six o'clock news;
the Father, Son and Holy Spirit – my life had not erased my
Catholic guilt. Instead, I found comfort in it, held it close.
Every time I was called bitch, punched, kicked or worse, I
took it and I held it to me like a shiny gold coin. A precious
gem. I built up a treasure trove of humiliation and payment
for my stupidity in that one year behind bars.

But I wasn't done. I still think of Jason, dream of Jason.
Daydream and fantasize and weep over Jason. I don't want
that. I do not want my heart 3,000 miles away in Long
Beach, California. I want it right back in my unbuff, too
thin, I'm-still-smoking-when-I-shouldn't chest. Right here
with me. Even if I never give it to another man as long as I
live. Which I won't. That much I'm sure of. Once I retrieve
my damn heart, I will never part with it again.

I take the number from Hazel, eat her horrible fiery
chicken bake and rice pilaf and head home well past dark. I
call Rob on my cell phone. A friend of a friend who has the
hots for me and is an easy piece of ass. 'So … wanna come
suck my dick?'

I figure it's straight forward. I can't lose. Rob can say
yes. Rob can say no. Rob can say whatever the fuck Rob

wants.

'I'll be there in a half an hour,' he says.

I actually feel that ball of nerves and worry loosen a little in my chest. Few things do it for me: sex; Hazel's humour; and the strong and unshakeable feeling that I will be doing something – moving forward – very soon.

I let Rob in and when I push him to his knees and thread my fingers through his short, short red hair, that knot of worry in my chest lets up just a touch more. 'You have a pretty face, Rob.'

He smiles, his pink lips bowing around my cock as I slide slowly and deliberately past his lips. Arching into the velvet moist heat of his throat. I try to be gentle but lose the battle as the orgasm grows, rushing toward me. A fireball, a heat wave. I groan and Rob laughs, the vibration setting me off. When he cups my balls, shifting them gently in his palms, I lose my battle and fill the perfect wet heat of his mouth with my come.

Rob sits back, eyes on me as he jerks his cock. A tiny, shiny thread of my come runs down his cheek. A pearl of it nestles in the corner of his mouth. Rob licks his lips and then his hips shoot up frantically and a geyser of opaque fluid arcs into the air. It rains down on my hardwood floor, gracing his knuckles with beads of white. I grin.

'So what's up, Kyle?' he asks, breath coming fast. His face is red and sweaty. His eyes glassy. His gaze strays to my prick again. We'll be going for round two after a beer or three and we both know it.

'I think I'm going to be a cowboy.'

'Cool.'

After we line up our dead soldiers, clear glass bottles in a row, bright green lime drowning in the dregs, we go at it again. This time, I push his knees high and fuck him. He's watching me. Big brown eyes staring up at me as I slide into his ass. But I won't watch him. I watch my dick disappear into him a millimetre at a time. I feel the hot grip of him on me. I look at the perfect split melon ass of his and I hear his breath ripping in and out of him like I'm killing him. I wonder if this is how Allen fucks Jason out in sunny California. And I wonder if I'll ever be sane again. And I realise as I start a hard, fast thrust that has me right on edge instantly, that I have a secret plan. I'll get my heart back one boy at a time. One piece at a time.

'Touch me, please,' Rob says.

So I do. I reach forward and work his cock with my spit-slick fist until I have to drop my head because I'm coming. I like Rob, so I touch him like he asks. But I never look at his face.

Chapter Four

MONTANA IS FUCKING HUGE. Did you know that? I know, theoretically speaking, but not for real. The sky seems five times bigger here than in the city. My boss, Nelson Sanders gives me a once over. About ten times. He doesn't seem to like the looks of me and that's fine. I don't like the looks of him much, either.

'It said on your resume that you sent through the computer that you did some time, son.' He says *son* like it's a curse and I almost laugh at "through the computer" instead of saying email.

'Yes, sir.'

'Am I gonna have any trouble with you?' His face shows ten more years than I guess his chronological age to be. He has the mangled hands and weathered face of someone who works outside all day and doesn't know what the fuck SPF means.

'No, sir. I did my time and I'm done with all that.' I mean every word.

He nods. 'You'll be working with Carson, then. Carson will take you around and show you what sections of fence need to be replaced. You'll learn this and that and when the visitors come for their vacations, you'll be able to take on your own.'

Who pays to work on vacation? This is beyond me but I nod. 'Yes, sir.'

'Listen to Carson but don't be like him. He can be a bit of a fuck sometimes. But he's young.' Nelson shrugs as if this explains it all and again, I'm biting the insides of my cheeks to make sure I don't laugh out loud.

'Yes, sir.'

'I'm in and out. I have to handle a lot this week. Worst possible week to have someone new coming in … but sometimes we can't control every in and out of life, now can we?'

I'm not really sure if he's talking to himself or me so to be safe I mutter, 'No, sir.'

'Anyway!' He slaps his gloves against his jean clad thigh just like a cowboy in a movie. 'Tad is around here somewhere. Tad is my *numero uno* and you listen to Tad the same way you listen to me. Got that?'

I nod. In my head, Tad is big and bow legged. A wrinkled, sun browned face and a moustache. Craggy mouth and a pack of smokes in his front top pocket. He'll be mid-fifties and in no mood for none of my shit. 'Yes, sir. I do have it.'

'Sit tight. I'll go find Carson.' He turns and off he goes, leaving me waiting by a barn under a too big sky.

It turns out that Carson *is* a bit of a fuck. He gets me behind the Jeep we use to drive out to the fence. He gets me back there and he says, 'You have a pretty mouth.' He says this to me as if I don't get the reference. Then I wonder if *he* gets the reference.

'Yeah, you too, cowboy,' I snipe. In the end it's me, getting Carson on his knees. And it's me making use of his pretty fucking mouth. It's odd to come with a huge sheet of blue sky eating up the horizon. That's all I see when I look out over his dark head, bobbing against the front of me. It's all I see, when I grab the tailgate to steady myself when the orgasm rips through me like a lightning bolt. All I see is sky.

We mend the fence and on the way back to base we see a man on a horse: tall; lean; blond hair that would look more at home on a surfer than atop a horse-riding ranch hand. He's heading where we've just been. I can see the frown on his face even from the shotgun seat of the Jeep. 'Who's that?'

Carson frowns. 'That's Tad. Asshole. He thinks he's such hot shit.'

I study Tad again. Forearms flexing thickly when he tugs the reins. Tan cheeks and corn floss coloured hair. Faded jeans, boots, and a plain blue shirt that looks like it would be soft as sin to touch. He is hot shit. I say nothing.

Dinner is in the big dining room, presided over by Nelson and his wife, Dot. Dot has cooked. How the hell she cooked for all of us, I have no clue. I don't care, either, because it is possibly the best meal ever. Roast chicken, corn, mashed potatoes, bread, greens, iced tea, milk, and rhubarb pie and pecan pie for dessert. The entire meal, Tad, who I think of as surfer boy, stares at me. Hard blue eyes like ice chips watching my every move. I'd be flattered if I didn't see the frown on his face.

After dinner we all pile into a truck owned by another hand, George. We go to *Dollars* and grab beers on draft for a buck a pop.

The busboy's staring and I'm staring back. Some country song is blasting out of the juke box and I can't follow it. I don't know who it is and I don't care. Because the bus boy has big hands and big brown eyes. He's bigger than me, but he looks down when I stare back. So there's my answer. I get to be on top. Or behind. Or pretty much however I want. I drink two more drafts and say I'll catch a ride back to the ranch.

Tad's over there frowning at me and I tip my baseball cap like it's a cowboy hat and smile. He doesn't smile back.

Eddie, the bus boy, has a teeny tiny apartment that makes me feel like I've been shoved into a pine box for Potter's Field. 'Want a beer?' he asks.

'Take your shirt off.'

He does. Peeling it off the instant the last word slips over my lips. I can hear him breathing. There's a green

15

handkerchief tossed over the lampshade. The whole room feels like we're under the ocean. He wants to kiss me, I can tell, so I kiss him. Really soft and then really hard. I run my fingers over the hard-on bulging against his zipper. His belly is flat and ridged and hairless. He smells like dish soap and cooking oil. 'Now the pants, boy,' I say against his throat and bite him hard enough that he stiffens. His whole body going rigid for a heartbeat.

He makes a sound in his throat that makes my cock hard. I take his belt while he bucks against my hand like he's trying to get off. I put his wrists behind his back and loop the belt high up on his biceps, securing them in a not too tight circle of leather. Eddie goes willingly, fuck – eagerly – when I lever him forward over the sofa arm. I open a drawer randomly and there's the lube and condoms. I work my fingers into him and his head tips back and his eyes slam shut and he's saying words I cannot hear but I can see his lips moving. My whole body is crawling with that anxious energy and I slip into him like I can hide from every problem I've ever had. And while I'm fucking him I am hiding. It all lets up and the world slips away.

His hips are wider than mine and my hands are so white still. They stand out like cartoon gloves on his sun- darkened skin. I watch my dick slip in and out, in and out and it calms me like a flesh and blood lullaby.

'Faster, please.' At the last moment, he throws in, 'sir.' His arms are bound and his dick is hard. Every time I thrust it rubs his cock against the padded arm of the sofa. I go faster and he starts to move and finally it all comes together and I am shooting my load and he is decorating his sofa with a pearlescent pattern that looks sort of like an eight when all is said and done.

Eddie wants me to stay. I want him to drive me home. He drops me at the end of the very long driveway with a pleaful look and a 'Call me.'

I say I will. We both know I won't.

Chapter Five

I DON'T SEE HIM until it's too late. My heart, despite my best efforts, swells too big for a moment and I get angry at the jet of fear that surges through me.

'You should watch yourself.' It's Tad. Even in the dark I can see that particular slouch of his. My mind's eye pulls up the image of that surfer boy hair and the shocking blue eyes. Cold and startling like pool water in August heat.

'Why's that?' I walk right by him, my boots crunching in the dirt and gravel under my feet.

'People might not like you whoring around.' His voice is barbed wire and smoke. I can smell him over the sharp green-smelling night air. He smells like leather and thyme and for some reason, in my mind, the beach. It must be the hair.

'And by people I assume you mean you,' I snort, and stomp, quite literally, toward the main house. I want my sweatpants and another beer from the small square dorm fridge. Then I want bed and sleep. Nothing can top heroin but sleep. Sleep is oblivion. It's so close to death and I love it in a dark possessive way. It lets me get rid of everything. Unless I dream. But that is what the beer is for.

'No. I mean the other men. Especially Nelson. Nelson doesn't like to know things. He's like a one-man military. Don't ask, don't tell. Only the caveat, don't let me accidentally find out, is in there too.' Tad runs three fast steps and grabs my arm. I'm not thinking. The last few years of this shit-eating life crash down around me and I turn, swinging before my beer soaked brain can mull it over.

Calm as can be, Tad catches my lazy flying fist and pushes it down to my waist. He holds my hands so I can't hit him. It's then that I notice that his breath smells like beer and candy canes and that there is a scar on his lower lip that makes me want to kiss him.

'Don't,' I say. I'm not sure what I mean. *Don't make me want to kiss you, Tad?*

'I'm not doing anything, Kyle. You're the one trying to hit me.'

'Don't make me feel like more of an outsider. I'm doing that all on my own.' I want to bite my tongue off to keep from talking. Why am I saying this to him? Why am I acting like such a pussy?

Tad leans in and his forehead is just a whisper from resting against mine. I can feel the heat coming off his skin with just the thinnest sliver of chilled night air between us. My eyes dart to his lips again and I have to force my gaze up to meet his. My heart is beating way too fast and my cock has gone from tired to hard as a rock and ready to go. Fuck.

'I'm trying to protect you,' he says. 'You're not in the city. People don't like promiscuity, period. There are a lot of people who haven't joined the current century. I'm just asking you to be smart. Don't let your addiction get the better of you.'

He smiles and I stagger back three steps. The moon is throwing bolts of white light against his platinum hair. His belt buckle catches a shard and light bounces off him like he's some kind of messiah.

'Addiction?' I have not been addicted to heroin for over a year.

'Yeah. To men. To the fuck-you attitude. To doing whatever you want whenever you want and putting yourself in harm's way. Men, sex, pain – pick an addiction.'

I haven't even been here a week. 'Fuck off,' I whisper, but it doesn't sound angry. It sounds scared.

'Just watch yourself.'

'Yeah.'

And then he shocks the hell out of me again. He leans in and grabs my shoulders, hauls me forward so I stagger and he kisses me. It's a hard kiss. The kind of kiss that is usually followed by rough, angry sex. He's not wooing me; he's sticking his tongue down my throat. Making a point. Doing what? Staking a claim?

His big hand slides the length of my cock and he presses his palm to my crotch so that bright red sparks go off in my darkened vision. He bites my bottom lip so that I jerk against his hand and he rubs me one more time to make his point. 'Do what I say. Got it?' he says, breaking from me.

'Yeah,' I say again. And all I can hear in my ears is my heart pounding and the crunch of his boots on the driveway as he slowly walks away.

In my bed, I stroke my cock slowly. All around me are snoring men. The dorm is just that: bunks in a big room, a fireplace and lockers. If I stay for more than a few months I can put my name on the list for one of the three private rooms occupied by long-timers. I jerk myself off as quietly as I can. I try to picture the bus boy, bent and bendable. Docile, pliable, fuckable. I try to do what I do so often. A nice body and a blank face. A parade of blank buff boys to get off to.

Instead, I feel the sharp bite of Tad's even white teeth on my skin. Feel his big hand rasping over the button fly of my jeans. I remember the involuntarily jerk of my hips when my body struck out to get more contact with him. In my mind, as my hands travels in an almost angry pattern along my hard length, I see myself sucking his cock. Long and easy and perfectly. With a clarity and tenderness I've not had, for what feels like for ever, I can so vividly see his hands in my hair and him bucking against my lips. I can see him fucking me and me fucking him. Teeth and tongues and cocks and bright blissful orgasms. At first I don't even realise I am coming. Then my hand is warm and my limbs are heavy and my heart hurts just enough to let me know I'm alive.

Chapter Six

WE WORK ON THAT damn fence all of Wednesday. It's raining and it's cold and the weather is so raw it makes you want to scream. Instead, we find holes in the fence and we patch them. The rain water drips in my eyes and down my collar. It makes my fingers shake and my bones sing. I wonder what it will be like when I am old if I'm feeling this poorly in the damp now. It's nice, though, too, the discomfort. It's nice to focus on the decrepit and painful bits of myself instead of just the sucking black hole that has lived in my chest.

Tonight, I will call Hazel and check in. I'll hear about her latest outings and her classes and how she still wants to lose five pounds. She'll fill me in on home. She'll make me want UTZ potato chips and Berger's cookies and all the things I adore that I can't get here and can only find at home.

'Hey, I heard you're a fun guy.' This from the other hand, Donald.

I don't like his tone, so I shrug. I'm not sure where he's going with this. 'I like to drink beer and I sing a mean *Ring of Fire* if you get me drunk enough,' I quip.

I bind the fence post tight and make sure it's straight. When we get back to the main house there are a list of repairs to do as long as my arm. Me, I just want a hot shower, a six pack and maybe a cheeseburger. Later, I remind myself. The point of this is change. Pain signals growth. I need to move on.

'I mean fun. You know, *fun*.' He stares at me and his

tongue drags slow and pink along his bottom lip.

Inside, right then, I'm at war. My cock jerks in my pants and I'm hard. I want to bend him over the damn fence and fuck him. Hard – so that he cries at the end. And I also want to punch him right in his pretty face and tell him he's mistaken and possibly retarded. Tad's words echo back to me from the night before and I clear my throat. 'I think you heard wrong, son,' I say softly and turn my back on him.

When we go back to the house to eat, Tad watches me from the far end of the table. I put my eyes down and eat my chicken salad. I drink my tea. I corral my eyes every time they pop up to try and see him. And every damn time he is watching me. Every damn time his eyes are on me as surely as hands stroking over me. My dick's hard, my disposition sucks and so does the chicken salad. I find an empty stall in the bathroom, lock myself in, get myself off. In my head, I'm on my knees for Tad. His hands in my hair, his cock in my mouth, his voice in my ear. 'That's my boy,' he says.

And I come.

When I come out of the bathroom, he's smiling at me. And it makes me think of how I used to look at Jason when I knew he'd been bad. I can count on both hands with leftover fingers how many times I let Jason fuck me. I prefer to top.

For whatever reason, my mind likes to fuck with me and Tad: me on my knees; me bent over; me not topping at all; me not being in control; me showing my weakness. I grit my teeth, shake my head, clear my plate and go on about my day, the list Nelson has provided in my jean pocket. Every time Tad's face pops into my head I blank it out.

'You're behaving, I see,' Tad says when he stops in the barn for a spot check.

'I'm not in the mood,' I say, but my heart jumps around like mad in my chest and my stomach bottoms out like I might be sick. Him being in the dusty cool barn with me is enough to set my head buzzing. I put my head down and keep pitching the hay. I have a few more things on my list including a busted glass pane in the back barn window. Local kids. At Blue Sky the term "hand" means you do whatever the fuck they tell you to. With a, "yes, sir," and a smile.

'No? You looked in the mood at lunch. Seriously, I'm glad you took me to heart.' He touches my shoulder and an invisible bolt of lightning flares in my body. I feel like I should be glowing, or have smoke rising off my skin. Or both. I shake him off and move a few paces away where I feel more sane.

'It's best to keep my wits about me. I knew I was wrong. You were right. I'm not ashamed to admit it. It's fine.'

He moves in again and when I whirl on him, panicky about what I will ultimately do if he touches me again, he raises his hands like I have a gun instead of a raging hard-on.

'Good. That's good.' I hear the tone he's using and it's the same one he uses on his horse, Pitch. A soft soothing tone that makes your muscles go looser. I bark out a laugh and toss my hat onto a nearby tractor. I run my hands through my hair and see that they're shaking.

'I appreciate the stamp of approval,' I say. I'm shooting for acerbic. I achieve breathy. What the fuck has gotten into me?

'You're an addict,' he says, taking a step toward me.

'Recovering,' I correct.

'Sort of. You've switched addictions.'

'We always do. You are always an addict of something. It's just that is it a socially acceptable addiction?'

'Like Home Shopping Network?'

I laugh. 'Yeah. Or church. Food. Whatever. As long as you don't get too fat. Then you have to be addicted to reality shows about fat people.'

'But you're all better now?' He has somehow come forward so that we are nearly toe to toe. It's like being mesmerised. The cobra and the snake charmer.

'Yeah. I'm fine. Thanks.'

'You're not here to run from anything?'

'No. Why?'

Tad shrugs his big broad shoulders and smiles. He reaches out and touches a single hay-dusted finger to my lips.

I stop breathing.

'Because you're bagging an awful lot of boys for someone who's all better now.' He pushes his fingertip into my mouth and I don't think, I suck the tip of his finger and wet it with my tongue.

'See, there you go,' he says and his eyes fall shut for a second.

I let him slip his finger in further and touch the middle of my tongue. I can taste sweet hay and warm skin. My cock is so hard I think I might weep. I don't. I suck his finger until he pulls it free, shiny and wet from my mouth. It's all me, I do it on my own. I don't let myself consider it. I reach for him and run my fingers lightly over the bulge showing at the front of his faded jeans. Tad says nothing. He's watching my hand and I'm watching my hand, too.

I see it in my head like a movie first. I drop to my knees and then I do drop to my knees. A physical echo of my internal thoughts. I open his belt, his fly, the flap of cotton that covers him. Tad's breathing speeds up and his cock springs free when I barely touch the fly of his boxers. I inhale the dark leathery scent of him and put my forehead to his belly. My mouth isn't touching him, but my breath is and his cock bobs like it's in a stiff wind. I almost smile at the thought but I don't. I don't because now I'm tracing the whole of him with the tip of my tongue. Gathering the salty taste of his skin and feeling his fingers starting to brush my hair. My hips shoot forward, thrusting at nothing at all. I take him in my mouth and Tad say, 'There he is. There's my boy.'

I think I might come right there.

The only other thing he says is, 'I've been seeing this in my head since they pulled up with you in that bus.'

Fuck me hard. So have I.

I suck him the way I like it; long and hard then soft and teasing. Then just big wet messy swipes of my swallowing gullet over his dick. He's pulling my hair so hard that tears are swimming out of my lower lids but I suck in air through my nose and run my tongue over the slick, velvety head of his prick.

'Jesus Christ on a cracker,' Tad says and comes, flooding my throat with the bright white bleach and saltwater taste of semen.

I put my head back down, catching my breath. Waiting. Then I get up and he's buckling his belt. He's smiling. He kisses me, open mouthed, tasting his own come on my lips and tongue. He holds my shoulders so hard I think his fingerprints will be there for days. He kisses me even harder before letting me go. 'Damn, Kyle. I …'

'Don't,' I say. 'It didn't mean a damn thing.' I leave the barn. When I walk across the field to find someone to give me a ride to town, his face comes into my mind. Sunny and rugged and perfect. I blank it out.

Chapter Seven

MY PROBLEM SWITCHES FROM Jason to Tad. I no longer struggle with ghosts of loves lost. I struggle with phantom wants and needs. Every time the night presses in on me and it's his face I see, I fuck another guy. Every time I can't shake the image of me on my knees for him and something swells in me, a mix of joy and rage, I get drunk. I spend my days focusing on the calluses and pain, cuts, abrasions, chores, errands, bruises and Nelson's lists. I spend my nights at the bar, telling myself I will not hook up with some other pretty sucker right before I drink one more beer and do just that.

Tad sits at the bar and watches me leave most nights. I catch him in my peripheral shaking his head and looking frustrated, angry and sad.

Tough shit. I told him it meant nothing and I meant what I said.

So why do I wake up with his image pressed in my mind like a perfect dried flower pressed in a book?

And now, a week past the whole damn mess in the barn, a guy is really working me. It's all hush-hush around here. God forbid anyone admit to liking dick. You just have to watch yourself. Don't be overt. Learn the rules and the lingo and the signs. This one isn't discreet, though. This one leans in and says in my ear. 'You've got a pretty ass, hand.' Hand is a common term around here, usually tossed about by the ranch owners or the higher ups – the uppity ones who have something to prove.

'Watch yourself, mister.' I sip my beer like nothing at all is out of order. But my pulse has gone up and the hair on my neck is standing like it's been teased by an approaching storm. 'I'm just drinking my beer. Move it along.'

'But I think we could have some fun, you and I,' he says. Now he's facing the bar mirror, not looking at me, but he's keeping his voice low so only I can hear.

'I think you're mistaken.'

'I've heard things.' He's older than me. Built wiry and stringy. Not much to look at but you know a man like that works with his hands and is nothing but barely controlled strength. Coiled up chaos with a wide stripe of anger running through it.

'Lies, I assume.' But I'm the one lying and I'm watching Tad at the end of the bar. His face is no longer mildly annoyed sadness. There is an agitation there. His body language is off. He's sitting forward like he's ready to spring off his stool. And his eyes are not leaving my suitor for even a moment. My nerves flare and my head pounds but now I want to know what's up.

The man to my right shakes his head, his dark hair shot with white is cut so close to his skull it borders on a buzz cut but isn't. 'See, I believe they are truths. They say you're new and you like it hard and fast and no strings attached. Which, just so happens, to be the way I prefer my amusements.'

"Amusements". I try not to laugh. I manage not to but I do smile.

'Sorry. Someone's been telling tall tales.' His leg presses to mine under the bar and I don't move mine away, I sit and wait, my eyes shooting back to Tad.

Tad is fuming. You wouldn't know it to glance at him, but if you really look you can see the flush in his cheeks and the glare in his eyes. You can see the muscles bunched under the tanned skin of his jaw and the way his mouth is turning down instead of up. His shoulders are high and tight

27

and he's got his hands fisted despite his uncaring appearance. He's trying to look relaxed but when I look at him I see frustration and fury. Tad catches my gaze and gives one nearly undecipherable shake of his head. No, he's telling me. That makes me turn to the man and say, 'My name's Kyle, mister.'

'Ahhh, and he comes to his senses. Name's Simon.' He puts out his sun browned hand and gives me a shake that is intended to intimidate. He presses my hand just so within his so that the fine bones rub and grind together. I don't react.

'Good to know you, Simon. So, what did you have in mind?'

Tad is shaking his head, those impossible blue eyes are flashing at me and I am doing my best to ignore it. I ignore him and the tug of worry in my gut. I follow Simon, who walks like a real cowboy, outside. When I pass Tad, he reaches out real fast. 'Kyle, don't,' he says.

I wave him off to prove how what I said was true. The barn meant nothing. Me being that way for him, nothing. Wanting to be that for him, nothing. The dreams mean nothing. The constant stream of him through my head all day long means nothing. If it wouldn't break my family's hearts and be the dumbest fucking thing ever, this would be the kind of thing that would drive me back to the drugs. Into the warm, welcoming arms of oblivion.

We're to the back of the parking lot, Simon and I, when the punch I do not see coming lands at my temple and stuns me. My ears reverberate with a high pitched whine and I shake my head. It does no good; the ringing intensifies and then bleeds into the sound of cicadas that don't exist except for in my head. He hauls me up and I stagger.

'Did I mention,' Simon says in the pitch black by the back of the lot, 'that I like to tenderise my meat before I use it?' His laugh is like smoke in my ears and there is a flash of white light and red noise in my head as his knuckles connect with my temple again. My teeth come together in a clack on my tongue and I taste blood. It's as red as the noise that fills mind.

'Hey,' I try. But the blood in my mouth and the roar in my head swallows up most of it so it's just my busted mouth spitting sound. I can taste dirt and bits of rock from my first face plant.

'Just a few more and we'll get on with business,' Simon says. Only he says it like *bidness*. His knuckles glance off my eye socket, skitter down my nose and connect with the spot right above my upper lip. My face is singing like a rotten tooth and I suck in a gulp of air and swallow blood.

He's pushing me down and my world is so fucked up: big looping revolutions in my body; vertigo that staggers me; Ears full of noise and face full of pain. My legs fold up like a ladder and I hit the gravel with my knees. My whole body is sore like when you have the flu. I know where this is going. Good news is, I am so far resigned right now I can't dig up the shred of self-worth to care. 'Mister,' I say. I can't get his name to come out of my mouth. 'Hey … mister. Look,'

This time it's a backhanded slap that rocks my head back. And my world does another hokey-pokey twirl. My eyes feel like they're spinning in the sockets all because I was too fucking stupid to keep my guard up. And too fucking asinine to just admit to myself how I was feeling about Tad. So I ignored his advice and the true heartfelt urge to admit my attraction and be with him. Instead, I left with this fuck-wipe and now he's going to treat me like a dog and maybe kill me if I'm lucky.

Simon shoves his hands in my hair and uses it as a handle. He yanks hard and my eyes fly open though my vision blurs. His jeans fill my focus. Just a field of dark blue denim right in my face. Rusty tan hands work his button and his fly and that fucker is laughing. But my head won't let me get a grip on up or down and the world won't stop moving. 'See, here the thing is, I am as straight as an arrow,' Simon growls. Even with my head pounding I wonder who he's trying to convince. Me or himself. 'But I do enjoy a good dalliance from time to time.'

It feels like I roll my eyes and I'm not sure until he backhands me again. 'Show some respect, boy,' he says and my head snaps back, rocks forward. I feel like I'm gong to be sick.

How the fuck did I end up here? I'm a pretty skilled fighter. I'm a pretty cautious person. Even when I'm trying for a hook-up, I'm smart. I never saw this coming. And my mind is running the movie of Tad. Shaking his head, looking worried, tense body pose. Warning me off, welcoming me in. Kindness. Smiles. Me down in front of him. The way he had touched me. All of it. All of it burns like a match point for me to focus on when I hear the tear of the zipper. 'A little. Fucking. Respect.'

Simon is yanking at his own jeans when I hear. 'Maybe you should practice what you fucking preach, Simon.' And then I see Simon's head snap back and his lip splits like a glistening red flower and blood is everywhere. He is falling, back, back, back and his goddamn cowboy jeans are tangled around his knobbly knees and he's done for. His head cracks the dirt and his eyes roll back. His chest is rising and falling so he's not dead. Too bad. Maybe I could help him out with the not dead part.

And I would, but my head is swimming and now Tad's face is filling my watery vision. He doubles and trebles in my liquid world and he smiles. 'There you are. How are you? You OK?' He touches my face and pain just ripples through me. Bigger and bigger circles of pain growing from the tiny epicentre where I have a screaming hot agony. A high small sound rocks out of me and Tad frowns. He looks angry and sad and like he might scream or cry or both.

'You stupid, stupid shit. It might not have meant anything to you, but it meant something to me.' He helps me stand, dips his big body in a graceful move and has me up in a fireman's carry before I can process. I hang there. Sorry. Sorry that I pushed him away. Sorry that I lied. Sorry that I was too prideful to ignore his protection of me. A sorry fucking sack of bones.

Chapter Eight

I WAKE THROUGHOUT THE night. A washcloth on my eyes, a voice in my ear. I'm on an honest-to-god fucking bed and not a rock-hard bunk so I have to be in a hotel or one of the long-term working man primo rooms we all bust balls about. I wake another time to my clothes being cut or ripped off and warm soft clothing being put in its place. Wake to pills being pushed into my mouth and water trickling over my sore, sore tongue. Pain sparks along the line where my teeth sliced muscle but the water is heaven.

'Try to sleep. It will be better.' Tad's voice. Right in my ear. Right up close so that it raises goose bumps on my beat and broken skin. I pull my body in against his warmth, making a comma of myself to mould to him. I feel his hard cock against my ass and almost smile, but my face shrieks in protest. His breath is soft and even but not deep. I don't think he's asleep even as I start to drift.

'What did you give me?' I notice the buzz in my head and the weight in my limbs.

'Percocet. I had some from a root canal. It will help. Trust me.'

'Don't take advantage of me,' I joke but part of me wishes he would. Right here, with me bent in against him. Weak and busted up and under his protection. I have that urge again to be less than strong in his presence. That it's OK. I shake my head and the world tilts. I groan.

'Knock it off and behave yourself.' His fingers are playing over the hair at the nape of my neck. His body is heating mine up so I don't feel so stiff and achy. 'Go to sleep, Kyle.'

'Not tired,' I slur. And I'm asleep before I can laugh at him for worrying so much.

I'm half awake in a twilight dream and it's Tad's face in my head. Tad kissing me. Tad touching me. Fingers parting me, sliding in, making my cock hard. Tad whispering to me. When I open my eyes, Tad is sleeping, draped around me protectively. I feel no urge to blank him out of my mind. No urge to drink or fuck stupidly or beat or rage. I lay there, his arm heavy on my bruises. A perfect welcomed weight.

I don't know he's awake until his lips touch the back of my neck. The sun isn't up but I hear showers running in the dorm wing. The ranch hands getting set for a day of rain, weanling calves, yearling calves, tending the horses and hay and heavy labour. What will we tell Nelson about me? Tad reads my mind, 'I'll tell him you got jumped last night at *Dollars*. It's happened before.' His cock rides the cleft of my ass and I press back to it. Liking the feel of him there.

I turn in his arms. A little panicky, a lot needy. He goes to kiss me and I pull at him, like I can lift him higher. 'Come up to me. Come up here to me. Let me, please.' There is that panic, crawling, crawling, crawling in my chest like a living thing. I don't quite understand it but I want to give him something. Anything.

His words run through my head haunting me. *It might not have meant anything to you, but it meant something to me.*

'Hey, easy, Kyle.' He smiles and something close to anger but much akin to sadness rears up in me.

'Come on, Tad. Come on.'

His fingers push to my cock, slip into the sweats he's dressed me in, touch me until I can't think. 'Calm down. Be easy.'

I arch into his hand. I don't know how to be easy. I've forgotten how. His lips come down on mine. So soft they're almost not there because of my bruises. I kiss him harder,

33

welcome the bite of the pain even as he runs his thumb over the head of my dick. 'Come on, Tad,' I plead. That spidery need fills my solar plexus but the rest of me is happy with his fingers and his touch.

'How about if we share?' His fingertips brush my balls and I forget to breathe.

'Share what?'

'No tops. No bottoms.' He says this to my neck, my shoulder, my collar bone. Then he's spinning so that I can access him and he can access me. I tug at his pyjama pants like a mad man even though my fingers are scratched and my jaw throbs and I breathe in the saltwater scent of him and take him in my mouth. His lips touch my cock at the same moment and my hips shoot forward.

It does mean something. I feel no rage, no ache, no emptiness. I feel his mouth on me and his warmth on me and there's safety. I feel safe. It's not long, this first time for us. It's been a long fucked up road to here and I have no patience. I just want him to come for me, and me for him. And then we can go from there. There's a lot to work out. I'm not sure I'm meant to be a cowboy. Not cut out for working horses or mending fences or the bullshit. But I am meant to be something. Someone.

I thrust to his lips, empty for him. I'm brave enough to say his name. I am someone. Not a blank.

FERRYMAN

Chapter One

'SO ARE YOU LIKE a handler, or what?'

Charon noticed his eyes underneath were smudged with what looked like kohl – fitting for a rock star – but he quickly realised it was simply fatigue. 'Perhaps. A bit. Not really.'

Graham Cooper of *Big Fuel* was reported to be surly, ornery, possibly alcoholic and drug addicted, rude, crass, and a sexaholic. He was reported to be a pansexual, unisexual, omnivorous, voracious and aggressive sexual hunter. Charon stared back as the younger man stared him down.

'What the fuck does that mean? And what's with the suit? And what kind of name is Charon?'

'Shall I start with the first question?'

Graham dropped like a tall lean stone to the ugly green sofa and flopped a denim-clad leg over the arm. 'Go for it, dude.'

Charon frowned. *Dude*. He'd have to get used to that. 'What *that* means is your record label wants someone to be at your … disposal should you need it while you're on leave.'

'Leave!' The young man snorted. 'Is that what they're calling it?'

'You're to regroup, Graham. Find out what you want. Your becoming a spectacle over and over again isn't good for anyone. Not you, not your label, not your fans.'

'Whatever. I'm here in my hometown USA and I'm

going to try to get my shit together. For me, though, not for them. Let's move on. What's possessed you to wear a fucking suit?'

'I like suits. They suit me.'

Graham chuckled and then grimaced when he realised that the man hadn't made a joke. His choice of words had been deliberate and sober.

'Ohhhh-*kay*,' Graham said. 'And Charon? That's a made up name, right?'

'No, sir.' Charon shot his cuff and straightened his tie. 'It was the name of the ferryman on the river Styx. You gave a coin and he ferried you across the river to hell. It was said that those who couldn't pay wandered for all eternity.'

Graham clapped. 'Awesome. I pay you and you're gonna take me to hell.'

'Your company pays me and I'll watch over you. And help you. I have no intention of taking you to hell, Graham. But I will be here as a resource if you need me and please call me Aron.'

'Why?'

'I prefer people not use my full name. It's a thing.'

'You have a thing?' Graham asked.

'It seems I do. Now what can I help you with, Graham? Anything? Now that you're back in your home.'

'Haven't been here since my mom died,' the younger man said, and for just a second Charon saw a small bubble of insecurity and fragility in the cocky man. Something in him stirred at that, but he did not mix business with pleasure. And though he found Graham Cooper both beautiful, intriguing and arousing as hell, he wouldn't touch him with a ten-foot pole. He fondled one pearlescent button on his suit and waited for Graham to answer.

'Did you hear me?' he asked.

'I did,' Charon said. 'My condolences, sir.'

Graham rolled his dark brown eyes and blew out a sigh. 'Fine. Whatever. Bring me a girl. Curvy and shapely with huge tits and plump lips. And a boy. Who looks like me. Got it?'

'Yes, sir. I'll do my best.'

'Do better than that. Just get it done. *Aron*.'

'Sir,' Charon said, and left as quietly as he'd come.

It was a quick phone call. Charon had handlers who had handlers who had handlers. It wasn't so much of an escort service as someone who could find young men and women willing to fuck a rock star for free. Or for tickets, as the case were. Graham was still spread artistically across his sofa when they arrived.

Charon studied the girl, an almost plump, large-breasted creature with lagoon-blue eyes and rose-petal-pink lips (natural) and long dark hair that brushed the waistband of her skirt as she walked. Her eyes flew huge and she started to jump up and down like a teeny bopper when she saw Graham. Her voice hit unnatural pitches as she squealed, 'I thought it was total bullshit! Total bullshit! But OMG, here I am and here you are.'

'Sit down and shut up,' Graham said not unkindly and she dropped her shapely ass in an easy chair as easily as a well-trained dog at the word "heel".

'This is Tonya, Graham,' Charon said.

'So I see. And this is?' Graham nodded to the pretty young boy with spiked black and blue hair. His eyes were rimmed with smoky grey, his lips almost true red in comparison with his pale skin. He was poured into skinny leather jeans and a red T-shirt that showed a wolf and Little Red Riding Hood. A black Edwardian vest and high top Chuck Taylors completed the uniform of the disenchanted.

'This is Freddie.'

'Freddie.' Graham rolled the word off his tongue as if tasting it. He nodded and patted the sofa next to him. When Freddie moved forward like a wraith, Charon stood and waited. The boy seated himself next to Charon's employer and sat frozen like a gorgeous statue. 'You sure are pretty.'

Graham leaned in and stroked the leather jeans like he was petting a house cat. The boy flushed, his pale cheeks turning blush-coloured in the span of a heartbeat. 'Thank you,' he breathed.

Charon didn't know if the boy was gay or bi or just didn't care either way. A sexual vulture, perhaps. But he saw that he was at least turned on by Graham's touch because a hard-on rose under the constricting leather pants like a hump. Charon had to hold his breath, bite his tongue, list chores in his head and count when Graham leaned in and licked the boy's lips. 'Kiss me,' he said and Freddie parted his lips and allowed Graham to slide his dark red tongue inside.

'Hey, what about me?' Tonya asked, crossing her arms over her huge breasts and frowning. A petulant child, a pouting minor in demeanour. She couldn't be more than 19 and as pretty as a china doll.

'We'll get to you in a moment,' Graham snapped at her. Charon watched her seal her lips shut and roll her eyes.

'Can you get it up for girls?' Graham asked the boy.

Freddie nodded. 'Sure.'

'Good boy,' Graham said, and patted the boy's supple cheek.

Chapter Two

CHARON WASN'T SURE WHAT *at all times* meant. The record label had instructed him to be on Graham Cooper like white on rice until he got himself straightened out. The younger man's bright blue eyes flashed at him as he kissed the boy deeply, thrusting his tongue into the wet recesses of his mouth. He studied Charon and grinned, obviously enjoying that he was watching.

It made Charon want to stay; it made Charon want to leave. 'Shall I ...'

'Stay right there. Do your job, Aron,' Graham said. 'Stand up,' he said to Freddie and Freddie did. 'Shuck 'em.'

The boy undulated like a human wave and peeled the impossibly tight leather pants from his lean legs. He toed off his shoes and kicked them across the floor. He stood there, naked, but for streaks of what could only be baby powder and his shirt and vest hanging in the way of his cock.

'Touch it,' Graham said and leaned back, popping his buttons, freeing his cock. He was all cocky and surly and gorgeous and Charon tried to study the ceiling but instead he studied the girl. 'You too,' Graham said to her, 'Hike up that skirt and touch your pussy.' He ordered it all as if he assumed it would be done.

And it was. She wriggled her skirt up around her waist and watched the boys. Her plump fingers playing over pink folds, her eyes glazed like she was drunk.

'Get down and suck me,' Graham said and Freddie dropped down to his knees. He leaned in, licking a wet line of spit from tip to root and Charon held his breath, praying to be released from the room. Not because he found anything disturbing, but because he found his new boss so intoxicating. Like a liquor calling to a drunk. The plush look of Graham's mouth, the lean ladder of his ribs as he peeled his T-shirt off to pinch one flat nipple then the other. He wore his sexuality like a badge. Charon waited.

The boy went down again, swallowing Graham, gagging on him. Impaling his haunted gorgeous face on Graham's long blushing cock. Charon shifted from one foot to the other, hoping that for anyone paying attention he merely looked bored.

Graham's eyes drifted closed and then fluttered open. Closed, open, closed, open until he wound his long fingers into Freddie's hair and said, 'Now turn around and lube up your ass. You do take it up the ass, don't you?'

'For you,' Freddie said. 'I'd do anything.'

'Good. We're going to play a game. I'm going to fuck you both at once. I'm going to fuck you and you're going to fuck her and I'll be fucking you both. And you look so much like me. It'll be like fucking my own shadow into pretty Tammy.'

'Tonya,' the girl corrected.

'Her too,' Graham said. Charon winced. There was a cruel edge to his new ward's voice. As sharp as a knife and probably as painful to the young woman.

She brushed it off and continued to masturbate with soft almost delicate swipes of her fingers. Graham watched – watched Tonya with atavistic glee, watched Freddie like he was dinner. When the boy turned and presented his ass – now glistening with some thick lubricant Graham had handed him – Charon thought to close his eyes, but didn't manage it.

Graham pressed his fingers along Freddie's flanks. He smoothed his palm, flat and rasping, over the curve of the younger man's buttocks. 'Eat her out,' Graham whispered and Charon barely heard. He did feel a crawling unease. He should leave, go, bolt, move. Instead he stood his ground, studying Graham's expression.

Freddie pressed his lips to Tonya. She promptly let her head fall back, long dark hair raining down the back of the easy chair she had draped herself over. She arched her ample hips up and thrust against his face with eager movements. 'Come on, like you mean it,' Graham said.

Charon shook his head, wondering if Graham's bravado was real or for show. Was this whole thing simply to make him feel so uncomfortable he feared self-combustion? If so, it was a lot of effort on Graham's part.

Freddie lapped at the girl faster, sucking her hot pink clit into his mouth, pushing his long pale fingers into her pussy and Graham moved in behind him like some sinewy predator and rolled on a condom. 'That's it, make that pretty girl happy. Pull up your top, Tammy.'

'Tonya,' she barely managed, so close to coming.

Graham just said, 'Do it.' He was playing with her, Charon was almost positive. The boy knew that girl's name.

She pulled up her top, her heavy breasts spilling free. Her fingernails, painted a chipped navy blue played over the puckered pink discs of her nipples, teasing them erect so they stood out like small erasers. 'Oh, God. That is so good,' she said. She didn't seem to be speaking to anyone in particular.

'Yeah, Freddie's mouth is pretty sweet,' Graham muttered, and pressed the sheathed tip of his cock to the boy's back hole. Freddie never moved but to arch his back and sit back enough to show that he was ready.

Graham's long lashes drifted shut, his rough hand clamped down on the boy's hips. He surged forward, biting his lip and Charon felt that swell-tug-jerk in his cock that meant he really needed to focus on something else.

Graham sank into Freddie, who pushed his fingers in more and more aggressive thrusts until Tonya bowed up under him and came with a big cry that made her tongue flash pink and wet in the low light. Then she shut her mouth, big eyes opening and looking a bit drunken.

'Now you're going to fuck her,' Graham said, and pulled free. He reached around Freddie and rolled a condom onto the boy's long hard prick. It curved to the right Charon noted with efficient interest. 'Safety first,' Graham said of his actions. Then, 'Go on.' He smacked Freddie once on the ass as if he were a horse and the boy entered Tonya with a slippery thrust and a moan.

Graham shoved back into the boy with no preamble and for a moment the trio stilled. A trifecta of pleasure at varying degrees. The other two – the visitors – waited for Graham to move and when he did they began to move as well. He gripped Freddie tight, his fingernails leaving blood red crescent moons in their wake. Charon noticed that one fingernail on each hand was painted black.

Graham bent his head and kissed the boy in the middle of the back. He took his time as he fucked and licked up the ropey ridge of the kid's spine. When his eyes grew dark and his movements jerky, he gasped once, sank his teeth in at Freddie's shoulder and came. Freddie capitulated, coming on a fierce startled cry and the girl joined in, her face still dazed and flushed.

The whole scene stilled, silent but for some barely audible panting. Graham withdrew, snapped off the condom, dropped it in a rattan waste paper basket and turned to Charon. 'Get them out of here.'

'But …' Tonya started.

Freddie simply stood as if resigned to his fate. He found his pants and pulled them on.

'Miss, if you will,' Charon said politely, indicating she get herself together.

'But …' she started again.

Freddie said, 'Hush'

Graham rolled his eyes, pointed to the door. 'Go.'

Tears welled in her eyes and then anger flashed, abrupt and brilliant. Her eyes cleared and she stomped out, breasts swaying, skirt still bunched around her curvy hips.

'You too,' Graham said to Freddie, but pulled him in for one last kiss. Charon noted that he nipped the boy's bottom lip hard when he was done. Charon did his best to ignore the own tug of arousal in the pit of his belly.

'Sir,' he said to Freddie and nodded to the door. Then he followed behind the two to let them out of the house. He locked the front door, made a call, assuring himself (so he could assure his boss) that they'd hear nothing more from Tonya or Freddie unless they were called upon.

When Charon was satisfied that the transaction was completed and neat, he went back into the living room. Only to find Graham drinking a water glass full of whiskey and smoking a joint.

'So tell me what kind of parent names their kid after the ferryman on the river Styx.'

'Graham, I doubt you're interested in …'

'Don't tell me what I am or am not interested in,' Graham snapped. So self assured, so smug for someone only in his mid 20s. Despite his demeanour, Charon counted down the days until he could be that confident. That assured.

'Fine. What would you like to know?'

'I already asked you. What kind of parents …?'

'My kind,' Charon interrupted.

'And what kind were those?'

Charon sighed. He sat on the arm of an overstuffed lounger and when Graham poured him a shot he shook his head no.

'Drink it.'

'No.'

Graham looked surprised. He sat back and said, 'What? No *sir* tacked on there.'

'That isn't part of my job. To drink because you tell me to.'

45

'What if I order you?'

'No.'

'What if the record label orders you?'

'Won't happen.'

'Why not?'

'I don't drink. They know that.'

'Since when?'

'Four years,' Charon said levelly.

'What happened?'

'Nothing good. So I stopped. Now on to my parents. They were scholars and of the literary persuasion and figured no one else would be named Charon. Thus far, they've been right. But I have had to explain my name on a daily basis for thirty-four years.'

'How old are you?' Graham asked, swigging his amber liquid.

'Thirty-four.'

Chapter Three

'SO YOUR PARENTS WERE artsy-fartsy and named you after a guy who shuttled dead people around after they had bitten the dust?'

'Correct.'

'And you don't drink?'

'Correct again.'

'Why is that, again?' Graham put the joint down and lit a cigarette with a lighter shaped like a penis.

'I prefer not to discuss it,' Charon said. He snagged the joint, pinched it out and put it in a coffee mug on the side table. 'Your employer prefers that you not do drugs, Graham.'

'They also prefer I not do Tonyas and Freddies but they can go get bent.'

'So you did know her name. Why did you keep messing it up on purpose?'

Graham shrugged but his face clouded over. Charon watched him war with himself, opening and closing his mouth, puffing his cigarette. Finally, he sprawled back and said 'I didn't want her to have any false expectations. God knows it sucks shit to expect one thing and get another.'

Charon felt he had hit a nerve. A clue to the erratic behaviour, maybe. 'Has that happened to you?'

Graham narrowed his eyes. 'Why don't you drink?' he asked yet again.

Ah, it was going to be tit for tat. In the infamous words of Doctor Lector *quid pro quo*. Charon caved. Just this once.

And just for this young man. 'I had some issues. I was a bit of a slut when drunk. And I liked being drunk. Got myself in some trouble. Got a lover in some trouble. He was emotionally ... *unstable* and ended up ...' He lost his nerve about there and Graham covered his eyes with a thin, pale hand.

'Did he off himself, Charon?'

'Yes, Graham. And I prefer you call me Aron. Now ... what experience do you have with shattered expectations?'

The younger man shook his head, lit a fresh cigarette off the first and ground out the smoked-down butt. 'They pulled me out of county fairs and back yard barbeques and talent shows when I was 13. I was going to be a rock star. Play the covers that got me noticed, write my own stuff, take care of family. All that happy bullshit from the Friday night movie. Instead, they hired some douche bag who wrote my music, slapped me in front of a band, moved me around, made me cover up who I am. There's more, but the point is, fame and fortune ain't always what it's cracked up to be. Neither is fucking a rock star. I wanted Tonya to know that.'

Charon nodded and watched the next swallow of amber liquid go down. It was nearly gone. He didn't even want to consider how many shots that tumbler equalled. 'I see. I'm sorry, sir. How long is your contract?'

'Well, to keep the money rolling in, the money that is currently paying for my sister's chemo, five more years. I'll be fucking old then.'

Charon couldn't help but laugh. He'd be 29. Five years younger than Charon was right now. 'I see.'

'But the worst is ...'

'What?' He almost wanted to ask Graham for a cigarette. Almost.

'The girlfriend clause. If I'm ever to be seen in public with a significant other, it's to be a girl.'

'I see, and that is upsetting because ...?'

Graham rolled his eyes and arranged his long limbs over the sofa again. He looked artistically placed, Charon thought.

'Because I mainly like dick, that's why. I mean, I'm not immune to feminine wiles or a sweet cunt on occasion. But I dig the dudes. And they have issues with that. Public perception and all.'

Charon sighed. 'And legally …?'

'Not much I can do. Oh I could fight the good fight, but they have an option to drop me should I become difficult. And then 17,000 paragraphs in legalese that explains what they deem *difficult*.

'And they hired me to watch you.'

'Yep,' Graham said. 'But you got me a guy. And a girl. And you did it well. So you're OK to me. So far.'

Charon gave a short nod.

'If I kissed you would you have a drink with me?' Graham asked, catching Charon off guard.

'I don't drink,' he said softly. He didn't mention the kiss but it was stuck in his head when he went to call in Graham's pizza order.

'Don't fuck where you eat,' he told himself while he waited in the foyer for the delivery man. Charon knew better than to mix business with pleasure. Even if it was difficult. For all his bravado and bluster, Graham was nothing more than a young man in a tight spot. A boy who'd thought all his dreams had come true until someone yoked him into a job and a persona that weren't his true calling. He was just another jaded rock star who liked boys instead of girls and thought pot and whisky and a big filthy mouth would change any of it.

When Graham pulled out extra paper plates and said, 'Sit and eat with me,' he did. When he said, 'I'm gonna get that kiss at some point,' Charon said nothing at all. He didn't trust himself to speak.

***

On the back porch of his childhood home, Graham popped a small white pill and fired up a cigarette.

'May I ask what …?'

'Vitamin,' Graham said and grinned.

The grin went straight to Charon's stomach like a fireball. He remembered the look of this young man sinking deep into Freddie, rocking his lean hips slowly like he owned the world. How he had commanded the girl, flattering and breaking her spirit all at once. Graham was a broken king, a wounded prince. He was darker than Charon had expected and something in that darkness called to Charon's own. But he had to maintain, behave, hold steady.

'I see.'

'Smoke?' Graham shook the pack at him and though he wanted one desperately, Charon shook his head. 'Don't smoke.'

'Don't drink, don't smoke, whatdoyado?' Graham sang in an impressive impersonation of Adam Ant.

'My job,' he said, hating how prissy it sounded.

'Oh, and I'm your job am I?'

'At the moment.'

Graham leaned in and walked his fingers up Charon's suit pant leg. He tiptoed his fingers like small feet until about eight inches from the cock Charon was trying so very desperately to control. Charon put his hands on Graham's one wandering hand and said 'Sir, please.'

'Do you work overtime? I usually don't dig daddies but you with the bald head and the piercing green eyes. The little goatee. The suit. The whole package screams *do me daddy*.'

Charon, who hardly considered himself a daddy, laughed softly. 'Well, I'm flattered, but I don't make grievous mistakes where I work. I don't mix business with pleasure.'

'So you won't fuck me? Let me fuck you? Fuck together?'

'That would be the pleasure part, Graham,' Charon said

softly. 'But I can't. I'm entrusted to watch over you. It wouldn't be fair to any of us, most of all you.'

Graham narrowed those eyes again showing his ire. Charon noted how long and luxurious his dark lashes were. Like a girl's and just as feminine. Graham was clearly unused to being told, no. 'Then I'd like for you to bring me two boys tomorrow. One that looks like me. One that looks like you.' He grinned and it was somehow cold and predatory, but gorgeous none the less.

Charon's stomach twisted on itself but he gave a brisk nod. 'Sir,' he said and rose. 'Now I think I'll retire for the night.'

'You do that.'

'Anything else you need, Graham?' Charon asked, smoothing his trousers.

'You already told me no about what I need,' Graham said and popped another small white pill.

'Graham?'

'Yeah?'

'Those won't help.'

'Oh, I know. But it sure is fun to see if it will.'

Charon took his leave before he did something dumb. Like forcibly remove the drugs from his new ward. He was here to monitor, not assault. He was here to protect what the record label viewed as a valuable asset, but he was not to interfere. So he went to his room and took a long hot shower. His body uncoiling and shedding the tension under jets of nearly scalding water.

When he came out, Graham was draped over his bed. 'Still saying no to me?' he asked, and stroked his cock with one hand.

Chapter Four

CHARON FROZE. HE CLUTCHED his towel in one hand and ran the other over his eyes, feeling weary and old and so tempted he couldn't even comprehend it. 'Graham.'

'I mean, I'm pretty fresh meat, don't you think?' His black hair – cut in a long romantic way that curled around his cheeks – looked nearly blue. It stirred up shadows on his pale skin. His blue eyes were ethereal in the golden lamp light. He turned to his side accenting a flat stomach, a thick thatch of pubic hair, a row of indentations along his abdomen that was more like an eight-pack than a six-pack.

'You're very tempting, Graham,' Charon said, weighing each word carefully. He was walking a very thin line. 'But I have to say no.'

'I won't tell,' Graham said. He ran his thumb over the tip of his cock and spread the small drop of moisture around the pink-pink skin.

'It doesn't matter. I don't mix fucking and working. It's a bad combo. Like oil and water. Or fire and gasoline.'

'Fire and gasoline works. It's hot.'

'And dangerous.'

'Sexy.'

'It destroys,' Charon said.

'So you think it'll destroy us? Me fucking you. You fucking me. Us fucking each other?'

'It would destroy our ability to work together,' he said.

Graham rolled to his back, flexed his feet, long thin toes pointed to the ceiling of the guest room. The whole house a

52

ghost of his childhood, his past. Charon watched him lazily stroke his cock as if it helped him think.

'What if I ordered you?'

'I'd quit.'

'Hmm. What if I begged?'

'You wouldn't.'

'But I want you,' he said and flashed those big blue eyes, shadowed underneath with lack of sleep or worry or both.

'I'm not a conquest. I'm not a trophy.' Charon sighed and then shivered. 'And, sir, I'm getting cold. I'd like to get dressed.'

'Fine,' Graham said, no real heat in his voice. He rolled off the bed onto his feet, enticing, young and limber. He stalked up to Charon and said, 'I don't get you.'

'Few people do.'

'Don't forget my order for the morning.' Graham grinned. He put his hands on his hips, his cock still rigid and very inviting. It was a struggle for Charon to keep his eyes above the waist. He wanted to let his eyes wander and skim at will.

'I'm about to send an email about it.'

'Good man,' Graham said. And lightning fast he moved. His upper body like a snake striking. He leaned in and kissed Charon full on the mouth. His lips hot, lush and invasive. Then he turned, chuckling. 'Told you I'd get that kiss.'

Charon fingered his lips and watched his employer waltz out of the room. His naked ass swinging like he owned the world. His body a masterpiece of cocky self assurance and the beauty of youth.

'Sweet merciful Lord,' he said and dropped to the yellow bedspread. The house had been left in its original form of décor he heard. The mother had died and the father and siblings had moved out. Graham had purchased the property and insisted it all be left as is. This bedroom had been a guest bedroom, but Charon had still found little bits of the

53

past strewn about. Some clothes in the closet, a porn mag full of buff men behind the dresser (Graham's he guessed), some stashed cigarettes long ago stale in the adjoining bathroom medicine cabinet.

He was sitting in Graham's past and it was serving a dual purpose. It was taming the musician and stirring the pot. One moment he seemed more stable and clear headed than reported by his employers, the next he seemed irritable and volatile.

And gorgeous.

Charon lay back, the towel falling open, a few stubborn droplets of water clinging to his thighs. He shut his eyes to try and still his heart some and it took a few deep breaths to get the galloping beat down to a fast thud. But he couldn't clear the flashing images of Graham fucking that boy. Of the forceful rocking of his trim hips, the elegant and cruel jut of his jaw and the curve of his throat. The way his hair fell like a curtain when he leaned in and bit that boy with sharp white teeth.

Charon found his hand on his cock. Traitor. It had wandered there on its own but when he squeezed gently the pressure was too good to move his hand away. It was too tempting to cave in and allow himself such a small secret pleasure. So he gave in. Long, slow strokes while playing his images over and over. The flex of Graham's ass, the muscles in his thighs, the small star tattoo done in nothing but black on his right hip. How his eyes had found Charon's as he moved and fucked and worked that boy over.

How he seemed to want to make sure Charon was watching.

Charon froze, his hand stilled and his heart banged. He squeezed again, pressing his flesh in his palm, cutting off blood and then letting it bloom back under his skin, until he could stand no more and let himself relive the warm press of Graham's warm lips to his.

He worked himself faster, begging his body to be done

with it now, to move past it and he came with a stifled groan.

It was only when his breathing slowed that he heard the soft *snick* of the door as someone in the hall pulled it closed.

Charon heard it, but preferred not to act. If it had been Graham, then he'd needed to see for a reason. Or he'd needed to prove a point. Either way, Charon was fine with what the young man needed to do. He had left being upset by small things such as spying years ago.

When his mind filled with Marshall, he pushed it away. Marshall was a thought for another day, for a time when he was utterly free to dive into the past head-first and wallow. Neither of which he wanted to do his first night on the job.

Charon booted up his laptop, scrolled through his address book and eventually found a contact he trusted. It was hard to find brokers in Maryland. Baltimore was a booming city, but here on the outskirts, past the city limits, in this little country-like home that reminded him of a farm, Charon had to weigh his options. Luckily, they were close enough to D.C. and Virginia to be catered to by some major players. Not to mention Graham was *the* Graham Cooper, that helped too.

Charon fired off a quick email that ended with, *send me two men tomorrow afternoon. One that resembles me, one that looks like my employer. Photos attached. I trust this is CONFIDENTIAL and expect you to operate thusly.* Then he attached a headshot of Graham and a random snapshot of himself from his photo file. He closed the computer, poured himself a soda and wished for that cigarette again.

Instead, he sat up in bed and read a John D. MacDonald mystery to pass the time. He'd watch TV but his mind felt kinetic as it was, TV would only aggravate the matter.

At quarter past twelve he went to bed. He had no earthly idea what time a man like Graham would go to bed or what time he'd end up rising. So Charon planned on being up and about at eight. It seemed like a safe bet.

Half asleep, he wondered how Graham felt being home, if he missed his mother, why he'd set his sights on Charon and how he'd moved so fucking fast to kiss him that way.

'Fuck me hard,' he said to himself. He stepped over a very unconscious Graham, who was spread out on the hideous couch that just seemed to get uglier, in Charon's opinion. 'What did you do?'

He didn't expect an answer, but Graham's eyelids fluttered and he snorted once before closing them again and going back to sleep. A glass bottle on the floor by his foot held about a quarter inch of amber liquid. Charon could only assume that Graham had consumed the rest. The ashtray (shaped like an oversized mushroom in keeping with the super seventies décor of the home) overflowed with roaches from joints and cigarette butts. It was a wonder Graham hadn't burned the house down as he slept.

This is what happens when you're not allowed to own who you are. For whatever reason, Marshall flashed in his mind – big and blond and smiling. Charon shook his head to clear the memory cobwebs. *That is what happens when you allow yourself too much leeway with your identity.*

'Cut yourself too much slack and you kill people,' he said.

Graham rolled but startled him by saying, 'I doubt you killed anyone, smart boy.'

Charon grunted, grabbed the ashtray and dumped it in the kitchen trash. The urge for a smoke from the night before faded fast with the smell of extinguished tobacco and ash. He dropped the ashtray in the sink and filled it with warm soapy water. Then he poured a huge mug full of filtered water and squeezed half a lemon into it. Then he rummaged in the cabinets hoping to find some pain relievers. Finally, he found a bottle that was half full and hadn't expired yet.

He set all that on the kitchen table to wait. Charon pawed through the refrigerator contents and found fresh eggs, milk, parmesan cheese and some button mushrooms. Someone had thought to stock the house for Graham before either of them arrived. There was no way in hell that rock star boy had bought all this stuff. He looked more like the kind of man who'd stock his kitchen with frozen chicken pot pies, cases of soda and snack cakes that would survive a nuclear attack.

When the omelette was done and the coffee had brewed Charon went in and nudged Graham with a toe. He didn't trust himself to lean over the boy or touch him. Even if he was mildly disgusted with his behaviour.

Part of him found Graham repugnant and part of him wanted to clean him up and hold him close and try and fix him.

You can't redeem yourself by fixing another broken person. Own what you did to Marshall and what happened. You acted, he reacted, he's gone. End of story ...

'Come eat, Graham?'

Graham flopped to his back, one tattooed arm strung across his brow to block the light. 'Oooh, what am I eating? You? And then you'll do me?' His mouth twisted in a semi-cruel smile and Charon felt his belly curl and his cock twitch. What he could do with that mouth.

'No, sir. Omelette, coffee, toast, juice, water and a big bottle of pain relievers.'

'My man,' Graham said and tried to sit.

Charon extended a hand and when Graham curled his fingers around his hand the stab of lust was sudden and staggering. He regretted letting Graham touch him. That might be the end of him if he wasn't careful.

When they stood eye to eyes, Graham brushed a coal black lock from his face and said 'So, did you place my order?'

Charon nodded. 'Of course.'

'Sure you don't want to cancel it and fill in for them yourself?'

'Sir,' Charon said softly, wearied.

'Fine, fine. Feed me, then. I'm starved.'

'Good, I made plenty.'

'What kind of pain killers are we talking here?' Graham asked over his shoulder. Charon watched his lean hips move in the baggy pyjama pants. His broad back was trim but extremely buff. Who knew you could get so many muscles lifting a liquor bottle and a joint. Charon shook his head feeling ancient again.

'Over the counter kind, Graham.'

'Damn.'

Chapter Five

THEY ATE TOGETHER AT the kitchen table in a shaft of sunlight. Charon thought they reminded him of something from a sitcom. Maybe one about two gays. Something a network would exploit and turn into slapstick. The damaged rock star and the self-restrictive bad boy turned good.

'You know,' Graham said chomping into a piece of toast. 'Just because he killed himself you don't have to punish yourself for ever.'

Charon swallowed a bite of omelette. What had been light fluffy wonderful egg had become a clump of sawdust in his throat.

Graham caught his look and said, 'I know what you're thinking. What the fuck could a guy like me, as fucked up as *I* am, have to say about your life and how to fix it.'

'The thought had crossed my mind.'

'How a guy who orders people like they're on a menu and drinks himself to sleep with a few prescription pills and pot chasers can give you wise input.'

'You score again,' Charon said, sipping his coffee – black, one sugar.

'Well, it's *because* I'm so fucked up that I can see the forest for the trees. You carry your guilt around like a piano strapped to your back. Dude, I can nearly see the outline.'

'Thanks for your input.'

'Look, tell me what happened. Tell me all of it. All the dirty, gory details. All the stuff you left out when you tried to explain it to other people. Even your shrink or the bartender the last time you got shit faced. Purge. It's good for the soul. And who am I gonna tell? *Plus*,' he went on, 'What better confessor than the most despicable bad boy in rock?'

Charon's chest was tight with anxiety and yet he said, 'You're not despicable.'

'But I'm not good.'

'That's your opinion.'

'And it's a good opinion.' Graham shovelled in a huge bite of omelette and Charon wondered how the boy didn't have a raging hangover. He simply seemed a bit sleepy. 'Now you know I'm right. You never told anyone the true story, did you?'

Charon studied his meal and pushed his plate away. 'No.'

'So tell me.'

Charon shook his head.

'Come on, what do you have to lose? Some guilt? Some of that weight on your back? I won't smoke any joints today if you tell me.'

'And no pills?' Charon asked.

'Dayum, man, you drive a hard bargain. OK. No joints, no pills. Now spill.'

'Give me a cigarette?'

Graham blinked at him. 'Seriously?'

'Yep. Seriously.'

Graham lit two, passed one to Charon. 'Here ya go, Charon.'

Charon let it slide and inhaled that first hit. His head swam and he felt nauseous, followed by a fast blip of pleasure, followed by a surge of tobacco scent and taste flooding his senses. He coughed once and decided to lay it out simply. 'Marshall and I saved forever to go to Mexico. We did the whole Ensenada, Rosarito, tourist trap deal. Gorgeous hotel, the ocean, stonework, big rooms, lobsters at dinner fresh from the ocean, red tile, pretty girls and boys serving drinks. And drink I did.' He cleared his throat and

60

loosened his tie just a bit. For once he wished he was addressing Graham without his usual suit of armour so to speak. 'I drank and drank and drank as we did the night club circuit. See, we were celebrating. My new job running a big bar in the city that I'd wanted so bad and Marshall coming out of the dark.'

'Is that like coming out of the closet?' Graham asked, not unkindly. He tapped his ash into the ashtray.

'No, he was a depressed man. He was kind and sensitive and funny and creative. He wrote, but he also read. For a living. He proofread for a small publishing company that also put out two of his books of short stories. He made very little but it helped his depression not to have to be out in the big bad work force day in and day out. He worked with a handful of people who treated him like family. And he worked hard to overcome his issues. And he had a sort of awakening right before we left. He had ditched the steady meds and just had a maintenance routine; therapy had helped his anxiety issues. He was happy … and excited. To try and be what he called normal.'

'Ah … and?'

'And we did the nightclub thing. We went from club to club, drinking and dancing. A big fucking deal for him. And as the night wore on, I got more and more drunk, harder and harder to deal with. I knew I had what I considered *a bit* of an issue.'

'Like a lion is a pussy cat,' he said.

'Exactly. But I didn't want to hear it from him. And I told myself I didn't. I worked in a bar full time for fuck's sake. This wasn't a TV show. You can't run a bar and be dry.'

'It would be hard,' Graham said.

'I tend to get a bit belligerent if I go past a certain point. I'm not a happy giggly drunk. And since we were on vacation and living it up and celebrating …'

'You went beyond that point.'

Charon sighed and rubbed his forehead as if he could

ward off the ghosts floating up in his memory.

'Yes. I did. And he went back to the hotel. He said he'd see me when I was hungover or sober, either one being more rational than in full-swing party mode.'

'More?' Graham poured himself some coffee and waved the warming pot over Charon's mug. 'I'm buying.'

'I'm good.'

'Go on, then.' The cocky, swagger had mellowed out to an attentive young man with a keen ear for listening.

'So I was out all night, drunk, I think I took something … none of that an excuse, mind you. But I picked up a guy and I spent the night with him. His name was Colin and he had curly blond hair. So fucking curly you could only describe it as spirals.'

'Ah, the cherub look.'

A short chunk of laughter burst from Charon and he rubbed his eyes. 'Exactly. So I spent all night with him and when I finally woke up at about noon the next day, the moment I opened my eyes … I knew I was fucked. I wasn't sure if we'd used protection. I didn't know where the fuck I was. I wasn't sure how to get back to the hotel and he was as high as a kite and out like a light and I couldn't wake him up to help me.'

'Wow. Bad, bad, bad. And I can say that because I've been there, sadly, and done that.'

'So I finally found my way back and he was crushed. Crushed. Marshall was in mid panic attack, he was sobbing, he was packing. He was livid and crushed and hurt and enraged. And he deserved every god damn emotion. And I tried to make him feel better, but that's hard to do when you smell like booze and drugs and fucking and some other guy.'

Graham nodded, lit two more cigarettes and passed one to Charon who had just crushed out the first. He didn't say anything, he just waited.

'He got the first flight out. I could tell his anxiety attacks were unreal but he didn't ask me for help or to come with him or to even come home. He left the hotel with a driver and he was pale and shaking when he did. I followed the next day. Figuring I'd give him the night to chill out. When I got back we tried to talk. And he was listening. He was considering all we'd had and I'd promised to get help and ...'

'Second chances, man. The world is built on them.'

Charon ran a hand over his shaved pate. He rubbed his eyes again realising he'd pay a million dollars to lie down and take a nap. 'I went to work that night. We'd made love, with protection and extra care to make sure he was safe of course. I'd made promises. I wouldn't drink that night. I'd be home as soon as the bar closed ... etc. I came home to find him on the sofa with a rag over his eyes. It was three in the morning and he wouldn't talk to me. When I asked what had happened he just pointed to the answering machine. It was him. Colin. Apparently I'd given him my number and he lived near us. He wanted to hook up.'

'So all your hard work was blown.'

'Well, I could have saved it right there. I could have deleted the message, blocked the number, called this guy and told him I wasn't interested. Instead, I tried to talk to him and when Marshall refused to hear me out ...' This was the part that stuck in his throat. The part that made him sick and heavy and sad.

'Oh,' Graham breathed. 'You didn't ...'

Charon said, 'I met him. Colin. I was with him again. It made sense at the time. I had fucked up, I was drinking, I had Marshall who I loved but refused to believe I just wanted to tell the guy to go away. I was angry at Marshall for not automatically trusting me. And I was angry at him for being suspicious and I met the guy to try and fix it. But again ... drinking. It all made sense in that state of mind. If he wasn't gong to trust me, why was I going to bother trying to be trustworthy?'

63

'And?'

'And more fights, more panic attacks. He wanted me out; I needed to find a place. Finally, he snapped one night and threw me out. Colin had called again and then hung up when Marshall answered. He just lost it. He threw all my shit out front and locked the door behind me. I slept on my friend, Lisa's, couch. Her twin brother lived with her and I shit you not I was almost positive they were fucking each other. But that's neither here nor there, it's just a snapshot of my life.'

'What happened?' Graham asked. His voice was low as if he could feel it coming. Charon could feel it coming – the memories he hated. Grief he'd tried to run from.

'I went by the next day before work. I wanted to try and reason with him. I wanted to explain that I loved him and I was fucked-up and I knew I was fucked-up, but I'd fix it. I loved him and I loved our life and one day I wanted kids with him and a picket fence and all that happy Hallmark bullshit from TV. But I did. I wanted it. And when I got there …' Charon broke off, swallowing convulsively as if that could steady the cresting wave of grief that was surging over him.

Graham started to speak, but Charon waved a hand at him and he went silent.

'I came in and found him in the bathroom. We rented that apartment because it was only four units. Each unit had something special and ours had exposed wooden beams. He hung himself. He'd been dead for hours. There was nothing I could do. The only thing I could have done was to have not been an asshole in the first place.'

'You'd been human.'

'No excuse.'

'We all fuck up.'

'Not like that.'

'So this is it? This is what you run from?'

'Who says I'm running?'

'It's just the suit, the demeanour, the way you carry

yourself. The no kissing policy,' he said, chuckling. 'Kidding, kidding.' He put his hands up and then dropped them suddenly. 'But seriously, you reek of a man trying to block out his past.'

Charon leaned in, a little angry, a little relieved, a lot exhausted. 'So what are you running from, Graham?'

'Me? Nothing.'

'Oh come on, they've hired a babysitter for you – me! You drink way too much, you use drugs, you mix the two – a death wish we both know. You smoke like a chimney and fuck like a whore. You have to be running from something.'

'Nah,' Graham said lighting a smoke, this time just one. 'I'm not running from anything.'

'What is it then? I'm not buying it.'

Graham levelled his blue-blue gaze at Charon and the other man had to fight his sudden urge to lean in and kiss Graham. To kiss him until it went way too far and they ended up twined around each other like human vines.

'Funny, I don't care if you buy it,' Graham said and grinned. 'But since you asked so nice ... it's not that I'm running from anything. It's more that I feel like when all is said and done, at the end of the day, I'll have no one to run *to*. So I fill my time.'

The doorbell rang and they both looked surprised, then annoyed. Charon glanced at the clock. Almost eleven.

'Who's that?' Graham asked.

'That would be your order, sir.' Charon stood and wiped his hands on the cloth napkin.

Graham pushed himself up and said, 'Feed them, will ya? I'm going to shower and shave.'

Chapter Six

CHARON FED THE NEW arrivals. One was so near to Graham physically he did a double take when he opened the door. His doppelganger was about ten pounds heavier, a few inches taller and was bald, not shorn. But it was pretty on the mark, Charon felt. Pretty close to home, in fact, on first glance too close for comfort.

'A drink?' he asked.

'A drink drink or coffee?' the fake Graham asked.

'Coffee, water, juice ...'

He shook his head. 'Nah.' His name was Jack but Charon knew that Graham didn't want to know.

'You?' he asked his double, whose name was Tom.

'I'm good.'

'So he's really the rock star? The real deal. Graham Cooper in the flesh.'

'Yes,' Charon said and was surprised to feel an ice pick stab of jealousy in his chest. He'd never admitted the whole truth to anyone about Marshall. He'd never gone that extra step to admit that he not only had the affair but then saw the guy again.

'Cool. I get to tell folks I fucked Graham Cooper.' The fake Charon was infuriatingly calm. Charon wanted to rattle him.

'He might ask to tape, is that an issue?'

The younger man paled but Tom just shrugged.

'He might call you different names,' Charon informed him.

66

Again a subtle shrug and this time Jack said, 'I've been called plenty.'

Charon wanted to ask them if they were paid escorts or whores or just star sluts. Instead he poured out three cups of coffee while they waited. Fuck it. If they didn't want it, they didn't have to drink it. It calmed his nerves to serve it. He'd keep them here where they couldn't wander or steal until Graham came. Then he'd run errands while they got down to business.

'Well, lookie here. It's like looking in a mirror,' Graham said. He was draped in the doorway in nothing but jeans slung low around his hips. His hair, wet and sleek, clung to his jaw. His lips were flushed as if he'd been chewing them with nervousness. Charon thought he was beautiful in his dirty kind of grace.

'Wow,' Jack said and stood so fast he tipped the chair over. The other Tom was much more calm. He stood and extended a hand.

'Hi. My name's …'

'Ah-ah-ah,' Graham cut him off with a hand up. 'Sorry, dude, I don't want to know.'

Tom gave a short nod, looked only a bit disappointed, and sat again.

'So, are we ready?' Graham asked.

The men looked at each other and then back at Graham. 'Sure.'

'Yep.'

'Good. Here in the kitchen's good. Go on and take off your clothes and start kissing.'

They looked confused for a moment. Even Charon was confused. Then the Graham look-alike said, 'What? Like … each other?'

'Yep. Chop-chop. Let's do it.'

'But Mr Cooper …' It was Tom the older voice of reason who now tried and he too was cut off.

'Hey, you were brought here to make me happy. Now

67

fucking make me happy or get out. Get naked and start kissing. Don't make me say it again.'

Charon leaned back against the kitchen counter to try and figure this out. Graham leaned back with him. 'Let's see what it would be like,' Graham said.

'What?'

'Me and you fucking.'

'We were supposed to fuck a rock star,' Jack said with a pout. But when Graham put a hand on his cock through his well worn jeans and nodded as if to show he was paying attention, the young look-alike got into it. He kissed the older man – the fake Charon – with increasing gusto until Tom couldn't help himself. He put his hand on Jack's head and pushed him down, showing with no doubt what he wanted.

'I like this part,' Graham said in Charon's ear and Charon felt the skin along his neck shiver. He watched, enraptured like his boss wanted, as the young man peeled back the fly of Charon's doppelganger.

Me too …

Jack dove in eagerly, he was all mouth and lips and tongue. Slurping and kissing. He sucked one ball and then the other as Tom swayed on his feet, his pants crumpled at knee level, his hand on the younger boy's hair. Tom watched with avid eyes the mouth devouring his cock, the hands stroking the insides of his thighs, the fingers that poked through his legs to probe at his ass. He chuckled and sighed and thrust with an eager rhythm.

Tom's eyes found Graham and Graham said 'I think you might want to reciprocate. He looks like he could drive nails with his dick.'

'Here?' Tom asked, his gaze finding Charon's gaze. In that instant, Charon saw how much they really did resemble each other but for the fine stubbling of hair along his scalp.

'Here. It's nice and sunny in here. Might as well take

advantage,' Graham said and popped his button. The copper zipper hissed when he drew it down and he pulled his cock free of his pants, stroking it once and saying to Charon, 'Don't worry, Aron, I won't order you to whack off.'

Charon managed to tear his eyes away only after seeing the blushed tip of his boss's cock. It all seemed to boil down to sex with Graham. Love, power, surrender, joy, anger. Sex was the key to him. Charon's eyes went back to the two men at the table.

Tom, his sex surrogate, had pushed Jack back so that he sprawled across the oval table. The yellow placemats has scattered like scared animals and one lay on the floor. His big hands yanked and tugged at Jack's zipper and he freed his cock with one smooth yank. He didn't stoop to suck him instantly. He ran his hands, big and callused, up and down the shaft until Jack made little gasping pleas that sounded like he was crying.

'Do you want it?' the fake Charon asked the fake Graham.

'Yes. God, yes.'

Graham squeezed his cock hard in his hand and bit his bottom lip. Charon risked a quick glance and then looked away when he felt the echoing tug in his own boxer briefs. How badly did he want to stoop and suck Graham into his mouth in that instant? How hard was it that he was standing within inches of him, his cock exposed, his heart on his sleeve. This was Graham's way of spelling out in aggressive and no uncertain terms that he wanted Charon. That Charon was a goal. Charon stilled his chaotic insides and took a deep breath hearing his almost-twin say 'Then, say it.'

'I want it,' Jack said, his gaze moving restlessly over his audience but then slamming back to the man he was naked with.

'What is *it* exactly?'

His mouth worked, but no sound came and finally, when Tom stroked the length of his hard shaft with nothing but soft fingertips the young man managed, 'I want you to suck my dick. Go down on me. Do it. Now.' The last was meant to sound bossy and dominant but it came out sounding desperate and pleading.

Tom chuckled darkly and took his sweet time, dropping to his knees on the cheery red tile floor. He took his own cock in hand and gave himself a few brisk yanks before sucking just the tip of Jack into his mouth. Then he rolled his tongue, wet and pink and long, over the tip of the boy until he danced like some marionette on the dinette table.

'My mother is rolling over in her grave,' Graham said out the side of his mouth and then again, like a snake striking, leaned in so fast and so fluid that Charon didn't see it coming. The kiss landed on the edge of his mouth where upper and lower lip met and the smell of lust and cinnamon coming off Graham almost made him lose his willpower.

Instead he watched it all play out. Watched Graham direct and stroke his cock and then he surprised him by putting it away and zipping his jeans. The bump of his erection so evident inside the faded denim. 'Now fuck him,' he said and they watched Tom, transfixed, as he rolled on a condom and worked his new lover to the point of no return before sliding home and rocking against him so his longish hair brushed the wood of the table like seaweed in a gentle tide.

They watched as the fake Graham leaned up and tried to touch any part of the patient and silent Tom he could. They watched, arms not touching, but standing close enough for Charon to feel the heat radiating off Graham like heat rolling off banked coals. They watched as Tom stilled, leaned between Jack's thighs and kissed him, wrapping his tight fist around Jack's cock as he barely moved, still buried deep inside Jack as he tried so hard to stay still but seemed to practically vibrate.

They watched the soft white eruption of come as Jack gave in and clutched the edges of the kitchen table like he

70

was drowning and Tom spread the warm fluid around his lower belly using his fingertips and Jack's own cock as a paintbrush. And then Tom came, in the understated way that Tom had, with a simple groan and his bald head fell forward in submission to his pleasure.

'You can go,' Graham said, and left the room.

They looked up, surprised, but Charon bid them goodbye and showed them out. He watched them link hands on the way down the walk. Maybe something good had come out of Graham's childish way of treating people like his own personal play dolls. Maybe they'd go out to dinner and start a nice romance. Maybe there was hope for them. 'Would be a hell of a story to tell your grandkids,' he said to himself.

Charon retraced his steps, listening to a TV that had been turned on. 'That was rather harsh,' he said, finding Graham in the living room lighting a cigarette.

'I was done with them.'

'They're people.'

'They're well compensated. We all know it.'

Charon swallowed and said nothing. His own dick was particularly uncomfortable at the moment, shoved into his under-things like a too large package in a too small bag. His mind supplied unwanted images of their look-alikes fucking. What had started as simply a hot scene had turned tender and intense and somewhat sweet when all was said and done. Which made it feel that much more voyeuristic to watch.

'Will you tell me what's wrong?' Charon tried.

'Nothing.'

'You need to manipulate me that much to be happy?'

'Who's manipulating you?'

'What was that?'

'Me trying to show you what it could be like.'

Charon was shocked. Was he for real? 'How long have you been in the business now?'

'Too long.'

'Was that some kind of wooing ritual? And why me?' Charon crossed his arms, feeling suddenly vulnerable for the attention and the intent of what he'd just witnessed. This was supposed to have been a straight forward job. Baby-sit a rock star and not let him act a fool. Instead he was trapped with a handsome man in his childhood home and fending off advances he more than half wanted to give into.

Graham shrugged looking pissed. 'I don't know. Why are we attracted to who we're attracted to?'

'Well you started off with a boy and a girl and moved on to look-alikes for you and me. I'm just confused.'

'I don't know!' Graham roared and stood so fast he knocked over the ashtray. Cigarette butts and ash went flying everywhere and he lobbed a fist at Charon as fast as he had launched his kiss earlier. Luckily Charon caught on and threw up an arm to block. He very calmly said, 'I'll get the dustpan,' and pushed Graham's arm down to his side.

The door bell rang, he watched him stalk off with a swagger that screamed, "Fuck you". Then he came back with an envelope. 'Here's your coin, *Charon*. The label sent your pay cheque via courier. Too bad I'm still trapped here in hell. When does the next ship leave?'

Charon didn't bother correcting him. That technically, he'd be ushering him to hell. But hell was right here. Wanting this man and not giving in. Knowing Graham wanted him and not giving in and suffering his ire for it. Being paid to care for someone he had developed sudden and irrational feelings for. This was not what he'd signed on for. This was supposed to be an easy job.

Charon went to get Graham for dinner and stopped cold. The door was cracked just as his had been the previous night. Charon let himself stand there and watch as Graham finished what he'd started earlier. Every part of him said to turn and walk away. Come back and be noisy. Announce his presence with the clomping of feet and calling out.

Instead, he watched Graham draped over the small double bed with the vanilla coloured quilt. Graham faced away from him and Charon was able to study the top of his dark head all the way down the long expanse of his bare form to the distant peak where his toes pointed skyward. He watched the late afternoon light play over every crest and valley of his body and the shadows the sun threw over his muscles. Charon studied how his lower legs tensed and his toes went taut as he approached release and the way he froze, entirely, before that final jerk that made him come.

Charon pulled back from the door when Graham started to cry. It was too hard to watch that without rushing in to help. Without pushing into the room and gathering the younger man to him and demanding he tell him everything. What hurt and why.

But he knew enough, just after a few days, to know that he'd be met with anger and resentment and resistance. Best to let the failed kiss and the failed punch fade into the background before doing what he was prone to doing now. Every since he'd fucked up so tragically with Marshall, he'd run around trying to save him over and over again. Trying to save every man that crossed his path.

It was his weakness and his strength. The trick was helping to save someone without harming yourself in the process.

Chapter Seven

'WHY DIDN'T YOU COME get me?' Graham strutted into the kitchen and pulled back the aluminium foil on his dinner plate.

'I called up, I thought you were sleeping,' Charon lied easily. Removing the foil, he took the plate and zapped it in the microwave for 45 seconds. He'd made manicotti, garlic bread and kale for dinner. He poured Graham a glass of wine without asking and then water with lemon.

'Well, I wasn't. I was just … killing time.'

'Sorry. There's tiramisu for dessert after if you like.'

'Got an Italian thing going on, eh?'

'My mother was Italian.'

'And your dad?'

'A mutt. German, Scottish, some Native American. A little French, we think. Just a normal mutt.'

'Ain't we all,' Graham said. He shoved half a manicotti in his mouth and then breathed out puffs of steam like a dragon. He washed it down with some wine and eyed Charon. 'So you opened up rather fast to me. Do you always run around spilling your heart to your employers?'

Charon picked an invisible piece of lint from his sweat pants. He'd put on his evening clothes and was considering a run. Not much of an athlete, he did enjoy running, especially when he felt chaotic inside. His stocky frame and natural bulk weren't suited to running, but his mind was. 'Firstly, you're not technically my employer, the record label is. Secondly, you sort of guessed it. I saw no need to be evasive and lie.'

Graham nodded, took a big bite of kale with vinegar and hot peppers and then resumed his puffing and panting. 'Hot as a motherfucker, but too good to stop eating it,' he said.

Charon smiled, pleased. 'Thank you.'

'Sorry about the whole pay cheque thing. You confided in me. Your name, some of your history and I threw it back in your face.'

Charon shrugged, though he was thankful to see Graham thinking that way. 'So you tell me. What's all this …?' He waved his hands around, unsure of how to phrase it.

'All what?'

'The boy and the girl. The men to fuck in front of us.'

Graham looked like he had to force his final bite down. Then he cocked his head. 'I like sex.'

'OK, lots of people do. But …'

'I rarely get a chance to connect with people. Let alone form relationships. Let alone the kind that lead to monogamous sex. Let alone the love kind.'

'That's a lot of let alones.'

'True. I've been alone since I signed on the dotted line. Plus told to hide my sexuality. Or as my label put it my *confusion*. My mom died and I barely got time to mourn. And everyone I hook up with … even the ones I feel close to …' He shook his head looking both heartbreakingly vulnerable and enraged all at once.

'Go on.'

He put his fork down gently. It was a scarier move than if he'd thrown it, Charon thought. 'I'm a trophy. Something to report. It's a matter of someone getting to say *I fucked Graham Cooper* not that they want to connect with me in any real way.'

'I'm sorry,' Charon said and stood to portion out something sweet for Graham, though he hadn't even finished his plate. 'How about your sister? Have you had time to be with her?'

Graham picked at a fingernail, peeling off a cuticle so that it bled. Charon handed him a napkin to wipe it away. 'She's with her husband. They have a little girl. They're all wrapped up in their little family and fighting her cancer. I send money. I send gifts. I see them on holidays if I'm not playing *special holiday shows*.'

'You say that as if it's in neon,' Charon said.

Graham grinned. 'It usually is.'

'What kind of cancer?'

'Leukaemia. She was bad, then remission, then it cropped up again. She said she's grateful she had Grace before it all started. At least she has her daughter.'

'Grace is a nice old-fashioned name.'

'She's too cute,' Graham said, and yanked his beat-up wallet from his pocket and presented Charon with a snapshot of a little dark haired baby with the biggest toothless grin he'd ever seen.

'Agreed. She is too cute. And your dad?'

'We don't jibe. That's all you need to know. The moment he figured out that I was gay with a mild tendency to throw a random girl in now and again he wanted nothing to do with me.'

'And when was that?'

'Junior prom. He caught me with my date who happened to be watching me suck her best friend's cock.'

Charon peeled a half moon of his fingernail away. 'More wine?'

'Sure.'

He leaned in to pour it and Graham leaned in and kissed him. Charon saw it coming this time. But he let it happen anyway. He made his mouth soft and accepted the kiss and the gentle wet nudge of Graham's tongue past his lips. 'I can't fix it for you,' Charon said softly. 'I'm not magic.'

'I know.' Graham tugged just a bit and rubbed his hands over Charon's shorn head. The stubble that had cropped up during the day whispered at the young man's touch.

'I'm not your father. I can't be a stand-in.'

Graham sat back suddenly, his face colouring with anger. He tucked two hunks of black hair behind his ears and frowned. He downed the wine in three gulps and stood. 'I'm not fucking stupid. I know who you are and who you aren't. But now I also know what you think of me. Thank you so much, Dr Freud. Call and get me someone rough for tomorrow.'

He tucked his wallet with the photo of a child he clearly loved back in his pocket.

'Rough – as in rough around the edges?' Charon asked, swallowing what felt like a small lump in his throat.

'No. Rough as in, tie me, whip me, spank me, make me beg.'

'Graham, I …'

'I asked, now do. That is your job. I'll owe you a coin.'

Charon watched him stalk out.

Charon disliked the man on sight. Tall and brawny, he had the over-inflated look of a gym rat. The run the night before had done little to settle Charon down. He wanted to tell Graham off and comfort him simultaneously. This guy was a jerk, Charon knew it the moment he opened the door and the guy – Michael C by name – gave him the once over and said, 'Well, you're sure as shit not him.'

'No, sir. Come in please. You can wait in the living room.'

Charon had also expressed to Graham that having these people to his actual home might not be the smartest thing. Graham had basically told him to go fuck himself. Charon knew that if something happened he'd feel horrible, but it wasn't his home and life was packed with hard and painful lessons. Sometimes it was the only way certain people learned.

'Where is he then?' Michael C's gait was cocky and proud and Charon had to suppress the urge to plant his loafer into the moron's butt. His jeans were dark wash and well fitted. His shirt, a black button-down with no logos or markings was nondescript, but screamed expensive. He had dark brown hair cut short like a punk and his eyes flashed brown and envious, the colour of old coffee.

'He'll be down when he's ready,' Charon said and did as instructed. 'May I offer you a drink?'

'You may. I'll have a bourbon, straight up.'

Charon inclined his head. He had already decided he'd get fired before he sat in on this particular sexual escapade. For one thing, he didn't know if it was rough sex in general or if Graham was the top or this jerk. Either way, he wanted nothing to do with it and if that meant being unemployed, so be it. He'd kept Graham at arm's length, but did care for the boy. And his attraction was real. He would not suffer another torture session watching sex of some kind.

'I'll be right back.'

'Chop chop, Jeeves,' Michael C said, as if that was the funniest fucking joke to ever grace history.

'Douche,' Charon said under his breath once he hit the dining room.

'Who's a douche?' Graham came through, dressed in dirty wash jeans and a black T-shirt for a local coffee brand.

'Your ... *visitor*.'

Graham shot him a glance over his shoulder, his black hair – still wet – licked at his jaw and his broad shoulders. 'You're just jealous. You want me, but are too stubborn to say.' He dropped a wink and Charon grimaced.

It was true. He did want him. He didn't want to say. He didn't even want to admit it, but what do you have when you add a damaged young man to a tainted older guy? Two fucked-up men, that's what. Broken plus broken equals broken. Plus you don't mix work and sex.

'I'll get his drink. Anything for you?'

'Nope. We'll be taking his drink out to the garage.'

Charon stopped, half in the kitchen, half in the dining

room. It was there, between rooms staring at Graham that he realised how much bigger the farmhouse was than he'd thought. The rooms seemed huge all of a sudden. Graham seemed so very far away. His eyes flew to the kitchen table in the big eat-in kitchen. He saw the ghosts of the fake Graham and the fake Charon fucking.

'To the garage, why?'

Graham shrugged, rolled his eyes like a surly teenager. 'Because I *want* to. There's a loft out there. It was mine before I left home. When things got bad between me and my dad.'

Charon cleared his throat. 'Oh. Shall I put together some food for you?'

Graham rolled his eyes again. Charon thought it looked painful, to roll one's eyes that dramatically. 'I don't think he's here to eat and I'm not hungry. Just get his drink and get invisible.' Graham turned his back effectively dismissing Charon.

He tried not to let it hurt, but there was a sharp tug in his gut and his heart. He ignored it. It didn't matter.

He poured the bourbon and brought it in. When he walked in Michael C was wrapping a piece of rope around Graham's thin wrist saying 'See, I know knots, little boy.'

Both men looked up at him and he felt anger and frustration stain his cheeks red. But he kept his voice level and did his best to swallow his anger. 'Here's your drink.'

'Sir,' the guy said.

'Pardon?'

'Here's your drink, *sir*.' Michael C sat back with the drink in hand, begging Charon to cross him. This was his primping and peacocking for Graham. He was showing his dominance.

'Very well.' Charon smiled, but did not repeat the words.

'Well?' Michael C said. He crossed his ankle over his other knee and bobbed his foot up and down, showing his impatience.

'Well, what?'

'Sir.' Michael articulated it with venom in his voice.

Graham was watching this back and forth with mild amusement.

'You can just call me Aron,' Charon said and turned to leave the room.

Michael stood abruptly, coming toward him, all manly rage and ire. Charon took a step forward to meet him instead of retreating and that threw the newcomer off. He said in a low, gentle voice, 'I wouldn't. I'm not submissive and I'm not dominant. I'm not into your games and I don't like you and I don't have to address you in any certain way beyond not calling you shithead. So I suggest that you back off. Right. Now.'

Michael C turned his back, grabbed Graham and said, 'Let's go. Where are we going?'

'To the garage.' Graham stood, shooting one glance at Charon, and then let himself be hauled away.

'You might have to pay for his insolence,' Michael C said loudly and Graham snorted as if he found that highly amusing.

The front door slammed and Charon released the breath he hadn't even realised he'd been holding.

Chapter Eight

HE HEARD THE BLOW from the expanse of driveway that separated garage from house. The sound of hand hitting flesh and then the sound of pain. He turned the water on in the kitchen sink and rinsed a glass that was already clean. They'd been gone about an hour and this was the first noise he'd heard. Charon considered shutting the windows but then the house would be stuffy and he'd be giving into his own jealousy. When he cut the water he heard the blows coming fast and furious now.

'How much pain is he into?' Charon said to himself and rinsed another glass. Maybe he could just leave the sink running until they were done. But knowing Graham and his stubbornness and Michael C's wounded pride that could be all day.

He shook out a cigarette from the pack on the counter, went out the kitchen door and stood on the small concrete porch. The stress of doing this fucked up attraction two-step with Graham was getting to him. He lit the smoke and winced when he heard another blow land. The wind tossed the trees and a few dead leaves skittered over the driveway. Charon watched the small white curtains on the top loft windows flutter in the wind. He hadn't even known there was a loft, let alone that Graham had once lived there. He listened and heard nothing but a small whimper and what sounded like a sigh.

Somehow, hearing but not seeing was worse than being present to watch the erotic action. He'd seen Graham the first night with a combo deal. He'd stood almost arm to arm with him to see a simulation of what they could possibly do together. And now he couldn't see what kind of pain was being inflicted on Graham and all he could do was fret and wonder. 'And smoke,' he muttered.

Charon heard soft noises and could only assume the fucking had commenced. He could also do nothing beyond swallowing the bubble of rage that presented itself in his chest cavity. But he was wrong about the fucking because there were a few more sounds of impact and then Charon froze, cigarette half way to his mouth, when he thought he heard his name. Uttered in pain. In Graham's voice.

Clearly he was imagining it. There was no way that Graham was in there, fucking and proving a point, and calling out to him. He puffed some more, anxiety crawling under his skin, but then he heard it again.

'Yeah, OK, so I look like an asswipe, so what.' Charon dropped the cigarette and bolted to the garage door. The big door was down, the small entry door was locked. He pushed his shoulder against it and shoved. Then backed up a few steps and really threw his shoulder into it. Luckily the lock was shoddy and it gave. 'Might as well go all out if I'm gonna look like an ass. Probably get fired too for interrupting the festivities,' he muttered to himself as he moved up the steps. Just in time to see Michael C belt Graham across the face.

Graham's eyes rolled in his head and he glared at Charon. A dribble of blood trailed from his nose and he said, 'Christ. What took you so long? I think what we have here is a true sadist. And not the fun kind.'

Michael C clocked him again and Graham sagged with his arms bound above his head with the rope the other man had brought. His eye was swelling, his nose leaking. He didn't look satisfied or turned on or any of that happy shit.

'I think you're done,' Charon said and rushed forward. He grabbed the man's arm on his next swing and when

82

Michael turned to react, Charon hit him square on the arch of an eyebrow. He felt something buckle and give under his fist and it felt good. It felt so fucking good to hit this moron. He hit him again and when Michael tried to land a blow, Charon caught him with an uppercut to the solar plexus and Michael sagged.

The power that Charon carried in his stocky frame was one thing; the rage he carried in his heart was another. 'I think I owe you a few more so you and he are even.'

Graham hung there, watching as if half asleep.

'Fuck you,' Michael said with a gurgly little laugh and Charon grinned down at him and hit him again.

He hit Michael C until the man didn't respond and his fist ached and throbbed like a fractured bone.

'Charon,' Graham said softly.

Charon was lost to him. He toed the other man with his boot and when the man groaned, he kicked him.

'Charon, stop.'

The voice was so far away. A ghost of a voice. A voice so faint it could have been Marshall's.

'Charon, help me. Get me down. I hurt.'

It was only the plea that peeked through his rage like sun peeking through a grimy window. 'I hate him,' he said, and spat on Michael C. The nasty, cocky, cruel, non-sexy motherfucker.

'I know. Me too. Now help me. Please.'

Graham had no swagger in his voice or his body. He went limp when Charon let him down. He wrapped his arms around Charon's neck with no urging and tried a joke. 'Hey, there. I'm not making the moves on you or anything. I know how you feel about that. Don't panic.'

When he smiled at Charon his split lip reopened and Charon winced in sympathy.

'It's fine, it's fine. Shut up and stop smiling. Your lip will get worse.'

'Christ. You think it can get worse?' Graham said. '*Here*

I am, broken and defective. Love again deflected. A long road ahead a short road behind, wanting you and going out of my mind ...'

Charon recognised the lyrics of one of his top hits and as he dropped down to catch him in a fireman's carry he said, 'You're not defective.'

'Dude. All the blood is rushing to my head. And it hurts.'

'Dude,' Charon said, but couldn't help but smile. 'I think everything is gonna pretty much hurt for a while.'

Graham blew out a sigh and let himself go limp. 'So what's new?'

Charon toed the infamous Michael C, who groaned and opened one swollen eye. 'You have ten minutes to get off the property of your own accord. After that I call the boys in blue to come help you leave. Time starts now.'

When he exited the garage the man was just sitting up.

'Graham, you can't be into ...'

'That is not what I am into. I don't think anyone is into just having the merry shit beat out of them. When he said I would pay for you, he meant it. I thought it was a joke. Teasing. Something to amp up the pleasure-pain deal. But no. He's just bat shit crazy, Charon.'

'Aro – never mind.'

'Oh, must be my birthday, he's letting me call him by his full name.'

Charon couldn't help but grin. He carried Graham to the master bath and stood him up. 'Should I go and check on that assho–'

They both heard the rumble of Michael C's engine turn over and Charon looked out the bedroom window to make sure he left. He watched him pull out fast; he'd exited so quickly he'd left the side garage door open.

'Good riddance. He wasn't even hung or anything,' Graham snorted. He laughed and then his face folded with pain from the movement.

'My God. Don't tell me. I don't want to know.' Charon

pulled the jeans off Graham, sticky and stiff with blood they didn't want to give but finally yielded. He had nothing underneath and no socks or shoes. His shirt had already been removed and welts had risen in angry pink and red streaks along his flanks and his back. His face was speckled--red and pink and blue and purple bleeding into each other along his jaw line like some exotic batik.

'Sorry. I know it was stupid. I didn't even like him. Rule number one of rough sex, you should like or severely dislike the person. You should trust them ...' He petered off, his voice wavering like had been drinking or was about to cry.

'Shut up and just let it go. You're human and you fucked up. It happens.' Charon turned on the shower and got it as hot as he could.

'Oh, look who's talking. The man who's still beating himself up over his long lost love. Must say, Charon, if he did that, he had issues to begin with. It takes some serious balls or some serious pain to take your own life. You have to have that in you to begin with. It just doesn't crop up because someone done you wrong like a country song.'

'Shut up and get in,' Charon said. He pressed his lips tight together and tried not to hear Graham.

'I can't. I'm tired. Everything hurts. I can't ...' He sagged on the toilet seat and put his hands over his eyes.

'Come on. You have to. We have to clean you up and see some of these wounds for real. Make sure they're OK. And ...'

'Look, if you want me in there, you'll have to put me in there. And fucking hold me up there,' Graham said. 'I'm so fucking tired I can't even focus my eyes.'

'You could have a concussion,' Charon said and pulled Graham to his feet. Graham pressed against him, his body warm and soft in spots. Hard and bony in others.

'Nope. I've had one. I'm fine. No real rocking blows to the head, just my pretty face. I'm just bone weary and beat to hell.'

'Get in.'

'Make me.'

Charon blew out a sigh. 'Really? You're still gonna be stubborn?'

'Yep.'

'Fine.' Charon picked him up a few inches off the floor and put him in the shower. Then he stepped in fully clothes and soaped a wash cloth. 'Now this is gonna hurt,' he warned.

Graham snorted, black humour twinkling in his eyes. 'That's what he said.'

'Christ. Hold still.'

Graham let him wash his face, the cuts on his shoulder, the welt marks. With all the water it took Charon a moment to realise that silent tears were rolling down Graham's face. 'I'm sorry. I'm not trying to hurt you.'

'Are you kidding? It's the best thing I've felt in a decade.'

Charon stopped. 'What do you mean?'

'Someone's taking care of me. There's nothing quite like it.'

That did him in. That broke him. Charon leaned in and kissed Graham's swollen lips. Graham winced and sucked in a breath, but parted his lips and touched his tongue to Charon's. Charon felt the heat of the kiss, the force of his want, in his cock, his heart, his belly. He held Graham close like he might break, as he was so broken already, and cuddled him. He kissed him just a bit harder and put his hands in that thick hair. The dark ringlets of black hair wound across his finger and felt so impossibly heavy and so amazingly light.

'Fuck me,' Graham whispered. He put Charon's hand on his hard cock and said 'Is there any doubt how much I want you?'

Charon allowed himself to wrap his fingers around Graham's erection. He let himself feel the solid velvet feel

86

of the pale skin and the smooth tip. He kissed Graham again and took his hand away. 'I will. In three days.'

'Three days!' Graham gasped, but he laughed.

'Three days.'

'Jesus. Talk about a dom. Fine, fine. What is three days?'

'We'll know it's us and not stress or lust or circumstances. No fucking for three days. That means me or any of your on demand, a la cart human toys either.'

'You sure are bossy for an employee,' Graham said.

'Sorry. Now turn around.'

'Oh, Daddy, why?'

'So I can wash your hair. My shoes are full of water and I have a hard-on I could chop wood with. We need to get out of here soon.'

'Then you'll feed me.'

'Whatever you want.'

'I think I love you,' Graham sighed and smiled. He presented Charon with his back. Charon didn't say a word because buried in their banter, he sensed a tiny grain of truth. A tiny seed he wouldn't mind nurturing, he realised.

It was the longest three days of Charon's life, but he did his best to pretend it wasn't. He did his best to ignore Graham when he walked through the living room in nothing but sweat pants, twirling a drumstick between nimble fingers. A pen tucked behind his ear, a pad in the other hand. The blue sweats the jutting knobs of his hipbones and Charon found himself wanting to press his lips to the fading blossoms of bruises along his jaw and on his body.

'Caught you looking,' Graham said and chuckled. He carried on to the living room and flopped on the sofa.

The next day it was faded jeans and a white T-shirt, a pinstriped charcoal grey vest from a vintage suit. He was singing to himself, whispering words in the gloomy light. The day was rainy and they were confined. Charon had offered a movie or a trip to the gourmet store, but Graham had begged off to write lyrics.

'Besides, you need to stay with me, I have a headache. It could be a head injury,' he said. His fingers, so talented on a guitar, were warm and gentle on Charon's knuckles as he traced each one and then slid the tip of his finger along each finger to its tip.

'You're lying,' Charon said, trying so hard to find his breath.

The split on Graham's lip was almost healed but when he smiled he still winced. He smiled anyway. 'Maybe, but you have to stay with me to be sure.'

Charon snorted.

'Plus, I haven't had a single joint in days, No pills. Just a few wines here and there and not even that many cigarettes. You need to watch me. I could go into withdrawal.'

'Dear God, you are a piece of work,' Charon said and barked out a short laugh. 'And I never asked you not to.'

'I know. I just don't need to is all. Not now. I had an epiphany.'

'What's that?'

'That I can't find what I'm looking for where I'm looking for it.' He touched each white fingernail on Charon's hands and Charon fought the urge to give in. After all, it was day two. What was a day and a half, give or take?

'Oh yeah?' He hated that his voice came out so challenged. Like he was fighting so hard to control it. But he was.

Graham turned his bottle green eyes to him and smiled, a big open smile that was somehow accented by the bruises and the marks. Charon had never seen him look more honest and direct and happy. 'Yeah. And I also figured that sometimes when you stop looking, something you've been searching for – like some great mythical creature – is dropped in your lap by fate.'

'Like what?' Charon asked, keeping his gaze pinned to Graham.

'A good man.' Graham dropped a kiss on Charon's shorn head and wandered out singing to himself all over again.

On a hunch, Charon called, 'What are you going to do when your contract is up?'

'I'm thinking a nice open solo career sounds good. Where I can be me. My real fans will follow me,' Graham said, popping his head through the door. Then he winked once and was gone, singing again.

Charon felt a burst of pride in his chest. Graham was thinking ahead and in a good way.

Day three dawned and Charon considered calling a truce. Simply saying they were done. Why force another full day? Why?

But he wanted to follow through. His urge to be with Graham had not faded, if anything it had increased. It seemed that way for Graham too. But Charon wanted to be sure. He wanted to be safe in the knowledge that it had not come from danger or the feeling of being rescued. No hero syndrome. No gratitude. He wanted attraction. And as he turned restlessly from one side to the other over and over again in his big empty bed, he let himself admit that he wanted another chance. Time had passed; he wanted a chance to be happy. He wanted a chance to let someone into his heart.

'Say love, Charon,' he said to himself but then he laughed. He was still shunning that word, even at his own request.

The door opened and a sleepy-eyed Graham peeked in. 'You awake?'

'I am. Listen, I know it's silly, one more day, but please give me the …'

'I didn't come to attack and maul you,' Graham said, pushing the door wide. 'I just brought coffee, is all. Jeesh, so suspicious.'

'Well, we have met. You were the swaggering, cocky, bossy brat when I arrived.'

Graham nodded. 'Still am, to a degree. I'll be the first to pout or shout or carry on when I don't get my way. But I also realised a lot of that was fear. And sadness. Funny, I don't feel so sad. Or angry. Getting the tar beat out of me changed things.'

'Well, it's a shitty way to learn a lesson,' Charon said, and took the cup Graham offered him. Black, one sugar, just as he liked it.

'True. But hey, sometimes the best stuff comes from the worst shit.'

'Still think I'm your ferryman through hell?' Charon asked.

Graham took his hand and squeezed it for an instant. He kissed the back of Charon's hand and let it go. 'My mother told me once that sometimes you have to go through hell to get to heaven. I've been hearing her say that in my head for oh ... about three days.'

'Gosh. Heaven? No pressure there.'

Graham grinned. 'None at all. You'd just better be the best lover ever.' But he threw his head back and exposed his long white throat, laughing. Charon felt his heart expand and for the first time let himself feel a bit of self-forgiveness for what he'd done. He was ready to let the past go.

Midnight. Midnight, midnight. Charon sat up, unable to sleep. What if Graham was sleeping? Did he really have so little willpower that he had to make it a midnight release, like a movie or a CD or the latest book craze.

'Yes, I have no willpower,' he said aloud.

'Good, I thought it was just me.'

Charon jumped when Graham entered. He hadn't seen the door swing open in the darkness and for old doors, they sure were oiled within an inch of their lives. They rarely ever made a noise when opened.

'You'll give me a fucking heart attack before we can ...'
He shook his head, his cock already hard at seeing Graham

standing there in his pyjama bottoms. Long black hair all unruly and sleep tossed.

'Fuck?'

'Yeah that.' Charon waved a hand at Graham. He sat on the edge of the bed, his feet on the chilly hardwood floor. They were sliding toward fall and it showed this far north in Maryland. He watched Graham move to him and thought he'd never seen anything more gorgeous to watch.

'I don't think this heart could have an attack. Soften a bit for me, maybe. Be a good daddy and not just boss me around in general, but in bed.'

Charon shook his head, suppressing a laugh. 'You're right. You are still a brat.' He slipped his fingers into the front of Graham's pyjama pants and took his cock in hand. It was hard already, as he knew it would be, and Charon swept his fingertips over the tip, making Graham jump and then sigh. 'I like the way you feel in my hand.'

'I like the way I feel in your hand too,' Graham said. His head fell forward and his pale face was blocked by a black wave of hair.

'Get down here. I want to kiss you.' Charon squeezed Graham's erection once and then released him.

Graham dropped to his knees and moved into the space between Charon's legs. He presented his face to be kissed and parted his lips when Charon probed him with a wet tongue. 'I think I might lose it if we don't …'

'Shh, patience is a virtue.'

'I'm not very virtuous.' Graham slipped his hand inside Charon's pyjama bottoms this time and it was his hand that found Charon's prick, hard and ready. It was the first time Graham had touched him and Charon felt like the floor was sliding away from him, like the world was tilting on its axis. When Graham wrestled his pants down and bent his head and pushed his lips to the head of his cock, Charon watched tiny little white lights appear in his vision. Then he remembered to breathe and sucked in a breath.

Graham ran his tongue over Charon. He licked his legs, his balls, his cock. He lapped and sucked until Charon had to bite his tongue to keep from weeping or babbling, maybe both. He was insane, he was drunk, he was drugged and losing his mind but in the best possible way. All from this man.

'Come up here. Before I come and ruin the whole fucking night.' When Graham stood, Charon yanked his pyjama pants down. His mouth found Graham in the near dark and he only gave him three teasing sucks before grabbing his arms and tipping him off balance. He had him on his belly then, yanking his hips high. The snap of the condom sounded like a shot gun in the dark and Graham squirmed, moving his long limbs like he was swimming.

'Hurry,' he said.

Charon lost track. It was just a chain of movements and sounds. His lips on Graham's flanks and his ass cheeks. Nibbling, licking, probing, moving. He laughed when he heard Graham laughing and said 'What's so funny?'

'I don't know. This is taking for ever it seems. I want you in me. But it also seems to be going all too … fast.'

'There'll be more. Tonight. Tomorrow. And after. If you don't push me away. If you let me stay.'

'If you don't run,' Graham countered.

'If we don't fuck it up,' Charon said. He slipped in, pushing fast for an instant so that Graham went taut under him and then he froze, buried deep, feeling the molten heat of his new lover around his cock. He reached under Graham, finding his dick and stroking him so that again, Graham wriggled like he was swimming in the sea. Charon pressed his lips to the back of Graham's neck, the thin body pinned under his bulk warm and supple and coveted.

'We won't fuck it up,' Graham said. 'We'll do it right.'

Charon was moving then, moving like he had no choice. Because he didn't. He had to move. He had to fuck. He had to be as close to Graham as he could get because the weight of those three days had crushed down on him now and he wanted to throw them off.

'Fuck. You made me wait too long. Too, too long.' Graham was laughing. The warm evidence of his release covered Charon's hand and he said 'Christ.'

That was it. He was done for. The secretive sighs and the silken feel of come on his hand. He pressed his hand to Graham's cock, providing more friction, unwilling to stop touching him as he came. His forehead pressed to Graham's warm hair that smelled of cinnamon and cedar.

'I made me wait too long, too,' he admitted.

They lay there, hearts banging and skin cooling. There was a silence that only came with satisfaction and affection. They moved without speaking and Charon rolled Graham in against him, making him the inside of the spoon. Graham pulled away for an instant, hanging over the bed. Charon had a moment where he feared he was going to get up and leave, but Graham sat up and handed him a coin. 'Here.'

'What's this? A penny?'

'It's my coin. I'm giving it to you for ferrying me through hell and helping me find something better.'

Charon fingered the shiny copper coin. The small amount of street light coming through the window illuminated one half of Graham's face making him look ethereal. 'That's not how the story goes,' Charon said.

'It can be our version,' Graham said and put his head on Charon's shoulder. 'Now put the money down because I'm ready for you again.'

'Brat,' Charon said, but he turned, kissed his young man.

'You know it, big boy,' Graham said with a dark little laugh. 'Now kiss me.'

Charon did.

REPORT FOR REPAIR

Chapter One

CHANCE BLEW OUT A sigh as the mechanical voice cooed to him, *'Please continue to hold ...'*

'Where else am I gonna go?' Chance growled.

'Here at Sunshine Gas and Electric your business is important to us. We have a staff of highly attentive operators at your disposal. Most waits are under two minutes ...'

Chance glanced at his watch. Six minutes had passed. As he waited, his bedroom was already starting to grow warm. He paced to the huge picture window that overlooked his backyard. Below, his nemesis had dropped another limb, once again successfully knocking out the power to his home as well as the rest of the block.

'I cannot fucking believe that assho–'

'Good morning, Sunshine Gas and Electric. This is Maria, may I please have your phone number starting with the area code?'

Chance recited it by rote. At this point he should ask for a direct line to his own personal highly attentive operator.

'And what's the problem this morning, Mr York?' Maria chirped. He could picture her all smiling and happy with pink lip-gloss and bright eyes. For some reason that image pissed him off.

'The tree behind me has dropped another limb,' he said, trying to keep his voice calm.

'I see. I'm sorry to hear that, Mr York.'

Chance ground his teeth together and pulled his T-shirt away from his chest. Already he was starting to sweat. 'Me, too, Maria.'

'I see by our records that this has happened before.'

'Three times.'

'And the house is still unoccupied?'

'Yes, that jackass has it up for sale. But he won't take down the tree.'

'I'm putting in a report, Mr York One of our employees should be there within the next three hours to reconnect your service.'

Chance blew out a sigh. Three hours. Three. Hours. It was August. It was ninety degrees at nine in the morning and the humidity was about a billion per cent. But three hours was better than four or five or more. 'Look, Maria, is there any chance they can send a cherry picker and a guy with a chainsaw to just lop the top of this damn thing off and call it a day? It would save us all a hell of a lot of time.'

'I do understand your frustration, Mr York, but that is not our responsibility. It's the homeowner's responsibility to have the tree removed.'

'I know. But that dip shi … sorry. That *person* is not in the house and really doesn't care if his decrepit dead tree keeps knocking out my air conditioning.'

Silence.

'I've put you at the top of the list, Mr York. You should have air conditioning within the hour. I hope that helps some.'

'I will take it, Maria. Thank you.'

'I wish I could do more, Mr York.'

'I'm sure we'll talk again,' he sighed. 'Unfortunately.'

Chance disconnected and went to make a pot of coffee. He could still boil water and he had his grandmother's old drip percolator in the china cabinet. It was something. He could pass the time until the tech arrived by watching his coffee drip slowly through the filter. The old fashioned way. 'Then I can eat beef jerky and hard tack for breakfast and pretend I'm a fucking cowboy.'

'Oh well *thank you*, Maria.' The man was tall and broad. He reminded Chance of a brick wall in Dickies. A bald, goatee-sporting brick wall. The tech's eyes were hidden behind black wraparound sunglasses. He shimmied up the utility pole like an ape man and Chance took a deep breath to stave off his lust.

It didn't take him long to reconnect the downed wires. MacGruder's dead-ass tree was basically hollow with dry-rot. But the limbs were heavy enough to knock down the small lines that fed power to the homes.

Chance held his breath, watching the man hover so high above earth to hook the wires up. Then the man held the pole with one hand, turned slightly and eyed the tree. He shook his head, lips pressed in a tight seam of disapproval.

'Yes, sexy, that tree is totally fucking dead,' Chance whispered.

The guy reached out with his free hand and swatted a small branch that promptly dropped to the backyard below. Like rotten fruit dropping to the ground, wood rained down and Chance shook his head. The pieces the tree dropped weren't necessarily heavy but they sure as shit wouldn't tickle if one fell on you.

He sipped his bitter almost cold coffee and when the man on the pole turned to eye him, Chance choked. It looked as if the guy was looking right at him. When the man tipped a finger salute and nodded to him, he knew he had.

'Damn damn damn.'

The guy pointed and held up his finger as if to say, 'Stay there. I'm coming.'

'Fuck,' Chance breathed.

Elvis sauntered in to see who his master was talking to. All 17 lbs of stout miniature dachshund waddled as he walked. 'That hunk of burning love is coming over here, Elvis,' Chance said.

Elvis snorted. He had sinus issues.

Chance's cell phone rang. 'Chance York.' He hadn't even read the display.

'I need you to... '

'I'll have to call you back, Rebecca. I can't right now.'

'But you are ...'

'I know. I know. I'm your personal assistant. That's what you pay me for. And you let me work from home. Blah, blah, blah ...' Lucky, he thought, that they were also friends.

Dead silence.

'Chance ...'

He could tell she was trying to keep her cool. Chance played the pity card. 'Look. That monstrous tree dropped another limb. I have no power and I have to go deal with the electric guy.'

'Oh. But Chance later can you just ...'

'Text me!' he yelled and hung up on her. The doorbell had just bing-bonged and his heart was going erratic in sympathy.

'Now we *deal* with the electric guy,' Chance said to Elvis. Elvis just snorted again. 'And I'll have to buy Becca a whole damn basket of Ruby's gluten free pecan muffins. To make it up to her.' His phone buzzed in his pocket and he knew it was the text he had requested, OK, *demanded*. He promised her, mentally, that he'd do her bidding cheerily for the rest of the week. Surely she'd forgive him.

The doorbell dinged again and Chance put a hand to his heart to still it. 'Mister Impatient,' he muttered, taking a deep breath. Then he tugged the door open to find tall, bald and surly standing there. And his heart promptly resumed its erratic state. 'Hi there.'

'Hello, sir. I've gotten your line reattached.' The guy stepped up onto the door sill and Chance took a step back instinctively.

'Thanks. It's really become a pain in the ass,' he blurted.

'May I?'

May he what? Chance thought for a moment and then he

nodded. 'Oh, of course. Come in Mr …'

'Todd.'

'Mr Todd. It's really hot out there.'

'No, it's just Todd.'

'Oh. Right. Todd. Can I get you a soda or some water?'

The guy looked torn which was comical, it was only a drink. Then again, Chance didn't know Sunshine Gas and Electric's policy on fraternizing with the clients. And what if he lost his mind and his manners and just kissed this guy? Begged him to do things he knew, just by looking at him, that he could do. What was the policy on that?

'I'd love a soda if you have one.'

'I have a ton. Come on in. This is Elvis.'

The fat wiener dog yawned and lay his head down on the hardwood floor. He looked very unimpressed. Elvis was the Zen-like calm to Chance's fidgety nerves.

'Elvis,' Todd said and followed Chance into the kitchen, his work boots leaving fine bits of grit on the floor. Somehow that grit was sexy, at least Chance thought so. Chance poured him a soda with extra ice and handed it over. He watched transfixed as Todd's throat bobbed once, twice, three times and the soda was gone. It begged the question what else could that mouth and throat do?

Chance cleared his throat, blushing like a whore in church. 'That tree is a nightmare. And I know you can't do anything about it legally, but my God, I'm ready to go over there with an axe and just start doing my Paul Bunyan routine.'

Todd's stern face broke into a crooked grin and Chance felt his heart turn over in his chest. He also felt his cock spring to life in his pants. He started running through his list of errands and chores for Becca. No use embarrassing himself in front of the help by getting a raging hard-on over a smile. Big bald Daddy was probably straight or taken or just not interested in the likes of skinny, pale, blond Chance.

'I'd like to see that. If you crack and go all caveman on

101

it, let me know.'

Chance saw his opportunity and said, 'And how would I do that? Call SGE and report myself as a crazed neighbour with an axe.'

Todd fished in his coveralls and pulled out a business card. 'You could. Or you could just call me and save yourself some time.'

Chance's cock became more demanding. Jesus. This man up close was a dream. Big, imposing and bald as Mr Clean. He smelled like summer air and hot tar and man. He smelled like fantasy sex and salty kisses and carnival rides. Chance had to force himself to stop sniffing. Even Elvis was staring at him. Their fingers brushed for an instant and his skin tingled with mild electric zings and pops.

'I could do that.'

'Good. Now about that tree.'

'What about it?'

'Well, it's dangerous, but not so dangerous.'

'What the hell does that mean?' Chance stared out at the towering oak. Once majestic and gorgeous now it was dry and gnarled and ugly. A tree from a Halloween movie or a horror flick.

'It means it's dead. So it is definitely a bad thing. But the limbs it's dropping *currently* are pretty dry rotted and eaten out by bugs. They weigh nothing. I was tossing them like kindling. Now I did break a rule ...' Todd broke off and stared at the toe of his work boot.

Somehow the small boy gesture made Chance that much more smitten. 'How so?'

'I tied the one really treacherous branch to the asshole's chimney.'

Chance blinked and snorted out laughter. 'You did what? Why?'

'Because he has to know how dangerous that thing is and I guess since he isn't living there to deal with it, it's no big deal. It could really do some damage, that big one. So if it does some serious damage, it'll do some serous damage for him.'

'Gosh,' Chance said, cringing at his goofy school boy choice of words. 'I hope you don't get in trouble.'

Todd took a sudden step in, crowding Chance. Chance liked it. His heart raced and his hands shook just enough to give him a jolt of want and arousal. '*Gosh*, we're told to secure locations like that to the best of our ability. If the homeowner isn't living up to his responsibility, we aren't required to remove the tree but we can secure it, cut it, top it even.'

Chance swallowed hard. At the word *top* he had a vivid pornographic mental flash of this big, bald man tying him to a bed and spanking him until he babbled. Then fucking him slow and sweet until he wept with his release. He shook his head. 'Top?'

'Chop the top right off. But that's extremely rare that they let us do that and even if I could, I don't have a crew today. Plus, I'm hoping jack wipe, over there, will man up and take responsibility.'

Chance snorted again. 'You clearly have never met Mr MacGruder. He'd eat his own toenails before he'd pay for something he could get someone else to pay for on his behalf.'

'We'll see. But I wanted you to know because the main branch. The big one that has heft is angled so that it's most likely, barring a huge windy storm, going to come down on your fence out there.'

Chance watched Todd's lips move. Heard how he said *bigun* instead of big one. Watched how his sunburned skin crinkled in certain spots when he smiled. And he almost leaned in and kissed him. But Todd leaned in fast and surprised him so much he gasped like a girl on a soap opera. His cheeks flooded with colour again and he bit his lip.

'OK,' was the only thing he could think to say.

'I'm telling you so that you can get help if you need it.

And so you don't go too near that thing or, perish the thought, stand under it. This is thunderstorm season. It could drop chunks at any time.

He'd moved his weathered face in closer until Chance felt sure he might have a heart attack. 'OK,' he said again.

Todd flipped his sunglasses up on his head and his eyes were startling blue. Cool and nearly translucent like water. 'Good. I'd hate to see you get hurt, pretty boy.'

'Pretty boy?' he stammered. Chance considered himself a lot of things, pretty wasn't one.

'Yeah, to me you are. You look like getting clocked with a branch might dent you. Break you even.'

There it was – another pornographic flash of being whipped. His body bowing under his new lover. His face a contortion of pain and pleasure. And then the mounting from behind. Fucking like animals. Kissing and sucking and biting and … 'I doubt it,' he said, trying to sound brave and strong.

'I don't doubt it,' Todd said and pushed a finger to his bottom lip. Chance stilled, tried to breathe. 'I'd kiss you but you could sue me,' Todd said and turned on his work boots and crossed the room in three big strides.

He turned, Chance still staring, moving slow, dumbfounded. 'Remember, Pretty Boy. Just call to report for repair.'

He shut the door when he left, his boots banging across the cracked concrete front porch.

'Aren't you going to ask me out? Kiss me? Do fucking something about this?' Chance touched a finger to his hard cock. But no one was there to hear him.

Chapter Two

'SO NOW THE ONLY way I'm gong to see him again is if another chunk falls off that fucking tree!' Chance barked at Becca.

'You'll see him,' she sighed. 'Now, personal assistant, are you going to fucking assist me or what?'

'What do you need?' Chance tried to sound interested but all he could see in his mind's eye was Todd's gruff face pushing so, so close to his but not delivering the desired kiss. He could still feel his warm fingertip on his lip. Chance could still smell the other man in his house. He was a big, bald sexy phantom haunting his humble cottage.

Elvis snored loudly as he dozed and Chance touched him with the tip of his tennis shoe. 'Hey, you lazy bum. You didn't do much to help me flirt, you know.'

Elvis opened his eyes, appeared to roll them, and then yawned widely.

'I need you to call and schedule my hair, my eye appointment and my gynaecologist appointment.'

'Eew.'

'Are you going to work for me or not, damn it!'

'Fine, you do not need to yell.' Chance took the details of what she needed. 'Got it.'

'And I need you to pick up that paint I ordered for the kitchen and ...'

'I so do not paint,' he said.

'I have seen your attempt at painting, Chance. Don't worry. I'd never ask.'

'Good.'

'Then wine for the dinner party, dry cleaning, grab what's in my post office box and you are done for the day. Free to daydream over the burly, bald SGE man. And take matters into your own hands ... heh.'

'I would never stoop to that,' he said. He was lying. Chance knew it, Becca knew it. He was, as she put it PH – perpetually horny –masturbation for Chance was about as earth-shattering as putting salt on his fries.

'Riiiiiight. You would never ever feature Todd the Gas and Electric guy in your dirty fantasies.'

'Never.'

'Ever,' she laughed.

'True story. Now let me go and do all your bidding, you wicked witch so I can come home and jack off and figure out how to ask him out. Or better yet, how to get him to ask me out. And speaking of ... why *didn't* he ask me out?'

'He's playing with you,' Becca said, and laughed. 'I like him already.'

'Damn.'

Chance hung up and made his friend's appointments, making sure to stop daydreaming long enough to mark the dates of her appointments in her online calendar and send her an update. Then he grabbed Elvis under one arm and kissed his greying dark head. 'I've got errands. I'll be back. You hold down the fort, you're in charge.'

Elvis looked thrilled.

When he got home after dropping off paint, wine, mail and dry cleaning to Becca's apartment he found Elvis, lying on the cool tile foyer floor. Because the power was out. Again.

'Motherfucker!'

Elvis looked up and grunted. Chance immediately said, 'Not you, buddy.' Anger flared making his upper lip break out with a fine sheen of sweat. But then he remembered Todd's card and his belly buzzed with excitement and his cheeks flushed with anticipation. He felt them, hot circles of blood standing out for all the world to see. His facial equivalent of a raging hard-on. There was no hiding it.

He dialled the number on Todd's card and waited, feeling nervous and light-headed as it rang. 'This is Todd.'

'Todd? Yeah, um, this is Chance? Chance York. You were just here a bit ago because of my neighbour's...'

'Did you go all Paul Bunyan on its ass?'

Chance grinned like an idiot. Todd remembered! He remembered it all. 'No. God damn, I wish. This, sadly, is just another drop of another branch. So I assume. All I know is I got back and my dog is lying here in the foyer where he never ever hangs out. But it's cool. And there's no AC running, no lights, no computer. No friggin' nothing,' he finished.

'I'll type it in as an emergency repair and be there as soon as I wrap up this new transformer.'

'Thank you.'

'You sure you didn't tamper with that tree, boy?'

Chance shivered when he said "boy". 'Nope. Not me.'

'Is the chimney still intact?'

'Hold up, I'll check.' Chance ran into the kitchen where he had the best view of the chimney. 'Still fine.'

'Damn it.' Todd hung up.

Now all he had to do was wait for him. No problem. Wait patiently. Not be horny. Not even give it a second thought. That he'd be here, again. Alone with him. Hanging on a giant pole, risking life and limb, playing with electric wires. Dangerous, dangerous, tedious work ...

Chance nearly broke his neck racing to his room. 'OK, just this one time. So I'm not all skittish and nervous and manic.'

He took himself in hand, stroking his cock softly at first but going firmer almost instantly. He held the image of Todd, feet positioned on those pinions on the pole, in his mind. He saw him in his coveralls and his boots, his shorn head shiny in the midday sun. His water-blue eyes hidden by those wraparound, bad-ass shades. His cock ready for Chance, or so Chance imagined.

'Mercy,' he sighed, his fist slipping up and down, up and down so that he heard the rasp of skin on skin. He felt the crawling, heated weight of orgasm low in his belly. Gritted his teeth, shook his head, remembered the hot feel of Todd's lips so close to his and then the way he backed off and left him wanting more.

His brain, bored with just how good looking Todd was, switched it up to Todd hovering over him, pushing Chance's legs wide, leaning between his parted thighs their cocks brushing with maddening friction. Then Todd planted a kiss on Chance's waiting lips, stood – tall and burly, naked in this daydream – and plunged his cock deep. Chance rocked under him, begging him, his hand warring with Todd's hand to be on his eager cock. Then Todd stayed seated deep and bent, impossibly limber, and sucked the tip of Chance's cock until he cried out and came in a long gush of release.

'God, in my head he's Gumby. Biker Gumby,' Chance laughed, coming hard to keep time with his fantasy. Then the doorbell bonged and he yelped sharply.

Downstairs Elvis gave one bored woof and then silence.

The SGE man was here. Todd was here.

'Here I am,' Todd said and grinned.

Chance had never been so grateful for having jacked off in his life. If he hadn't, he would have been managing an erection he could have done sword battle with. 'Here you are. Is it up?'

Todd's eyes drifted low and he grinned wider, his smile very much a predatory leer. 'Don't know. Is it? We can work on that if you …'

'God, I meant the line.' Chance blushed hotly and felt stupid for it. 'The line, is the line up?' But then he glanced around and saw that his computer light was still off, his AC wasn't running and the digital clock on his cable box was dark.

'Not yet. I wanted to let you know that I'll be over there. And then I'll be back to get your feedback on your service.'

'Pardon?'

'We have these things we need to ask people to fill out now. You rate your service. You tell them how you like me.' The big man chuckled and leaned into the crack in the doorway. Instead of shutting the door, Chance pulled it wider, wanting to allow more of Todd into his home.

'Oh,' he said. His mouth was about two inches from the pink lips of a man he very much wanted to kiss. Not just kiss. Kiss hard and then maul like a grizzly in heat.

'So … how do you like me?'

It occurred to him to say *naked* but instead Chance said, 'Just fine, thanks. I like you very much.'

'Yeah?'

'Yes.'

'I'll be back. You can prove it.' Then he turned and all Chance could see was broad worker-man back. All Chance could hear was his own heartbeat.

He rushed into the kitchen and parted the white curtains to watch Todd mount the pole. Then he laughed to himself. 'Mount the pole, Jesus, Chance. You are such a pervert.'

He was near the top with the electric line looped over his shoulder like a thin black snake. It was a damn good thing, Chance realised, that the stupid wire had a lot of give. From his kitchen perch he could just make out the gnarled tip of the tree branch that had fallen since Todd left this morning. No thicker than his arm, it looked like it was reaching for *his* repairman with haunted, gaunt fingers.

'My repairman,' he said on a sigh.

He watched Todd's big arms flex as he looped the line around its securing hook. Then he watched, nearly salivating, as the big man reached out with one long arm and knocked down a few dead limbs that hung there like wooden

109

icicles. They hit the ground with a soundless clatter since the windows were shut and at that moment the air conditioner jumped back to life.

'Nice,' he said. 'I give you five stars.'

It was only a few moments later that the doorbell rang again. This time, Elvis didn't even bother to bark.

Chance counted his steps to the front door so he wouldn't appear too eager. One hot workman, two hot workmen, three hot workmen ... four. When he opened the door, fully prepared for the man on the other side, his blood leaped anyway. 'Wow, that was fast. Thank you, thank you. It gets hot in here fast,' he said and then felt his cheeks grow red again. He had to get a handle on this blushing thing.

'I bet. OK, I'm done. I just need you to ...'

'Come on in. Out of the sun. You're sweaty,' Chance said, and heard the lust in his final word himself.

Todd smiled, but it was only half a smile. An ornery kind of smile that twisted Chance's stomach into nervous knots and made his cock forget that he'd already gotten off today.

'Very,' Todd said. 'But I have to bolt. I have an affair to get to.'

'Lucky guy.' Chance meant to say it in his head but somehow it popped out of his mouth, too.

'More like "lucky nephew". I am speaking to a very bored, very energetic group of second graders in about an hour. Career day.' This time when he smiled it was lovely and heart warming and Chance felt his heart expand in his chest.

'Wow. I doubt they will be bored.'

'Hope not.' Todd pushed his sunglasses back and there were those water-blue eyes again. 'Now – about how you like me.'

Naked

'Right. I'll get you something cold and you pull it out.'

Todd chuckled.

'The paperwork. I'll be right back.'

Elvis pranced after him. Usually a trip to the kitchen meant food. He wasn't very happy when he found his master pouring a cold glass of tea for the new person. 'Soon, I promise, buddy.'

Elvis didn't look convinced.

'Here we go. Nice and cold since you're so hot.' He heard himself two beats later again and froze. 'My God. I can't seem to say anything clean around you at all,' he said and sighed.

Todd took the glass, running jut the tip of his finger along Chance's finger so his skin sang with the touch. 'I'll take it as a compliment,' he said and again downed his drink in three easy gulps. 'Here you are.'

Chance barely looked at the form. He ran down the list giving his new crush all five stars. Then he put 'Super fast and great service!' In the comments section and handed the yellow and white slip back.

'Wow, a clean sweep. Thanks. Glad you liked me so much.'

Todd leaned in close and Chance's lips shivered with excitement. 'You're welcome,' Chance managed.

'Again, I'd kiss you but you could …'

Chance grabbed a hold of the big tan face and yanked Todd forward. He heard the other man's heavy boots clomp on the hardwood floor as he tugged him off balance. He pushed his lips to Todd's warm lips and kissed him hard. Their tongues darted out to dance against each other and Chance tasted the cold, sweet tang of tea on Todd's lips. 'I know. I could sue you. You could sue me. But I'll risk it,' he mumbled and kissed harder, forcing himself to forget that he'd been the aggressor. Not the norm for him.

Todd's hands found his waist and he hauled Chance forward so that they were hip to hip, pelvis to pelvis, cock to cock. And both were hard. Then he pushed Chance back again and said, 'I have to go. I can't disappoint Tyler, but call me. Since you like me so much.'

'But I …' How do you say you are used to being pursued, not the pursuer? And was Becca right? Was Todd fucking with him?

'You have my card still – right?' Todd traced one callused finger along Chance's jaw and Chance felt his body erupt in goose bumps.

'I do.'

'Then use it when you're ready.'

Chapter Three

'JUST CALLED TO SAY thanks, baby cakes! You did a great job. And to see if you've heard from your uber manly man yet.'

'He came back. And climbed a pole,' Chance sighed, sinking down on the front porch glider. Elvis was still giving him the stink eye for not forking over a treat.

'Was it yours?'

'Har har.'

'You mean it wasn't yours and you had to watch! Of all the ner ...'

'Becca!'

'What – more tree fell down?'

'Yes.'

'*And?*'

'And then he came in and I gave him a drink like last time and he teased me about kissing me and me suing and ...'

'And!'

'And I kissed him.'

'Ooooh, you went all alpha male, Chance. Good for you.'

'It felt weird.'

'I bet.'

'What is that supposed to mean?' he barked.

'You are a bit of a princess,' she said.

'Jesus.'

'It'll be good for you. Get the old blood going. What did he say?'

'To call if I wanted. I had the number.'

'Are you going to call him?'

'I don't know.' Chance blew out a breath. 'You know me.'

'Yep, princess.'

'Shurt it,' he growled.

'Call him,' she said.

'But why? Why is he torturing me?'

'He's fucking with you. Pushing you. I like him, I told you.'

'Because you are a sadist.'

'Maybe he is, too,' Becca laughed.

'Oh. My. God.' Chance hung up to the sound of her laughter.

Three times. He'd masturbated three times and still couldn't shake the idea of Todd from his head. The sun was down and a thunderstorm had blown in, fast and hard. Chance watched his arch nemesis, the tree, sway and dance and dip in the wind. For the first time ever he stood there praying for it to drop a limb. Maybe the big one. Maybe the one that would tug down part of the chimney too. Then he could not only call Todd with a good excuse, but he could also be the bearer of good news that his plan had worked.

Instead the fucking tree decided that would be the perfect time to not drop a limb. Not even a twig.

'I swear it knows I want it to drop something,' he told Elvis. Elvis rolled his eyes.

'I'll never be able to sleep thinking about him. No one's gotten in my head this way for a very long time. Like *ever*,' he admitted.

Elvis snorted like a pig and wagged his tail once.

'I really need to get some friends since I seem to bore you,' Chance said.

Elvis yawed.

He tried watching a mindless movie on demand. Some

shoot 'em up flick full of ripply beefy men who blew things up and tossed out catchy one-liners. After ten o'clock, he was tired but wired. A horrible, horrible combination.

You tell them how you like me. He heard it in his head and said to the dog, 'Naked. I like him naked. I mean, I assume I do ...'

He dozed off on the sofa and woke to pounding rain and lightning. The power flickered off and on and he rushed to the window to see if the tree had dropped any of its limbs. Nothing.

It was midnight before the thunderstorm passed. Chance cradled a micro brew and nursed it. When it became clear that a) the tree was stable for the time being and b) his reoccurring hard-on wasn't going anywhere any time soon, he made a decision. He set his alarm for five and rolled over to try and sleep.

Sleep he did. Of course his dreams were riddled with nasty naughty hot dreams of a certain SGE worker and he woke up with his hand shoved in his pants getting himself off, but that was a minor detail.

'Elvis, stay here. This is dangerous work.' He gathered his painting ladder, a construction helmet from a previous job and the limb cutters his uncle Jerry had given him as a housewarming gift (and he had scoffed at, for the record). Thank God the previous neighbour had put a connecting door in the fence that separated MacGruder's yard from his. Whoever owned the home before MacGruder had been friends with the Tomlins who'd owned his home previously.

'Here we go. One gas and electric man coming right up.' Chance got to the third step on his painting ladder and it wobbled a bit in the wet yard. Two legs had started to sink and two hadn't. Mud squelched up around the rubber stick-grip feet. 'Just one good whack and ...'

He took a swipe at a medium-sized limb with his cutters and the whole ladder trembled a bit. At about five feet long, the cutter sported a sharp metal jaw on the business end for grabbing and lopping off small and medium branches from the ground. He didn't want to cut them, though. That would be obvious. He wanted to knock them down as if the storm had done it.

'Fuuuu-uuuck,' Chance said. 'Why can't you be normal, asshole, and just call and ask the man out.' He took another swing. 'Grow some balls!' Another swing.

Birds tweeted in the early morning air and the sky was just starting to turn that lavender colour he liked. 'Be a man!' Chance chided himself and finally connected with the tip of a smaller branch. A dry cracking sound hit his ears even as he tumbled off the ladder and he smiled. And yet the damn limb stayed on.

'Oh my God. Why?' He gasped. For weeks now the oak had dropped limbs if a butterfly flew by. Now he was playing the world's most demented game of whack the piñata and nothing.

He lay there watching the sun streak the lavender sky with blue and then shots of gold. Chance sighed, trying to regroup with a new game plan when the branch gave way with a snap, it snagged the trim black electric line on its way down and tossed it to the middle of the yard. Then it came down on his shin. It was heavier than it looked.

'Motherfucker,' he growled, but grinned anyway. Then he limped home, dragging his ladder and his limb trimmer with him.

'Don't even,' he said to the dog and plopped on the sofa, dropping an ice pack he kept in the freezer on the growing knot on his shin. 'I have succeeded. No matter how many war wounds I might have.'

The dog grunted, wagged once, waited for food and went back to sleep when he got none.

On top of the growing knot on his leg, Chance had a huge scratch up his arm from the fingers of the branch and one on his cheek. He had a knot on the back of his head where he'd collapsed and the helmet had hit his head. 'Who gets injured

116

by a hard hat for fuck's sake?' But he grinned again like a madman and dialled the phone number on the card he clutched. Chance ran his fingertips over the raised words "Todd Lewis".

A sleepy voice said, 'This is Todd. What is it? It better be good.'

Chance's voice deserted him but flashes of his dirty wet dreams came rushing down on him like a mental rain of smut. 'Um … hi, this is …'

'I know who this is. Did it drop another one?' He sounded more awake now and Chance pictured him all yummy and hot and naked in a bed full of tousled sheets and overstuffed pillows. Morning sunshine shooting through the window and glistening on his muscles. Did he have a tattoo? Where was it? What did it say? What did it mean? Would he let Chance kiss it?

Chance jumped when Todd said, 'Hellooooo? You there?'

'Yes. Another limb is down and the power is out.' There he hadn't lied. He didn't say another one fell. He said another one was down.

'You weren't out there going all Paul Bunyan were you?' Chance heard the sheets rustle on the other end as the object of his desire sat up in his warm, mussed bed.

'Nope. No axe,' Chance said. There. Again, he hadn't lied. He was getting good at that.

'I'll be there in about twenty,' Todd rasped, his voice still a bit sleepy. 'Be ready for me.' Then he chuckled once and hung up.

What did that mean?

Chance scurried up to take a shower. It would be cold without power, but so be it. A cold shower might be exactly what he needed.

He hadn't even put on his uniform and Chance did a double take. In a short sleeved plain white T-shirt, faded jeans and

117

work boots, the man looked sexier than he had in his work coveralls if that was possible.

'It's up.'

'Is it now,' Chance said, but again his cheeks flared hot. He had to get better at banter. 'Come on in. Coffee?'

'Magic word. Right up there with food and sex.'

'Well, I can offer you food.'

'And?' Todd turned fast in the short, thin hallway, his water-blue gaze pinning Chance.

Chance swallowed hard. He had the urge to blurt the truth. Instead he said. 'And I … um …'

Todd took a step in, crowding him to the wall, pinning him in. When he spoke his lips hovered over Chance's. He could feel Todd's warm breath and smell toothpaste on his mouth. 'Don't you want to offer me sex?' He grinned.

'I …'

His big hands clamped down on Chance's biceps and he held him there physically. Pinned him to the wall and pushed his back to the louvered door of the coat closet. When Todd's lips touched his Chance felt his body go limp like he might faint. He'd never felt more boneless but for a particularly nasty bout with the flu. He stood there, perfectly powerless and opened his lips to let Todd's tongue bully his. The kiss deepened and the bigger man stepped in even further, his chest and belly pressed to Chance's as the slats of the closet door pressed his back.

'Don't you?' Todd asked again.

'I do, actually. But that is so slutty,' Chance said, accepting soft baby kisses that made his skin tingle and his nipples go hard. His skin buzzed and thrummed and all the small hairs under his hairline rose up in a wave.

'It's the damndest thing,' Todd said, his fingers caressing the hard ridge of Chance's cock. Chance didn't let himself think, he pushed his hips forward to place his hard-on more firmly in Todd's capable hands.

'What is? What is?' he chanted.

'That branch looked like it has been whacked down. The splintering was all wrong.'

Chance stilled and Todd laughed against his mouth, the rumble working through his lips and his throat and chest. 'Really? How odd.'

'Really odd.' Todd pulled the top button of Chance's jeans and yanked. The whole row proceeded to pop one after another in capitulation to the newcomer's strength. 'You know what was more odd?'

When Todd's hand slipped inside Chance's jeans and boxers his breath disappeared. Chance tried hard to draw a deep breath and failed. He felt like a fish out of water, gasping and begging for more air. 'What? Dear Christ, what?'

Todd's hand started a slow but persistent rhythm on Chance's cock and Chance groaned like he was dying. He thought maybe he was dying. But what a fucking way to go.

'What's even more odd is the guy next door to that house who saw, and I quote, "*that loony who lives behind me out in the backyard in a hard hat hitting limbs with a stick*".'

'It was a tree pruner,' Chance corrected as Todd relieved him of his pants. 'And it's your fault.'

'How so?' Todd now tugged. He tugged him from the hallway into the kitchen and leaned him back against the giant butcher's block that was Chances' pride and joy.

'You could have just asked me out like a normal person.'

'And miss all the fun?'

'I …' But Chance had nothing good to say so he tugged at Todd, yanking at his T-shirt where he normally would have tugged at hair. He kissed him, arching up to try and come in contact with the man in all his entirety.

'Condoms? Grease?'

'Grease?'

He laughed. 'Lube. Something to make us all slippery and dirty and …'

'What makes you think I'm going to fuck you?' Chance

119

asked.

'You have no pants on.'

'And.'

Todd cocked his head and frowned. 'Bend over.'

Chance caved then. He pointed to a drawer and said 'There's a travel kit in there. It's all inside.'

'Don't move.'

Chance listened to Todd scrounging through the drawers. He felt the cool kiss of fingers to his opening and the warm kiss of lips to the back of his neck. 'No preamble?' He laughed, though, because truth be told he needed no preamble. He wanted Todd to take him as he imagined Todd took men. Hard and fast and frightfully good.

'Do you need some wine and maybe a cigarette?'

'No,' he breathed.

Todd's zipper growled and Chance turned his head to watch. The big man shucked his jeans and tugged his boxer briefs down revealing a spectacular erection. 'Do you need me to woo you?' Todd asked, rolling on a condom. He slipped one callused hand along his length and winked at Chance.

'No.'

Todd pinned him with a stark gaze. 'Do you need me to fuck you so your knees give out?'

Chance's mouth went dry, but he nodded. Here in the early light, in his pretty kitchen, with the pole-climbing behemoth, all he could do was nod dumbly.

'Good boy,' Todd said and dropped another wink before taking a big hand and pressing Chance's back until he bent over the rough wood butcher's block with his hands splayed like he was under arrest.

Todd squeezed his ass cheeks and Chance snickered, he couldn't help it. But then a loud smack filled the small kitchen and a split second later a line of pain danced over his buttocks. 'Don't laugh. You've got a sweet ass. Perfect for spanking,' Todd said.

120

Chance laughed again, sure he was joking, but instead he swallowed his chuckle because Todd smacked the other cheek harder than the first. Heat seared up his ass and down his flank. 'You're not kidding?' he gasped.

Todd delivered four more blows and Chance found himself pressing his cock to the hard edge of the butcher's block to gain friction. His pulse was trip hammering and his ears rang.

'Fuck no, I'm not kidding.' Three more slaps and the pain sang, hot and white through Chance but when Todd reached around him and grasped his cock, working him with a firm slippery fist, he thought he'd come right there. Or die.

'I see that. I've never been spanked. Tied up, yes. Spanked, no.'

'Is that so?' Todd said against the back of his neck and his skin tingled so much he shivered.

'Yeah.'

'How about whipping?' Todd asked Chance, circling his hole with the tip of his cock.

Chance shook his head, holding his breath, waiting for the invasion of heat and flesh. Instead, Todd circled some more, the lube making his gentle ministrations slick and maddening.

Todd shook his head, gripping the wood, begging in his head for Todd to slide into him and fuck him senseless. He managed a soft, 'No'.

'Caning, flogging, paddling?' Todd teased. He entered Chance, just the tip, just enough to send Chance's poor body into a flurry and an uproar.

'No, no, no.'

'We can fix that. Soon, if you behave,' Todd said, and gave Chance a smack and on his gasp, he slid home, entering with a rough thrust that made Chance gasp a second time. Todd's hand worked his cock and Chance held on for dear life as the bigger man rocked against him.

'Yes, please fix that,' he babbled. He moved back to

meet Todd's thrust, feeling the heated swirl of pleasure roll through his belly. His fingers shook with his nerves and arousal and he wished he could kiss Todd. Instead, he laid himself flat like a human banquet for Todd to enjoy. He sprawled his fingers on the oversized wooden block and heard Todd grunt.

'Damn, you look so fucking perfect like that. So vulnerable and ripe for the picking,' Todd said.

'I am ripe for the picking.'

'Let's check your stem,' came the gruff voice and then a laugh as he reached under and squeezed Chance's dick so hard Chance saw spots, but when he released him, the pleasure rolled over him fast. He felt hot and flushed and so ready to come he could weep.

'My stem is ready.'

'Christ, you're pretty. I'm glad you decided to assault that tree.'

'I would nev–'

'Save it.'

'Yes, sir,' Chance managed as he lost his battle and started to jerk under Todd. The orgasm slammed him as surely as the tree limb had slammed his leg and he blew out a gust of air.

'Fuck. You had to say sir?' Todd growled and his fingers bit into Chance's flanks, pressing white crescents in the flesh and anchoring him tight. He came with a final buck and a huge sigh and then his forehead was pressed to Chance's slim back.

Chance felt a kiss dropped there, just a warm flicker of lips on his spine and then Todd was pulling free of him. He turned fast, feeling anxious and clingy but worried too that if he didn't speak. 'I … wow.'

Todd dropped the tied-off condom in the trash. 'Wow, indeed.' Somewhere in his jeans a beeper sounded. 'Gotta get that.'

Chance eyed his muscular legs, trim waist, the bruise on

his right knee and the scar on Todd's left thigh. His body was a roadmap of years and stories and time. Chance wanted to hear every story. Know about each battle wound and each blemish.

'Gotta go. There's a big ass maple down on Kittredge Road. They need a bunch of us.' He hauled Chance forward brusquely and kissed him hard. 'Thanks for the morning pick me up. Don't go getting a concussion out there, OK? You get hit on the head, even by a little one and you're toast.'

'Remember my hard hat?' Chance sighed. He sought another kiss and was rewarded with a hard press of soft lips to his, teeth clacking his, a tongue bullying his tongue until he felt his cock stir again.

'How could I forget?' Todd laughed. He offered one more kiss, put his jeans on and smacked Chance on the ass. Hard.

This is it, Chance thought. This is where he asks me out.

'Call me if you need anything or to report for repair,' Todd said and left Chance gaping like a fish once again.

The front door snicked shut, the dog looked up and Chance said, 'Son of a bitch.'

Elvis went back to sleep.

Chapter Four

'YOU JUST NEED TO chill out. You're all torqued up after Allen and you can't be that way. This guy isn't Allen. They all aren't Allen. He convinced you that you couldn't do anything, so now you believe it. I think it's good that you have to be the pursuer guy. I think you need that.'

'I hate it.'

'You can do it,' Becca sighed. 'What are you doing for me today?' she asked. She was pregnant, recently married and running her own skin care line. Busy didn't begin to cover Becca.

'I don't think so.'

'Honey, when we were in college you used to pick up men left and right. You barely had to speak to them. You were a pro. Now look at you, convinced you can't pick up a guy who's already been there, made himself clear that he wants you *and* banged you? What do you want, an engraved invitation?'

'Maybe.'

'Are you looking for a more permanent job?'

'I like what I'm doing for you. I'm good at it, too. Aren't I?'

'Yep. Usually. Unless you're thinking with little Chance and are all preoccupied.'

'Har, har.'

'But yes, love, you normally are the bomb. I think you should have like three high end clients and be their bitch and run yourself ragged and charge mad fees.'

'Done and done. I am a good organiser type person,' he said.

'You are. Now go back to your mental space from college and get that man to kneel before you and beg you for your favours.'

'I think with this guy it works the other way around,' Chance said, brushing back the curtain and eyeing the tree. He switched the phone to the other ear and then poured the last of the coffee left in the pot.

'You mean he wants *you* to kneel?'

Chance heard the deep murmur of Becca's husband, Shawn, in the background. He worked with his new wife running the promotions end of her line. He still did some of his accountant work, but mostly freelance and only during tax season.

'Pretty much. I'm sure Shawn loves hearing this.'

'He asked that I let him leave the room before he was struck deaf,' Becca snorted.

'Gee, thanks.'

'It's not you. He doesn't like to hear dirty details about anyone. Now back to your whip cracker.'

'Seriously. He's a top, babe.'

'Does that bother you?' she asked.

'Nope. Sweetie, you know damn well when it comes to the bedroom I am a total bottom.'

'A bottom with a great bottom,' she giggled.

'Christ, now you sound like him.'

'Told you I liked him,' Becca said. 'Now will you call him?'

'Any bad weather due today?'

'Maybe late this afternoon,' she said.

'We'll see then,' Chance said and hung up. Then he proceeded to do Becca's grocery shopping, stop by her apartment, put it all away, leave her a whole bundle of real estate and vacation brochures she'd asked for. He also walked Nips her cat because Becca was a lunatic who

125

walked her fat, old cat on a leash around the block. Then he fed all the birds she insisted on feeding.

'Good thing her business is booming,' he told Nips. 'I'm so efficient, I'm going to cost her a fortune.'

Nips did a good Elvis impression by shutting his eyes and going to sleep.

His phone rang again as he was leaving. 'Chance,' he said, hopeful because he didn't recognise the number.

'This is Becca.'

'Oh.'

'Sorr-eeee.'

'I thought it might be him. Foreign number.'

'Ah, it's Shawn's phone. Sorry, babe. But I did call with good news.'

'Oh yeah? What's that?'

'Severe thunderstorms tonight,' she said.

Chance laughed but in the pit of his stomach something tingled. He heard Todd say to him, *Bend over.* Remembered that perfect sublime moment when he came and the burly repairman followed suit. God, he could feel the warmth of Todd's lips on the back of his neck if he focused hard enough.

'I'll cross my fingers for you,' she said. 'Oh, give Nips a piece of cheese!' Then she hung up.

'Nips, you fleabag, wake up and get your cheese.' At the word "cheese", the giant calico unfolded himself and bounded after Chance. 'Cheese whore.'

So he was sitting and praying to the rain gods that it would dump and the winds would blow and that treacherous piece of shit tree he normally feared would drop branches like leaves.

Allen had been a good boyfriend in most respects, but not very supportive in others. He'd often treated Chance like he didn't know what he was doing. From cooking an egg to calling a repairman for a sump pump. After a bit, Chance

126

had let him do it all and had worked in a retail flower store. Something he enjoyed.

'You have no creativity,' he'd said.

Chance had creativity, but it was more with stuff like flowers and time management, but Allen was a painter and viewed that as nothing more than frivolous time wasting.

It was Becca who had offered him the assistant job. It was Becca who had insisted he run so much of her life like it was his own and keep her in ship shape. It was Becca who had given him his self confidence back. And it was Becca who had said "dump him" when Chance had finally stressed how unhappy he was with Allen.

Now he was back in his house alone stalking the electric man and praying for rain damage. Chance grinned. 'But I feel all tingly and alive. Or maybe that's just approaching lightning.'

The phone rang and Chance jumped. 'Hello?'

'Big storm coming. Be careful.'

'Todd?' Chance's heart skittered in his chest.

'The one and only. I just wanted to make sure you weren't running around out there under the tree in a hard hat with a big metal rod.'

Chance felt laughter bubble up out of him and he tried to clamp his lips shut. He failed. 'No. I won't be doing my human lightning-rod routine. Don't worry.'

'Good. Gotta go.'

'But wait! That was…'

But Todd was gone.

Chance made himself a grilled cheese and tomato soup. He poured a huge glass of red wine and watched the winds rise and toss the trees in the neighbourhood like girls in hoop skirts. The leaves undulated in a wind he could not feel but could see.

Little spitting rain flecked the clean window glass and the old frames rattled with a burst of thunder.

'Come on …'

The tree rocked and swayed. Something that in the past would have had him a nervous wreck, instead he held his breath, praying for something, anything to drop. Nothing.

Chance went to bed with a big glass of wine, a mystery novel and a short simple prayer to whoever might be listening that the power would be knocked out. He fell asleep reading and when a huge crack of thunder at two a.m. was followed by Elvis barking his ass off, he crawled out of bed, stiff and groggy.

'What is it?' he yawned. The light in his room was still on; the digital readout on the cable box glowed red. 'What is it, you fat wiener do …'

A knock came and Chance jumped. It was the middle of the night. He had no idea who it could be. His insides warred, part excitement, part fear. He pushed his eye to the peephole only to see an eye peering back at him. He couldn't tell what colour it was but he bet it was the same colour as clear clean water reflecting a pale summer sky.

'Hello?'

'Can you let me in before I get fried by a rogue lightning bolt?' Todd demanded.

He undid the chains and opened the door. Todd stood on the threshold unmoving and dripping wet.

'What are you doing here?'

The light in the foyer that he kept on all night flickered as the wind gusted and the rain increased in volume.

'Hello to you, too,' Todd said.

'Come in, come in.' Chance took a step back, but Todd didn't move.

'I don't want to date anyone.'

Chance frowned. 'OK. Well … has anyone asked you to date them?'

'You know what I mean.'

'I guess. I think … not really.'

'I don't want to date anyone, think about anyone while I'm eating, showering, working out or folding my clothes.'

'I …'

Todd bullied on, 'And I don't want to worry about anyone without power or maybe being under a big ass tree in a huge storm. I don't want to wonder what someone is doing or wearing or thinking. And I certainly don't want to obsess over the feel of someone's lips.'

A small puddle of water formed on the tile of the foyer. Wind tugged at Chance's lounge pants and he considered pointing out that he was letting all his AC out, but instead kept his big mouth shut. He was so stunned that random rogue thoughts kept popping into his brain. But he pressed his lips together and nodded.

'I don't want to be here.'

'I see.'

'Can I come in?'

'Of course.' He took one more step back to prove his point.

Todd came into the house just enough that Chance could shut the door. 'I'm wet,' he said.

'I noticed.' Chance grinned but the smile went unreturned and he glanced around for a towel or a blanket.

'Were you sleeping?'

'Yeah. I was waiting for … the tree. Hoping …'

Todd laughed. 'You are weird, you know that?'

'So I've been told.'

'You know, I'm out of relationships six months now. I had to do everything. Always the aggressor. I didn't want to come here.' He said it again but instead of sounding angry, he sounded tired.

'So that's why you tortured me with the whole "call me" thing.'

Todd shook his head, said nothing, continued to drip.

'Let me get you a towel,' Chance said and hurried to the coat closet. He grabbed a beach towel from the tote he kept there year round. When he returned, Todd was watching droplets of water splash the red tile floor.

129

'It gets exhausting, always being in control.'

'But you like to be?' Chance wiped off the other man's shorn head gently. Like Todd was breakable. Because at that moment in time he damn near seemed to be.

'But not always.'

'I get it.' He unbuttoned Todd's blue work shirt, dropped it on the floor. He towelled the dampness from his skin and then kissed a line from nipple to nipple. Then a few more kisses from chest to belly button. When he spoke again, Todd's voice was rough.

'Oh, you get it?'

'Yep. I like to relinquish control. But not always,' Chance said, tugging the silver belt buckle and then popping buttons. 'Once in a great while I like to take matters into my own hands.'

'Yeah?'

'Yeah.' Chance slipped his hand down into Todd's jeans, closing around his cock with a firm fist. It felt good to touch him. The warm heft of his sex in the palm of Chance's hand. Chance's own cock went hard in the span of a heartbeat.

Chance tugged the wet denim down until he couldn't get it any further and Todd helped him. Then he wiped his magic towel along all the flesh revealed. His lips followed suit and wherever he wiped, he kissed. Small kisses, long kisses, gentle and hard. He kissed each inch of Todd who seemed to sway on his feet.

'Is that what you're doing now?' Todd threaded his fingers through Chance's hair and tugged just a bit. Not enough to hurt but enough to get his attention.

'Trying.' He pushed the other man a bit and Todd turned his back to him. Chance wiped each buttock slowly and followed with his lips and tongue. He parted Todd's cheeks and kissed and licked the moist skin in smaller and smaller circles until he rimmed the tight bud of his anus with the tip of his tongue. When he pushed his hand between Todd's legs and felt him hard and ready, his pulse jackrabbited.

'You're doing a good job.'

'Thanks. Now turn around.'

Todd turned, his erection standing out like a handle. Chance laughed softly and grabbed it, pushing his lips to the tip before Todd could even get his balance. He slipped his mouth slowly up the shaft so that those big hands flew back to his shoulders, his hair, his face. Todd made a soft noise and then a deeper one. His hips rocked slowly as he thrust against his lover's face.

'Don't move now, or I'll stop.'

'Now that's not ...'

Chance tsked. 'Now don't argue or we're done here.'

'You're getting the hang of it,' Todd growled.

'Still.' Chance tilted his head so he could look Todd dead in the eye as he went down further, taking the full length of his cock into his mouth, his throat, until he couldn't breathe and didn't care. Tears sparked in his eyes and he sucked in a deep breath through his nose.

'If you had any fucking idea how hot you looked doing that ...'

He sucked hard, and gave a brisk stroke with his hand and then pulled back. 'I plan to see how fucking hot you look doing it for me,' Chance said matter of factly.

'Oh do you?'

'I do.'

Todd frowned but then his face softened in a smile. 'We'll see.'

'There's no, "we'll see". Shut up and let me make you come.'

'Yes, sir,' Todd said but he snickered at the end. No one thought that he was really the one to follow orders or that Chance was the one to give them. But for this moment in time, with the flashing lightning and the rolling thunder, they would play it that way.

'That's more like it.' Chance went down again, dragging his lips and his tongue, relishing each slippery moment of friction between cock and mouth. He sucked in the warm rich taste of Todd. Sweat and clean clothes and smoky flavours that made him think of cigars and autumn.

Sometimes a cigar is just a cigar. And sometimes a cigar is a cock ... That's what Becca always said and it struck him as so funny he started to laugh even as he slid his mouth slowly along the hard length of Todd's dick.

'Don't laugh for fuck's sake. It's vibrating and ...'

He cupped Todd's balls, squeezing gently, letting them slide around a bit in his palm before squeezing again. He played his fingers over his inner thigh and behind Todd's balls.

'Fuck me hard,' Todd gasped.

'Later,' Chance said and smiled.

'Hunh. I plan to bend you over and ...'

He pushed his finger into Todd's ass, one hard smooth push and he was in and cutting off the bigger man's words. He fucked him slowly with first one finger then two, the hot smooth flesh letting him enter, gripping up around him. Chance's mouth never rested, he was kinetic. Cheeks aching, eyes watering, nose full of the sexy scent of Todd. When Todd grabbed his hair and tugged and began fucking his mouth for real, he let him go. Chance gave up the illusion of power and sucked for all he was worth as Todd rammed all the way home and came with a roar that rivalled the thunder. Then he dropped to his knees in the foyer, still wet on his eyelashes and brows and kissed Chance.

'That was pretty good for a first time in charge.'

'I've been in charge before.' Chance kissed him back, touched his face, relished the salty taste of his kisses. 'But not with certain people. People who make me ...'

Todd's hands were on his cock, stroking him. Chance found himself moving forward in a rocking motion to get more contact. To get more touch.

'People who make you what?'

'Nervous. Jittery. Electrocuted.'

'I electrocute you?' Todd's eyebrow shot up and he froze.

'In a good way. You make me feel like I'm gripping a live wire.'

'Wanna feel like you're dying? But in a good way?' He pushed Chance back on the hardwood floor and covered him with his body.

'Fuck yes.'

'Good. Here we go.'

Chapter Five

TODD'S HANDS WERE STILL cool from the rain as he tugged down Chance's pyjama pants. He pushed Chance's legs high, so high they nearly kissed his shoulders. His mouth was as warm as his hands were cool and he kissed Chance's chest, darting out his tongue in silken strokes, leaving wet trails on his skin. His sharp teeth clamped on first one nipple then the other. Chance danced under him, wanting to move but trying so hard not to. 'Stay still now. I'm going to take my time.'

The storm howled outside, lightning flashing against the dark windowpanes, creating disco flashes of light. Todd dragged the flat of his tongue down the middle of Chance's chest – what felt to Chance like the middle of his very being – until he hit hipbones. Then he licked each sharp ridge, dragging out the moments where Chance held his breath and prayed for contact. The feel of that tongue on his cock, on the tip of him, down low, on his testicles … just on him.

And hold his breath he did. He watched the meagre light glow on Todd's shaven head. Watched the cut of his jaw and the angle of his nose and the pink tip of his tongue dart out to draw invisible blazing lines on his skin. 'Say please,' Todd said.

Chance shook his head. Bit his tongue. Refused.

Todd shrugged, his hands lacing around Chance's ankles. He held his legs high and wide, he kissed the back of each thigh and then lower still with his demanding kisses. He nipped Chance's right ass cheek and Chance jumped, blowing out the breath he'd been holding. 'Jesus.'

The sharp stab of pain bled into a warm yellow pleasure and Chance sighed. Todd moved his hand, darted his tongue to the tight ring of his anus and then promptly bit the other cheek. Chance jumped again, his cock so hard he thought he might pass out. That burst of pain that became malleable and turned to pleasure had him damn near vibrating.

Todd drew out the torture, kissing all around Chance's sweet spot. He kissed and licked every place but his cock and Chance shook his head in frustration. 'All you have to do is ask,' Todd chuckled. He touched a rough fingertip to the very tip of Chance's cock, gathering the small dot of pre-come. Then he gazed up at Chance with those liquid eyes and licked his finger.

'Fuck. Fine. I cave, please.'

'Please what?'

'Suck my dick!' Chance wheezed, feeling like he might laugh or cry or possibly a combination of both.

'Hmm. I'm not sure if ...'

'Todd!'

One more dark laugh and Todd dipped his head and took him in. The inside of his mouth the closest thing to heaven Chance could imagine. Or maybe it was partly the strong, powerful hands holding his ankles like they were little twigs, fragile and easy to break. Or maybe it was the shaved head and the ethereal eyes or the deep gruff voice. Or the speech that he gave showing how much he didn't want to be here and yet he was. Maybe it was ... but he broke off then because Todd pulled Chance's cock free of his mouth and licked him from front to back and then did it again. He wormed a rough finger into Chance's ass and pressed and prodded and fucked until Chance cried out.

'Please!'

'Bossy.' Todd had mercy. He returned to his wet ministrations and when Chance came, he smoothed the come along his shaft working each final spasm like it was the first. Then he dropped a kiss on the top of each thigh and said, 'Well, I'd better …'

Chance started to shake: hurt; rage; anger – whatever you wanted to call it or a combo deal. 'NO you won't. You'll go get in my bed and stay here.'

'What if I say no?' Todd asked, sitting up, rubbing his head, watching the small light flicker and frowning.

'What if you do? I guess I can't stop you then,' Chance said, sighing. He was very tired suddenly. 'I guess if you want to go you can go.'

'Do you want me to go?' Todd asked, looking almost angry.

'Fuck no.'

'And you don't mind me staying?' His face was unreadable, but Chance thought he saw anxiety there.

He remembered Todd's tale about his past lover. About always being in charge. About how tiring it was. So he said, 'Get your ass upstairs, I have extra clothes in the bureau and unopened toothbrushes in the linen closet.

'I …'

'Do it.'

Todd nodded once and rose, offered Chance a hand that he promptly took. Todd tugged him to standing and hugged him, his kiss was soft but still demanding. 'Thanks,' he said, so low and so fast that Chance wasn't sure he'd actually heard him right.

So he said nothing. He just tugged the bigger man's hand and led him upstairs.

'What do you mean he was gone?'

'He was gone. How many ways are there to take that?' Chance ran a hand through his hair and felt the wave of anger that threatened to wash over him. 'He told me pretty much up front that he wasn't in for a long haul.'

'Yeah, but to leave *that* fast …' Becca trailed.

Chance drew ever darkening circles on the notepad where

he'd made out his list for the day. After a moment he realised that at some point he had switched to drawing dark rain clouds. *Paging Doctor Freud, please come to the front desk and bring your cigar ...*

'I don't know what to do. Maybe there's nothing I can do. Maybe I need to chalk it up to a ONS and call it a day.'

'An ONS?'

'One Night Stand,' he said.

'Is that what the kids are calling it these days?'

'No. They're calling it fucked up.'

'Ahhh, well I feel horrible. I think that you should do whatever makes you feel best.'

'Tie him up and drag him home and fuck him until he begs?'

Chance heard a groan and then Becca laughed. 'Did I mention you were on speaker phone?'

'Sorry, Shawn,' Chance sighed. 'Gotta go. My boss ... she is a slave driver.'

'Yeah, I'm so cruel. Call me if you need me, hon.'

'Will do.' Chance hung up. No use fretting it. It was what it was.

'It's sad, though,' he told Elvis. 'We could have been good together. No note. No nothing.'

Elvis sighed and Chance put his sneakers on. He had all kinds of running to do for Becca from picking up the crib that had just arrived at the baby store to returning library books. And lucky him, the sky had opened up and more fierce storms were rolling through. By the time he got to his car, he was soaked. Five steps from the door had turned him into a drowned rat.

He started the SUV and his phone ring. Without bothering to check the number he said 'What did you forget now, you shrew?'

'A note. An apology. Something.' Todd's voice was darker than usual and that was saying something. Chance broke out in goose bumps from the cold and the shock.

'Hey, what happened?'

'I left.'

'I gathered.'

'I'm all fucked up.'

'I know. I can tell.' Chance chewed his bottom lip and then added 'But if it's any consolation, so am I. I think everyone is in their own way.'

'I can't get past it right now. I'm really attracted to you. Really. And I like you. Which is odd.'

Chance barked out a laugh. 'Really? How so?'

'In case you haven't caught on, most folks annoy me.'

'Nooo. You?' He smiled as rain pummelled the vehicle.

'It's been a while since I even thought to show up at someone's house in the middle of the night, let alone to do it. It's been a while since …' Here he broke off. All Chance could hear was him breathing.

'Since you?'

'Enjoyed it that much? Fucked? Gave in to someone. Wanted to be submissive to someone. Had that urge, need, desire. Jesus, pick one. Mix and match.'

'OK. Well, come by. We'll talk about it.'

'No.'

'Todd, we've had very little besides power outages and fucking and I still feel drawn to you.'

Todd made a gruff sound but said nothing.

'Just come talk to me. Like … what's your favourite colour?'

'Blue.'

'Favourite food?'

'Steak.'

'Favourite movie?'

'Patton.'

'Favourite smell.'

'You. After last night…'

He hung up.

Chance put his head to the steering wheel and fretted.

138

'How do I always get the complicated ones?' What had started as mere attraction seemed to have potential to be so very much more. And yet, he was dealing with a gun shy man who took stubborn to a whole new level.

'I usually get to be the stubborn one,' he said aloud and started his errands. It would take some time to figure this out, but Chance knew he would. Bottom line was he was a stubborn motherfucker and if there was a way to get Todd to hear him out, think this over, he'd think of it.

At Becca's house, he struggled up the front walk with the crib and managed to wrestle it inside. Then he put the library books Becca had asked him to get when he dropped off the load that were due. A mountain of baby books went sliding down the hall as they cascaded from his arms. 'Shit!'

His brain was in overdrive. Doing his list, pondering Todd, hearing the echo of his dark smoky voice in his mind. He felt haunted and wired and half crazed. But under it all was a low level peace that made no sense. As if he intuitively knew it would all work out. 'Cuckoo,' Chance sighed and ran to get the few groceries he'd bought.

'Nips, I have brought a crib. And some books and cheeeeeese!'

At the word "cheese" the giant calico uncurled himself from an oversized decorative bowl he was prone to sleeping in and pounced on Chance. 'Finally! Some affection.' He sat on the floor feeding bits of cheese to the cat and finally decided what he needed to do about Todd.

Lightning flared and thunder boomed and the lights flickered before cutting out. The sump pump beeped and so did the carbon monoxide detector plugged into the outlet. Becca's house had become safe city since she'd found out she was pregnant. Then everything came back on before another big rumble of thunder that shook the window panes in their frames.

'At least the weather is on my side,' Chance said.

Chapter Six

'AND THERE'LL BE MORE storms tonight for sure.' The newscaster turned to the camera, his awful tie pattern dancing with glee as it wigged out the TV cameras. 'Look for rain, rain and more rain and some pretty heavy winds and maybe some severe lightning in certain areas. A good night to stay inside. This is Dan Bartenfelder reporting for *News 11.*'

'Thank you, Dan!' Chance said, realising he needed to get a boyfriend fast because the only people he talked to any more were Becca, the TV, Nips and Elvis and three of the four weren't actual people.

The ten o'clock news was done, the wine had been drunk, the plot had been plotted and he was ready to roll. He patted his pocket and felt the heft of the cuffs there. Another ex had been a cop and had left a few treasures behind such as cuffs, a blue work shirt and what Chance thought was a can of pepper spray but wasn't sure so he just left it sitting in the closet. He had nothing to do but act now.

One more shot of liquid courage … He poured off a half glass of wine and downed it like a shot. Then he hit speed dial on his cell and waited while it rang.

'Todd.'

'Power's out again.'

Silence. Then, 'Maybe you should call the …'

'Come on, man. Don't leave me hanging,' he said.

'I just think that …'

'Do you hate me?'

140

Todd sighed. 'God, no. Not even close. Which is the issue.'

'Look if you still like me even just as a person, don't put me through all that shit. Come help me out. I won't bother you again.'

'You aren't bothering me. In fact, I like you too much. I'm not ready to like anyone as much as …'

'Save it,' he growled, trying to spur Todd into action by being short with him. 'If you don't want me, fine. I can't change that. But at least help me out. I have no power and an old fat wiener dog who wants AC.'

'I'll be there in ten.'

'Just meet me in MacGruder's yard.'

'Why?'

Why? Whywhywhywhy …

'Because I want to point out another limb that's scaring the shit out of me since you'll be here. And I won't see you again after,' he added, just for the guilt effect. Hey, he wasn't above a good guilt play.

'OK. I'll be there soon.'

'I'll be out back.'

'It's pouring down with rain.'

'I won't melt.'

Chance cut through the back yard and stood near the gate. When they'd installed it they hadn't gone for an old boring chain link gate, they'd done a scrolled iron gate with an archway for ivy. Years and years of ivy crawling up the gate had turned it into a magical organic structure. Chance clinked the handcuffs against it to hear the solid clunk. He noticed his hands were shaking. If Todd was backing off because he felt too much, it was a good sign in a lot of ways. And he'd made it clear that he'd been in a one sided relationship. Something Chance totally got. So it was Chance's opportunity to show Todd just what he was made of. That he was multi-faceted.

And mildly cuckoo …

He shook his head and waited, the rain pelting down but luckily no lightning for ages.

He heard the truck and then the main gate to MacGruder's back yard. 'Hello?

'I'm at the gate,' he called.

'The lines look like they're up!'

'Hurry!'

If he caught Todd off guard he'd be good. If he had any warning at all, the bigger man could surely overpower him.

'They're up,' Todd breathed trotting into view.

'I'm stuck on this gate,' Chance said, not making eye contact. He was sure that if he looked Todd in the eye, he'd know something was up.

'What the fuck is going on? The lines are fine, no branches are down and you're stuck to a gate?'

'In the wrought iron scrollwork. I have my sleeve caught and …'

Todd got close, reached for him, small bits of light filtering from the nearest streetlamps. When his arms got close, Chance snapped on the cuffs. They connected and closed with a soft, sudden *snick*.

Todd looked up, confused, angry, shocked. 'What the fuck?'

'We need to talk' Chance said and looped the cuff through the wrought iron gate. It was an act of God getting the other hand caught up and cuffed. Todd made a swipe at him with his free hand, Chance ducked it and got right up close after wrestling it into the handcuff. 'We're going to talk. And you're going to behave.'

'Or what?'

'Or I can leave you here,' he said and grabbed the cell phone clipped to Todd's belt. 'Just until you calm down enough to be rational.'

'I'm going to bust your ass when I get out of these.'

'I count on it, but I also plan for you to fuck me when you're done. And then I'll make you dinner. And we'll go out. Like sane rational men who do not run away when they like someone.'

Todd frowned. He looked so angry Chance was grateful he was chained up.

'Well.'

'Well what?' Chance asked.

'Well, what are you waiting for? Talk.'

Chance blinked, panicking a bit as the rain continued to pummel them.

'Well?' Todd grunted, testing his bonds.

'Well, you put me on the spot!' Chance said, yelling to be heard above the wind.

'*I* put *you* on the spot? I am handcuffed to iron in a storm!' Todd yelled.

'There's no lightning,' Chance reasoned.

'Right *now*.'

'If it comes I'll undo the cuffs. I promise.'

'Don't want me battered and fried?'

'No, I just want you to listen.'

'I'm listening.'

'Why did you run from me?'

'I'm not ready. Now are we done with our feelings?'

'No.' Chance stalked closer and put his face to the other man's. 'We're not done. Look I feel a lot for you. Rational or not. I can talk it out … fuck it out … shit, I'd be willing to duke it out, but running?' He blinked, bit his lip and then 'Well, that's a pure pussy move.'

Todd narrowed his eyes at Chance and thrust his jaw forward. 'Undo the cuffs.'

'No. Tell me why.'

'I told you, I was always in charge. Sex, movies, books, food, all of it. I want a partner, not a kid. And it was a long fucked up drawn-out nightmare to extricate myself and I. Am. Not. Ready.' He yanked at the cuffs so hard Chance feared he'd hurt himself. Then Todd roared like some angry animal. 'Undo them!'

'No.'

Todd went still and that made Chance more nervous than the brutish show of strength. He held his breath and waited but Todd said nothing.

'Now, I'll admit I am a bit of a bottom, a sub, easy going, along for the ride, however you want to put it. But I also know what I want and for some insane fucked up reason I want you. Even though you ran, even though you're lying to me when you say you can just walk away. I think there could be ... something here. And we should at least see. Even though you are gruff and angry and surly and annoying stubborn. So you tell me ... would your ex have done this? Taken the situation in hand. Made you angry and provoked you to get you to listen and to get an answer?'

Todd clenched his jaw hard and Chance knew it was sinking in. He was making his point. The wind howled, driving the rain almost sideways and Chance stumbled under the sudden gust. Over them the tree groaned with a creaky moan and both men looked up. 'Let me out,' Todd said, his voice no longer angry but anxious and urgent.

Chance looked unsure, but then the storm seemed to calm a bit and he shook his head. 'Not yet. I want to drive my point home, first.' He dropped to his knees and his fingers fumbled and flicked at Todd's jeans.

'Jesus Christ, are you trying to get us killed you crazy mother ...' But his words dropped away like pebbles off a cliff. Chance slipped his lips along Todd's shaft, licking and nuzzling, sucking and kissing like his life depended on it.

He felt like it did.

'I didn't want anyone. Well - maybe a fast fuck. But I want to know you more. More than just the guy who climbs my pole.' His own words caught up to him and he chuckled even as he sucked Todd's balls slowly. One and then the other as if he were savouring a sweet treat instead of flesh and blood. The fear added to his thrill and he could only imagine what it was doing for Todd.

Todd groaned, almost against his will, thrusting up to slide his cock inside the loose slippery fist. Rain pelted them both, driving Chance's pale hair to his head so it looked like a skull cap. His shirt clung to his lean form, but the fear lived on, sizzling along his skin and making his pleasure that much more.

'I like this. I really do. And you're right. I was wrong to bolt. I wasn't prepared … I mean, I thought I'd fuck you, pet your dog, be on my way. Not have you flitting about in my head like some wraith I couldn't shake. But this storm is getting worse and this tree is unsafe and …'

'In a minute,' Chance mumbled, sliding his mouth low. His throat full of Todd. His head bobbing like he was in some odd form of prayer. He knelt there, looking both powerful and humble. A dictator and a supplicant.

'God, I wish I could touch your hair. I'd brush the water from your face and hold your chin and hold your jaw while I just fucking thrust deep.' The wind whooped and the tree swayed and there was a very audible snap and crack. 'We won't be fucking or dating or any of that if we die,' Todd grunted. 'You have to let me go.'

'One hand. This fucking tree has lasted a few storms now. I'll let one hand out.'

Todd shook his head. 'You are a stubborn ass, you know that?'

Chance grinned, nodded, unlocked one arm and then Todd grabbed his face. 'Listen to me. You need to.'

Chance was nodding and grinning and he pushed his lips to Todd's dick, his velvet tongue tracing the veins and outlines of flesh and blood and arousal. 'I know. Just come for me and then we'll go in. We'll go in and get dry.' His hands stroked the skin inside Todd's thighs, between his legs. His fingertip teased at the tight ring of his asshole and then stroked the perineum like a small instrument. Todd thrust, moving his pelvis, his pulse beating like a war drum in his throat so hard that Chance could see it if he looked hard.

'OK, fine. I'll come,' he growled.

'I don't mean to put you out,' Chance snorted.

'Shut up and suck,' Todd growled. He gave in and pushed Chance's blond head down between his legs. Rain dripped from his fingers, his nose and his eyelashes. He watched his new stubborn lover suck him deep and when he gulped over his cock, his throat convulsing, eyelids fluttering, Todd came with a rough sound.

His knees shook a bit, he felt light headed and he said, 'Now uncuff me.'

Chance reached for him, the small key pinched between his fingers and the sudden snap and pop filled their ears. The limb clipped Chance neatly over the right ear and he dropped. A wet sack of laundry shaped like a man. Todd made a shocked sound and he dropped to his knees in the now-muddy back yard. He stretched to his limit, just managing to snag the small cuff key with his big fingers. Then he worked the cuff, water and fear and panic making his fingers clumsy. His heart filled his throat and he searched Chance's still form for his cell phone muttering, 'Wake up, you goof. Wake up. I don't want you to be hurt. Christ, why are you so accident-prone?'

Tears pricked at his eyes and he angrily brushed them away, telling himself they were just rain.

He dialled emergency services, rolling Chance to his back to check his vitals for the operator.

Chapter Seven

'IT ALL LOOKS GOOD. We're gonna hang here for a few and let him sit. Make sure no headaches appear, dizziness, vomiting.'

'All that fun stuff,' Chance interjected.

Todd frowned at him and shook his head. The EMTs walked to the front of the ambulance and climbed in to update the radio operator.

'That was really fucking stupid,' Todd said. He sat on the back bumper and wrapped a hand around Chance's wet ankle. He squeezed and Chance took a hit off the oxygen he probably didn't need at this point.

'What can I say? I'm not the most shrewd at romance. Anything to get my man.'

'You could have been hurt. Had this stupid ass tree not been so dead and so dry-rotted you could have been killed. That could have been a much worse knock on the head.'

'Life isn't life without one or two hard lessons,' Chance sighed. He snorted and then coughed from the oxygen.

'I'll give you a hard lesson,' Todd said, shaking his head. He patted Chance's leg. It wasn't lost on Chance, how he couldn't stop touching him as if to reassure himself that he was in fact OK.

'I'm counting on it.'

Todd leaned in then, surprising Chance, and kissed him hard. He played his tongue along Chance's tongue, sucking it gently until Chance hummed with pleasure. Then he kissed the tip of Chance's nose and pulled back. 'They said you have to stay awake for quite a while and I'm to watch you.'

'Oh, baby.' Chance blew a kiss and rolled his eyes. Then winced for a second, his head hurt pretty good from being clipped by tree debris.

'But no strenuous movement. No stress.'

Chance sighed. 'Of course. Foiled again.'

Todd leaned in for one more kiss and put his hand for just an instant on Chance's fly. 'Oh, I think we can think of something. Trust me, I'm nothing if resourceful.'

Chance echoed himself. 'I'm counting on it.'

Epilogue

Six weeks later

'YOU'D BETTER BE BACK by the time the baby comes!' Becca yelled.

'I'll be back in plenty of time, dear. Do you know that man hasn't had a vacation in two and a half years?' Chance threw yet another pair of jeans in his duffle. You could never have too many pairs of jeans to go hiking in the country during leaf season.

'That would make anyone uptight,' she said.

'True story.'

'And the tree?'

'Tree is down. That limb that clipped me was the final straw for him. He had to come out one too many times to deal with it, but when it assaulted his *boyfriend* that was it.'

'Oh, darling, *boyfriend.*'

'You heard me, sister.'

Becca laughed and Chance grinned.

'So what did big, bald and surly do?'

'Oh, he might have helped it along a bit. Got it so it was leaning precariously and the whole neighbourhood threatened Mr MacGruder with a law suit if his cheap ass didn't get it down.'

'How did Todd do that?'

'Now what kind of personal assistant would I be if I couldn't keep confidences?'

He nearly heard her roll her eyes. 'Fine. One day you'll

tell me.'

'One day perhaps. But not now.'

'Brat.'

'You know it.'

'Have fun,' she said.

'Oh we will. It promises to be a wet, slippery, hard, hot, fun, sexy, coupling kind of trip.'

Chance heard a groan. Becca said, 'Did I mention you're on speaker?'

UNEXPECTED

Chapter One

GIOVANNI WAS THRASHING AROUND to death metal when I first saw him. I'd pulled flush to his broken down, beat-in white pick up truck and he was pounding out an imaginary drum solo with his left arm in a dirty white cast. I laughed and in the back seat Annabel responded to my laughter.

Something made him turn. Something made him swivel that lean taut face my way and grin. I wondered briefly if he was a crack addict or some kind of addict. He had that tense rubber band feel of someone running two speeds faster than everyone else.

But no, that was just Giovanni.

'Like, I cannot believe you motioned me over,' he said.

'It was a little unlike me.'

'I bet. I don't peg you for the pick up kind of guy. Why'd you do it?'

I told the truth. 'You made me laugh out loud.'

He worked at a home improvement store, I handled remodels. He liked Italian and I liked Asian food. But we both agreed the other had a valid point. We'd run through some niceties while we ordered our treats.

Giovanni licked at the shaved ice in its white paper cup and something warmed low in my belly. He caught me staring and he stuck his tongue out further to me. A blue raspberry-stained offering of slick muscle surrounded by dark blue teeth.

'Caught you, Charlie,' he said.

I laughed again. Something about Giovanni made me

laugh. Made me feel light in the centre of myself where I'd felt heavy and tense for way too long. Again Annabel gave a sharp little cry – a little bubble of joy bursting in the late fall afternoon.

'Yes, you did. You caught me. Good?' I nodded to his shaved ice, changing the subject.

'Good.' He settled his intensely clear brown eyes on Annabel and said, 'So, are you gonna tell me who this cutie is?'

Intuition reared up and I tapped his cast with my fingertip. 'I'll tell you about little Miss Annabel if you tell me about this.'

There was a flash of unease over his handsome face and my body hummed with interest. Interest in him, interest in his story. Something told me that he had not gotten that cast playing air drums.

'Fine.' He bit into his shaved ice and it made my teeth ache just to watch it. I shivered and he winked. 'But you first.'

'This is my daughter.' I shrugged and licked my lemon ice as if to say *end of story*.

'And?' He rolled his hands at me to carry on. His mouth was wide, his eyes flashing. He was a ball of energy lit by some unseen generator. 'I'm going to guess you might possibly be a … oh … homosexual?'

I snorted at his tone and his goofy facial expression. 'Correct.'

'And most of the homosexual men I know do not have kids. Unless they're older and did the whole denial deal. Or adopted maybe.'

'No denial here.'

'Well, how did …' Giovanni leaned in and touched Annabel's' nose and she squealed at him, 'this doll baby come to be?'

I blew out a sigh, setting down my lemon ice. Suddenly cold sugar and syrup didn't sound so good. I had to get used to this. Every guy I flirted with, every guy I talked to, every guy I potentially wanted to fuck would want to know about my daughter.

'Ready? Because I'm going to do it fast like a band aid.'

'That bad, man?' Giovanni asked

'Not bad. Just ... it was unexpected.'

Giovanni gave a brisk nod. 'Got it. So ... go!' He tickled Annabel's toe and she wiggled in her carrier.

'Annabel's mom is my best friend. For most of my life Mariah's been my rock. So, when she came to me and asked if I'd ...' I waved my hand.

'Knock her up?'

I blinked at him but then nodded. 'Yeah. She wanted a baby, couldn't afford invitro fertilization. Didn't have a guy in her life she wanted to, as she put it, spread a gene pool with. So she asked me. "Let's get drunk, fuck and I'll have a baby. You can be Uncle Charlie and I'll be mom and the kid will be none the wiser".'

'Sounds very modern and reasonable,' Giovanni said.

'I thought so too.'

'So what happened?'

'We got drunk and we fucked.'

'Who'd you picture?'

'Andy Garcia,' I said.

'Nice.'

'Thanks. Anyway, we actually had the stars aligned and it worked. She got pregnant on the first try and Annabel was born.'

'Cutie too,' Giovanni said and undid her strap. My heart stilled for a moment and then beat wildly in my chest. But he seemed to know what he was doing even with the cast. And Annabel, all agog over a new person, grinned and drooled and cooed like she'd known him for ever. 'I have a niece not much older than her in case you were wondering.'

Air flooded my lungs and it was only then that I realised I'd been holding my breath. 'I was. Sort of. Not a lot.'

It's amazing how fast you can go from unwilling father to overprotective worrisome dad.

'Liar. So go on,' he said to Annabel but was addressing me. She squealed and bashed him in his blue lips with pudgy fingers. At six months old my daughter was a featherweight boxer.

'She developed PPD – post partum depression,' I said. I said it slowly as if tasting the words. Then I flicked the edge of my shaved ice cup so that it scooted across the wrought iron table inch by chilly inch.

'And she bolted?'

I sighed before I could catch myself and ran my hands through my hair. Dark hair fell across my eyebrows, into my eyes. I needed a haircut but I kept forgetting to get one. I forgot damn near everything but what Annabel needed at any given moment. I usually remembered my remodelling appointments, so that was good.

'She bolted. You guessed it. It was too much for her. She didn't want the meds, she couldn't handle the baby. The crying, the sleep deprivation, the post partum itself. It was the perfect storm. She just left one night. Asked me if I could spot Annabel so she could go on a date and poof! The next thing I knew I was getting a phone call from her and she was in California staying with friends.'

'Cali's a long haul from here.'

'I know.'

'Her family?'

'No interest. Her mom's pretty much a drunk. And they're both hardcore practicing Catholics who think babies born out of wedlock are a sin.'

'And babies born with hom-ee-sex-shul daddies. Dear Lord.' He drew his words out in the ways of a fire and brimstone preacher and bounced Annabel so she gurgled.

'Right. Bingo. Give the man a cigar.'

That's when Giovanni turned to me and said quite bluntly. 'I don't know about a cigar but I bet daddy deserves a blow job. We'll see what we can do later when little ones are down for long naps.'

I swallowed hard, coughed, felt the surge and thump of blood in my veins, my cock. When was the last time I'd felt my heart stutter and my stomach roll over with that excited, almost sick feeling? Too long to remember.

For one brief heart-stopping second, I touched the small dark hairs on the backs of his fingers. His cheeks went rosy and his eyelids sort of dropped like he was stoned. 'Dude.'

'Shush,' I said. 'Now tell me about the arm. What happened there?'

He handed me the baby so fast I feared I'd drop her and his face changed in the span of a heartbeat. 'It's nothing really.'

'Yeah. I bet. Convince me of that.'

'I fell down the steps.'

'Ah, see, I suspected maybe you walked into a door.'

He grinned at me, changed his mind and took Annabel back. It was like a game, *Pass the baby!* But I gave her over easily. Giovanni's teeth were still blue and slightly crooked in the front. Just crooked enough that I wanted to lean in and kiss him. The baby bopped him in the face.

'That's a black eye, anyhow. Not a busted arm.'

'Do tell.' I picked at a small hole in the knee of my jeans. This is when I would have lit a cigarette. But I'd quit. For me and for Annabel. No smoking around the baby! I could hear my mother in my head.

'Do we really need to do this? We just met. This borders on water torture.'

'Do you trust me?' I wasn't sure why I'd asked that. It would be perfectly understandable if this man said no.

Giovanni cocked his head, his long dark shock of hair falling in his face for an instant. 'Yes.'

My heart staggered a little in my chest but I said, 'Then tell me.'

'My ex did it. There. But you knew that, didn't you?'

157

I gave one short nod so as not to spook him. 'Glad to hear he's your ex, though.'

'Well, damn. I'm slow to leave when I think I'm in love. I'm not stupid, though. I won't stay with someone beating on me.' He pulled his head back fast, realising maybe just how much information he'd just given away.

Annabel was staring, transfixed at this stranger, a hunk of his coffee coloured hair caught in her pudgy hand. She yanked hard like she was trying to rein him in. I winced but Giovanni didn't.

'I'm sorry,' I said.

'Don't be. He was an ass. When he hit me so hard my knees buckled you'd think that would end it.' He shrugged his thin shoulders and bounced my child on his leg. 'But no. He always was an overachiever, my John. So he kicked me down the stairs.'

Rage, hot and swift, filled my chest and my hands bunched into fists. Hitting the likes of funny, kinetic, sexy Giovanni was beyond my scope of thinking. Hitting his ex seemed totally doable.

'What the fuck?'

'I know! What the fuck? But that was the wake up call I needed. They say all addicts have to hit rock bottom before they get it. I was addicted to that man. And when he did that and then stepped over me to leave the house and go out and party with the boys, I knew that I, Giovanni Rustici, was spread out over my rock bottom. And I was bleeding on it too. So for the time being I'm living with my sister.'

'Can I take you out?' I blurted.

He blinked at me. His warm brown eyes unbelievably trusting for someone who was still wearing a fresh cast. 'We are out.'

I shook my head, losing my battle not to smile. 'On a date. A proper date. Just the grown-ups,' I said and watched Annabel start chewing on his stubbly chin. 'Sorry. She's teething I think.'

'Dude,' he said, grinning. 'My face is totally clean.'

I walked him to his truck, Annabel cradled on one hip, goggling at a group of kids who were rushing toward the shaved ice stand.

'You seem like a very good dad. Maybe a wee bit overprotective,' he said.

'Gee, thanks.'

'But good.'

'Thank you.'

'But stressed.' He stared at me.

'I won't necessarily argue that. It's been a bit intense this year.'

'But you're doing it and that means you're a good man. You're pulling your shit together. For her.' He nodded to the baby who was still watching the big kids with a determined kind of concentration.

'I'm trying.'

'So when do we go on that proper date …?' He pushed a card in my pocket. My cock responded by twitching with want and blood. A huge rush of need slid through my veins and I tried hard to breathe. 'We'll see what we can do about giving Daddy some stress release, yeah?'

He kissed me. It was soft and fast, but his warm pink mouth touched mine. His tongue twitched out and electricity coursed over my skin and into my bones. My twitching cock became my hard cock and I realised that I wanted this man with an aggression I couldn't recall feeling before.

And he came along when my life was a ball of chaos rolling perpetually toward an uncertain destination.

'Yeah?' he demanded again, breaking the kiss.

I was powerless to do anything but say, 'Yeah.'

'Good,' he said and patted my cheek before climbing in his shitty truck and tearing out of view.

Chapter Two

'YOU REALLY NEED TO let go. Don't you think?'

I could only nod. I had absolutely zero words for Giovanni right then.

'I can help you with that. Let me help you.'

Another nod from me and I watched him advance on me, his eyes glittering in the low light. He was really quite beautiful. More beautiful than handsome. Leanly muscled, pale with that dark fall of hair. Those bottomless brown eyes. He licked at the corner of his mouth and his tongue tipped a small chocolate dot of a mole. My cock got stiffer and the air in my lungs rippled like a scarf in a breeze.

'Help me.'

'Good boy. You do take direction well, though I don't peg you as a bottom ... or a top.' Giovanni ran the tip of his finger along the hard ridge of my cock and I found my hips rising in an invisible tide of air to meet his touch. I shut my eyes to steady my mind. It was whirling like a child's top and the world was rocking to some invisible rhythm fuelled by excitement and arousal.

'Maybe you're a bottom *and* a top. We can share the top. We can share the bottom.' He slipped his hand into my jeans, took me in hand and simply held me. My flesh beat with a steady rapid pulse. My ears rang with the force of my blood.

'Maybe. I'd like that. Both, equals,' I babbled.

'But for tonight, let's help you let go.'

Another nod from me and I willingly fell into the kiss

when his lips found mine. Sweet and wet, his mouth tasted like blue raspberry icy and cigarettes. His tongue tangled with mine and he crushed his body to me, the hump of his cock rubbing the length of me until I started trembling like I had a fever.

'Stay still, baby.' He pressed his cast to my chest, pinning me to the wall, his kiss growing harder. 'Don't move a muscle. Do not move.' His free hand pushed at my jeans, my boxer briefs. He wrestled my clothes into submission while dropping wild kisses on my lips and jaw and neck. I moved up against him – desperate for contact, needy for love, for sex – for a good strong fuck. Top or bottom, no matter to me.

But the feel of that cast mashed to my chest – flush to flesh and blood and bone – made me want to be bottom. Made me want to please Giovanni, see him smile. 'Please … something. Just please,' I said.

'I like to hear you say please.' His hand wrapped around me and he started the slow, maddening stroke along my length. The rasp of his hand on my cock, the sound of his breath in my ear, my head was light with the smell of us. The feel of him. The proximity to release was enough to make my stomach sick with anticipation.

'Please.'

'Good boy. It's such a nice word when you say it.' He ran the tip of his thumb over the weeping eye of my dick and the added slide of fluid made my knees weak. For as lean and angular as he was, he had a full, lush mouth that met mine in velvet heated kisses.

'Please, I am a good boy, Giovanni.' I found his eyes with mine. Wondering what he saw when he looked into my deep blue ones. Did he see the comfort and understanding I saw in his? Or did he just see pretty eyes? Wolf eyes, as my mother called them.

His tempo increased and my hips slammed up to meet him. My fingers gripped at the wall for purchase I didn't

161

need. I wasn't even moving, but I clutched at the wall. I chased his lips with my mouth to get another kiss and he pressed that cast down hard pressing the air out of me and kissing me at the same time. It was as if he were pushing the air from my lungs to suck it into his body – soul eater, heart eater, lust eater. Maybe he was magical. No matter, he could have all three: my lust; my soul; my heart. He could have me. I just didn't have the balls to tell him.

His hand flew and I thrust into his hand, greedy little jerks like I could fuck him where he stood. He laughed in my ear and the small hairs on my neck tingled. 'Such a greedy little boy, Charlie. Are you trying to fuck me? Do you want to *fuck* me?'

'Yes.'

His hand flew and I felt that tightening blissful heat that always came right before I lost my grip and shot. 'Slut.'

'Yes.'

'My slut?' The hand stilled and my heartbeat filled my ears, my throat. My head was thrumming with it. I tried to move my hips and Giovanni said, 'Ah-ah. No moving.'

I stilled, wanting to weep I was so close. Somewhere I thought I heard the baby cry but then the sound faded.

'Your slut,' I said. 'Yes.'

'Say you're my slut. Tell me. Say my name.'

'I'm your slut, Giovanni,' I said. It fell off my lips easily. Like dropping a coin in a wishing well. An effortless toss and it was out there – tumbling shiny and graceful through the universe.

'Good. Now you get your reward.'

When he finally moved his hand I had to curl my toes in my shoes to keep from coming right there. 'Oh,' I said. What else was there to say, really?

'Come for me. Come for pappa.'

And I did. I came, my hips shooting up and forward. My lips went numb with the force of my orgasm and I tried to fight his strong arm on my chest to touch him. Finally my fingers found purchase on his lean hips and I felt the warmth of his skin through his T-shirt and jeans. 'Fuck,' I said.

'Next time,' Giovanni said, looking up at me. I was about 25 pounds heavier and a head taller than him, but when he wielded that cast and his words, I was powerless against him.

Annabel started to wail and I said, 'The baby is crying, Gi.'

'Then I guess you should wake up now.' He leaned in and stole one more kiss

I woke to the monitor's racing red lights; the arc of Annabel's cry clearly visible in the dark. My cock was hard enough to break glass and my pulse pounded in my ears like a muffled drum. 'Fuck.'

I sat up, dizzy, disoriented, raging with anxiety and arousal. 'Fuck!' Then my brain kicked in and I yelled, 'Coming, baby. Coming, Bell.'

It was four a.m. and there was no way in the world I was going back to sleep. Not after that dream. I fed Annabel her bottle, keeping my movements soft and muted, my voice barely a whisper. I wanted her to sleep some more. I *needed* her to sleep some more. My life had hit a point of action. I had to find the balance so that baby and I were both happy or I would crack. Right now I was living for nothing but my daughter. It was time to give a little consideration to myself.

That consideration came in the form of Giovanni. The first person to spark my sexual interest and do something to my heart – it twisted sideways a bit in my chest when I thought of him. Picturing his face could make my body tingle with a thousand invisible sparkles of light.

'Goodness, but I have it bad,' I told the baby. She made soft sucking noises, her little eyelids drooping from being warm and dry and fed. Her long dark lashes swept her pristine skin and my heart twisted in an entirely different kind of way. She was worth the discomfort of unexpected radical shifts in my life. She was worth more than my life itself.

'Back to sleep, baby cakes.' She didn't fight me. She pushed one plump hand under one plump cheek and a small snore escaped her.

I tiptoed to the kitchen and started a pot of coffee. My small green and red and gold kitchen, decorated by my mother when I moved out on my own. Her Mediterranean heritage had clearly been in mind. The Columbian roast dripped nearly black and slow as sin from the percolator. I was wired but tired and impatient for caffeine but I knew the brew was worth the wait, so I waited.

'Hell of a dream to have – to wake up to. Hell of a want I have for that man.' I was talking to myself, tapping my fingers on the counter. My cock rose, hard and eager, after having to give up hope of release upon awakening.

My mind – so fertile with imagination – insisted I could feel the rough bite of his cast on my chest as he pressed me into submission. His hand on my cock. His lips on my lips. The coffee machine hissed and spit and I pushed one shaking hand into my pyjama bottoms. When I grasped myself, I made a sound low in my throat I'd rarely ever made. Pure unadulterated need. It was a naked, scary sound. To realise I was that urgent to be with someone after so long.

'Fuck.' My hand made quick work of it. The dream had primed the pump and I filled in the rest. Giovanni giving more of himself, more pleasure, a round two if you will. I played the scenario out in my head. After jerking me off with his hand, he dropped to his knees. Took my semi-hard length in his pretty wet mouth and started to suck me slowly.

He had a girl's mouth when he sucked cock; I'd noticed it right away. A pretty pink mouth with those full lips that curled up into an almost kewpie doll pucker. How bad I wanted to shove the head of my dick over those pretty pink lips and feel the mystical humid wetness of the secret recesses of his mouth.

In my mind's eye, I pushed just the head past the seam of his lips and when the velvet wet heat of his tongue licked at me, I lost my cool. I grabbed his long, chocolate coloured hair and forced myself further in. Back over the plush cushion of his tongue until his brown eyes grew wide and sparkled with unshed tears.

His hands – with those elegant long fingers – found my legs and he held me there. Not pulling me in, not pushing me away. The arm with the cast rasped at my legs because he couldn't really hold me. And then Giovanni was surging forward, swallowing me, gulping me down, sucking me so that my knees shook like a broken wind-up toy and my heart felt fit to burst through my chest.

'Fuck,' I said again, my fist flying with furtive dry whispers as the coffee pot hissed like a demon crouched on my counter.

I squinted my eyes tight to push out the reality of my small, dimly lit pre-dawn kitchen.

Giovanni pulled back, sucked just the tip of me, pressing his tongue to the single small slit in the helmet of my dick. He grinned at me and I lost it. Seeing the flash of white teeth and pink lips and silken tongue. I wanted to flip him and fuck him or offer myself. I wanted it all but more than anything, I wanted to feel Giovanni in my arms. I wanted to feel my hands on that quicksilver body of his. All sinew and movement, like something from the sea. I wanted to know what my hands felt like tangled in the smooth mass of his hair and what his heart felt like when it raced under my hand as I pressed my fingers to his smooth chest. I wanted to know what his mouth tasted like after he sucked me.

I came hard, my hand a pathetic stand-in for the man I was suddenly so infatuated with. But it was something. I had barely mustered the enthusiasm to even get myself off these last few weeks but now I felt half sick, half giddy with infatuation. It was a good feeling. It made me feel alive.

I cleaned myself up and made myself a cup of coffee, my

body still pleasantly loose and soft from the orgasm. When I closed my eyes I felt yellow all through my soul – the colour of buttercups and sunshine and lemonade. Internally, I shone with a warm colour that soothed me, just from this man. I made it through three Nickelodeon Jr. shows with Annabel, my breakfast, her breakfast, two diaper changes and 16 emails until I couldn't stand it and I dialled Giovanni's number.

He must've had caller ID because he answered, 'Well it's about damn time Charlie Nacht. What took you so long? I couldn't get you out of my head all night.'

I smiled at the phone. 'Yeah, I kind of had a similar problem. When can I see you? I need to see you.'

'Oooh, sounds urgent.'

'It is.'

'What's so urgent?'

'I need to kiss you again,' I confessed. *And then some.*

'Don't spoil me already, Charlie.'

I handed Annabel a black and white plush block and she grinned at me. A huge toothless grin that made me grin back. 'What do you mean?' I asked, confused.

'That's so fucking romantic. I'm afraid I'll get used to it.'

'Maybe you should.'

'Be still my heart.'

'Be still mine,' I said, remembering my dream. The air in my lungs seemed to solidify and my cock twitched in my jeans. I needed to get my head on straight. But I said 'Still got that cast on?'

A moment of silence and then 'Um … of course. Why?'

'I'll explain later.'

'Promise?'

'I do.'

166

Chapter Three

'TELL ME ABOUT HIM.'

'Ma …'

'Don't Ma me! Tell me.' My mother took Annabel and started to change her clothes.

'Ma, I just put those on her.'

'Hush. I bought her something.'

She handed me the baby's T-shirt and slipped a fresh one down over Annabel's pink all-in-one. The new one said, *IF YOU THINK I'M GORGEOUS YOU SHOULD SEE MY GRANDMA*. I rolled my eyes, but my laughter was genuine.

'See, that. Look how nice. Now tell me.'

'Marie, Marie, Marie,' I tsked. But I sat at the table and let her pour me some iced tea.

'That's Ma or Mamma to you. And to you it's Grandma!' Annabel smiled and made a cooing noise and my mother gave her a teething cookie.

'He's handsome. He's young, probably too young for the likes of me.'

'You're 30 for God's sake, not a 100.'

'I bet he's 25 – 26 at a stretch.' I picked the hole in my jeans, wishing for a cigarette.

'Enh. Not so bad. There's ten years between your father and I. Is he handsome?' She looked so avid, I felt a little sad. How long had it been since my mother grilled me over details about a guy?

'Very. He's lean and dark.'

'Black?'

167

'No. Dark like olive skin, dark hair, dark eyes. Italian.'

Her eyes lit up and I smiled. 'Oh my. Fabulous. Not that I …'

'Yeah, yeah, not that you care. Marie *Fratelli* …'

'Marie Nacht nee Fratelli,' she snorted. 'Stop teasing me. Good kisser?'

'Ma!'

'Oh come on. Did you kiss this Italian beauty or what?'

My mother is the only person alive who can make me blush. Heat flooded my face and I picked even harder at that shred in my jeans. 'Stop it.'

'Tell your daddy to tell me, Annabel! Tell him to tell Grandma. Confession is good for the soul. Even if it's to your own mother.' A shadow crossed my mother's face, probably realising that Annabel might never have a mother to confess to. It broke my heart to watch hers break. Mariah had been like a daughter to my mother. My mom had always wanted a girl and for years she had one in my best friend. When Mariah left we all lost – Annabel a mother, me a best friend, my mother a surrogate daughter. It was a lose-lose-lose situation.

I found myself spilling to her so that she'd feel better. 'OK. One kiss and it was nice.'

'Nice? *Nice* does not a love affair make.'

I pushed a hand over my face, gritted my teeth, but then I forced myself to speak. 'OK, ma. It was hot. He was a really good kisser and I got turned on for the first time in a long time. And I asked him out. Which is why I'm here. I wanted to know if you could play overnight babysitter tonight. So I can go out and stay out late and have some fun.'

'Yes!' my mother said, clapping Bell's hands and then she leaned in, nose to nose with my daughter and said, 'Maybe Daddy will get lucky.'

'Christ,' I said. I have weird, weird family. Fabulous, but weird.

***

'Here I am, cast and all.'

I took him in, standing there on my doorstep. His white button down was open three buttons showing his thin chest. He wore a thin leather cuff and blue jeans that had seen just enough abuse to be cool, not enough to be sloppy. His tan boots were also well used, well worn, loved but pretty pricey. Big dark eyes flashed at me and my stomach dropped to my feet.

'Come on in. Cast and all,' I said as an afterthought. 'I'm running behind. My mother came by to get the baby and ended up, apparently, needing everything the baby owned just in case. I'm almost ready. Wine?'

'Wine's good? Is it a nice Chianti? Is it lush and full bodied and *sexy*?'

'Sexy?'

'Yeah, isn't that stupid? That's the new adjective for food and wine. Things are spicy, tangy and sexy.'

I grunted, moving back to the small powder room off the bathroom. I put a comb through my wheat coloured hair and spritzed myself with a little cologne. 'Spicy, tangy, zippy, maybe but I'm not so sure about sexy. Maybe strawberries dipped in chocolate. On a good day. If I were drunk?' I smiled at him in the mirror and felt his fingers trip along the leather of my belt. My heart stilled and I watched him watching me in the mirror.

'Steak is not sexy,' Giovanni said. His voice was a soft hand on me. His voice a silken stroke. 'Not even Manicotti is sexy.'

'What is?' I asked. I tried to swallow but I had something wedged in my throat. I think it was my heart.

'You. You are sexy.' He tugged my belt and I stumbled back two steps. The room so small I was on him before I could process my movement. He wrapped his cast to my chest, embracing me from behind. His head peeked over my shoulder so we both stared at our reflection in the mirror. The hand I couldn't see was in the back of my belt, holding

169

me. Anchoring me as if I would bolt. 'You are very fucking sexy. All I could thing about last night. All I dreamt about.' His mouth pressed to my ear lobe and I shivered.

'Me too,' I confessed.

'Tell me about the cast.'

But he must have had some kind of inkling. Some sixth sense or some idea because even as he said it, he tugged the cast up hard over the cage of my chest and my cock stiffened to the point where the single burning thought in my mind was getting off, getting close to him. Being with him. However he wanted me, I was there.

So I told him. I started from the beginning and I watched his face. Watched his eyes grow liquid and his mouth grow pouty. The hand tucked in the back of my belt slid lower so that his fingers trailed over the skin along my lower back. My body pebbled with goose bumps and there was a moment where his touch felt so intense that I could not get my tongue to work. I could not swallow or blink or move. I was frozen in that moment where his fingers pressed hot and insistent to my flesh and all I could see or feel or smell was Giovanni.

'So it went something like this?' he said to the side of my neck. And then he turned and pinned me to the wall. The cast pressed to my chest and my heart fought back with a raging beat that made me light headed.

'Something like tha …' I lost my words when his uninjured hand had its way with my belt and jeans. When he took me in his grasp, his fingers impossibly cool for a second before heating, I shuddered as if I were already coming. He never stopped watching me, his big eyes taking in everything I did. Every inhalation, every twitch, every blink. He kissed me and his hand squeezed my cock and I made a sound almost like I was crying.

'My dream was a bit more intense. My dream was us fucking. My dream was me fucking you and then you fucking me. Everyone got fucked. Everyone was happy.

And you smiled and when you smiled for me …' He paused, running his finger tips along the length of me only to take me fully in hand again and squeeze so that I thought for sure I would come but didn't. Felt for sure my knees would buckle and dump me on my ass, but they didn't.

'What?'

'When you smiled for me it touched your eyes. You looked happy. For real. Not someone walking along the edge of happy and flirting with it, but honest to God happy and I had done that. I had made you happy. And when I woke up I jacked off to that thought alone. The thought of kissing you and the thought of making you happy.' Then he did kiss me. A long, hard kiss that made small silver and pink sparks go off behind my closed eyelids. I saw colours in his kiss.

'And?'

'And it was the best fucking orgasm I've had in years.'

'Yeah?' I moved my hips so that I slid into the loose circle of his fingers. I tried to touch him but much like in my dream, he held me at bay with the rough cast and his unexpected strength. Such a deceiving man – whip thin but fearsomely strong.

'Yeah.' He grinned at me and my heart jumped as if it might stop right there. 'Then I fell asleep and had another dream.'

'About what?'

'Me and you.'

'What about us?' I asked. My voice was high and thin and almost comical.

'About me doing this,' he said and he dropped to his knees. Right there in my teeny tiny little powder room, he leaned in to touch his lips to the tip of me and I mewled softly. An embarrassing but honest sound. At the very last second he said, 'Sorry we're moving so fast. I'm normally not so quick on the draw with a new beau. Though I haven't had a new beau in a billion years.'

171

'Me neither. It's OK. It's better than OK. I feel …'

He paused, his tongue a fraction of an inch from where I wanted it. From where I needed it to be. On my body. Giovanni cocked an eyebrow and said, 'You feel what?'

'Happy,' I admitted.

I stared, letting my body and soul relax into his deep brown gaze. Mesmerised by the honesty and sensuality there. Staring at Giovanni was like taking a warm, long bath with your eyes.

'Sweet talker,' he said, and swallowed me down.

Chapter Four

I ALMOST LOST IT on the first suck. When his lips and tongue and then throat took me in, gripped up around me like a moist prison. I almost shot my load and ended it right there. But I managed to keep my hold by biting my lip and watching the coffee brown waves of his hair shimmer in the soft light. I counted to ten and I wondered how many calories were in oatmeal (I'd had it for breakfast) and when I no longer felt like a 14-year-old boy ready to lose his control, I touched Giovanni.

His hair parted for my fingers the way I hoped his body would part and open for me one day. The thick mess of brown swallowed my hands and I tugged so he grunted, the vibration shooting up through my dick to rumble my belly. It almost tickled. I almost laughed. I wanted to laugh anyhow from the sheer joy of watching his mouth suck me in.

'You're so easy to please,' he teased, not looking up at me. He kept his eyes averted, long lashes swept his cheeks. He looked like a painting by some master. Some genius. Gorgeous.

'Not normally,' I admitted. 'You please me. It's as simple as that.'

'I don't want you to come.'

'No?'

'No. I want you to almost come and then tell me, OK?'

'Christ. I'll try, Gi. I have to tell you …'

His tongue did a lazy tour of the tip of my cock and I

173

hissed like his mouth was made of fire. 'Yeah?'

'You're awfully good. And you're awfully present ...' I thrust gently, a small rocking of my hips that pushed my penis a little deeper into his mouth each time. He smacked my thigh with the fingers on his unharmed arm.

'Sneaky boy. And what do you mean present?' He did look up then. Seemingly bottomless eyes that made me feel pleasantly heavy and unbelievably light all at once. Eyes that said I could fall for this man. That I could actually be in love. Feel all the things I'd always wanted to feel but had never quite managed simply because on a whim I'd waved him over to a shaved ice stand on a warm day.

'I mean you're in head. Filling my head. Deep in my brain. I dreamed about you. I thought about you. I almost can't stand watching you down on your knees for me without coming, for God's sake.'

His smile made my fingers tingly and numb it was such an overwhelming glimpse of happiness. 'Wow. You really are giving me a big head.' Then he laughed and squeezed my cock, both of us getting his unintentional double entendre at the same moment. 'Will you try?'

'I will.'

He bent his head again, his dark hair curtaining his face from me for an instant. 'Almost come, but don't come. Almost come, but don't come.' He repeated it like a mantra and the words shimmied up through my core into my heart. All that vibrating was going to have the reverse effect of his words, but I watched him and I felt each silken slide of his tongue on my shaft until I felt like I might scream if I didn't come.

'God, fuck, now,' I said. 'I'm almost gone.'

He was a tangle of long limbs and cast, white cotton shirt and denim. A swirling mass of leanness and then he was on his hands and knees, his shirt only half off, handing me a foil packet over his shoulder. 'I'm not a slut, but this is how I want us to be. I want it to be today. Right now. I don't

174

know why. Can you not ask me why?'

I nodded dumbly, working the condom down over my cock. I would never ask him why, because I felt the same. Like we were sealing something. Starting something. Kicking off a big event the way a football game starts with a bang of players running through paper and shiny coins tossed high in the air. That made me smile and I drooped to my knees, the soft navy blue throw rug tickling at my skin. He held the edge of the vanity. His hand was shaking.

'Help me with this fucking buckle and jeans. It's a pisser trying to do all this when your' nervous horny and wearing a cast.'

I took my time and undressed him, not letting him do any of the work. Every time he moved to try and help me I said, 'Still. Be still. I have this.' I dropped a kiss along his flank, his back, the tiny knobs of his spine lined up like little bone soldiers under his flesh.

I ran my finger along a small coffee stain of a birthmark low on his back. It looked very much like a coffee ring but smaller. I kissed it too.

'They say that birthmarks are where you've been stabbed in a former life.'

I kissed it again. A small piece of my heart broke hearing his tone. Something told me that Giovanni had seen a lot of pain. I don't know about past lives, but in this one. I rubbed my cock along the back of his thigh, the air in my tiny close bathroom fragrant with the smell of sweat and sex and latex.

'So you were stabbed in the back,' I said. I pushed the head of my cock to the small pink star of his anus and heard his breath hitch when he answered me.

'Yeah, most likely. I'm pretty sure I've been stabbed in the back in this life too. More than once,' he said, and waved his cast in the air.

I pushed but did not enter. Licked his birthmark and kissed it once more. 'I'm sorry.'

'Don't be. We all have hard lessons to learn.'

'I know. But they still suck.'

'And not in a good way.'

'Amen. Now under that sink is some lube.'

'Spit will do.'

'I don't want to hurt you.'

'I like pain.'

'Next time,' I said. 'Now get it.' Pain and pleasure and games, tops and bottoms and in betweens could be later. I wanted this time sweet. I wanted this time to be long and lazy, lush and decadent.

He handed it over and I used so much we both laughed. 'I'm going to slide into that restaurant like I've been greased!'

'You have,' I said. But then I was sliding into him and we both forgot just what the fuck we were laughing at. We were both too busy with the fucking at hand.

Each thrust had me gritting my teeth as I watched him struggle to breathe. He was powerless to jack off. His good hand held him steady, his bad arm folded under him, useless and dingy white in its plaster cocoon. I reached under him to find him long and hard, his skin hot in my hand. He sighed.

'It's like coming home, Charlie,' he said.

'I know.'

'What's it mean?'

'I don't know. Maybe in a past life …'

'Don't say you stabbed me,' Giovanni said, his body shaking with his laughter. But then he thrust gently into my hand and his ass flexed around me and I almost knocked the whole deck of cards down by coming.

'No, no. I could never hurt you. But maybe I was there to tend to you after. Maybe I was there to …' I groaned. I gripped him tight as if that could stave off my release but the orgasm just kept rolling towards me. A big boulder of a climax that would not be put off any more.

My hand flew over his cock and he whimpered. Over me, he was in control, under me, he was malleable. I had never

176

met anyone quite like Giovanni Rustici before. And I think that's because there just weren't many out there.

'Maybe you were there to what?' he asked, and I felt the warm splash of his come on my hand as I lost my battle and came with him. Thrusting hard but controlled against his precariously balanced form.

'Put you back together after,' I said. 'Maybe I was who you ran to.'

'I'm sorry I had to have my way with you,' Giovanni said.

I almost snorted wine up my nose, but bit my tongue to keep my composure. My mother had raised me to be a gentleman at the table. Especially when in a nice Italian restaurant. I couldn't stifle the smile, but I did swallow the loud burst of laughter.

'Wow. It's OK. I don't mind being taken advantage of.'

I'd pushed him into a shower and climbed in after him. There'd been no more fucking, but I think my hands had been on Giovanni more than myself. I washed his hair after washing mine, soaped him from head to toe until he'd joked "*careful, I might slide right down the drain,*" to which I answered, "*then I'd dive in right after you*".

How could anyone hurt this man, I wondered, eyeing his cast. But I forced my eyes back up to find him studying me.

'So I sleep with bad guys who hit and you get it up for lonely women who want offspring.'

'And then get to keep said offspring. But I love her, my Annabel.'

'I know you do.'

'I don't want any doubt of that.' I felt a huge amount of guilt for even having to articulate it. What did that say about me as a father that I had to reassure people that I *wanted* my daughter?

'There is no doubt to anyone paying attention when you are anywhere in the vicinity of Annabel. By the way, it's a lovely name.' Giovanni picked up a perfectly fried sliver of calamari and popped it into his lush mouth. My cock responded with a lazy twitch, my stomach warmed with lust.

'It means easy to love,' I said. I chose my own piece of fried squid and ate.

'Then it's accurate too.'

'Pretty much. She's intoxicating.'

'Like her father.'

For whatever reason, the hardest man in the world to embarrass found himself blushing for the second time that day. 'Shh. Don't.'

'Don't what?' His knee pressed to mine under the table. He didn't move it, or tickle or twitch. He simply pressed his warm knee to my warm knee. The pressure and the presence were staggering. I had never been so aware of my body before. Each nerve and molecule of flesh responded to the contact until I felt whole and fresh and light.

It had been a long time since my chest had felt light. For months I had carried a ball of dread and stress and guilt around in the general direction of my solar plexus. Now I felt it loosen and my eyes filled with tears I tried desperately not to shed.

'Just don't,' I said.

'Why are you getting upset?' He leaned in so that mere inches separated us and I could smell the spicy redness of the wine on his breath.

'I'm not.' It was true. I wasn't upset. What I was feeling was akin to relief, not sadness or grief.

'You look like you're going to cry,' he said.

'I might.'

'Don't.' He looked so worried I felt bad but my throat had narrowed with emotion and I felt partly liberated and partly stupid. I couldn't explain. Not yet.

'It's OK,' I said. 'I promise.' I rose so fast I almost knocked the chair over. I walked fast, my stride eating up the red and white imported Italian tile until I reached the men's room door. I entered, found I was alone, locked the door and wept like someone had died. I think someone had. The me who had been white-knuckling life for the last six or so months. That guy had just gotten his ticket punched.

I didn't know who this new guy was. The one who wanted to lean across the dinner table in public and kiss his new lover. To taste the salty spicy briny taste of seafood off Gi's mouth. This guy who wanted to put his hands on his shiny new infatuation in very inappropriate ways whenever the urge took him. I didn't know who this new guy was, the one staring back at me from the mirror. The one who had those same wolf blue eyes but with a new kind of shine and joy in them that hadn't been there before. I didn't know who this guy was, but I welcomed him.

Chapter Five

'SO LET ME TELL you what I think about what's in your head,' Giovanni said. He pushed himself back from the table as our waitress delivered his slab of homemade lasagne and a fresh salad.

'Do I want to know?' I picked at my own stuffed shells and finally took a huge bite, basil and tomato and Ricotta filling my mouth. I hummed low in my throat, the pleasure of the taste not lost on me despite the huge emotional waves washing over me.

I felt relief, giddy, sadness, joy. I felt absolved of all my sins of bad fathering and forgiven for every thought of wishing I had not given into Mariah. Fatherhood had not been something I looked down on or thought ridiculous. It was just not something I felt suited to, and being suddenly solely responsible for another human being had felt utterly and staggeringly heavy. A weight I felt I dragged around like Sisyphus rolling his rock up the hill forever.

Now I felt somehow OK with my ineptitude at being the perfect parent. I felt simply like myself. Imperfect and a bit goofy and often too serious, but good. I was a good person. I wasn't sure how Giovanni highlighted that with just his presence so that I could be aware of my perfect imperfection, but he did. And I was not only smitten, I was grateful.

My mother once told me that true love was when another person made you feel completely like yourself and it was still OK. True love was when you loved someone so much that you found you could also love yourself fully. My mother's pretty fucking smart, if you ask me.

'Probably not, but hey, it's a party. I know you carry a ridiculous amount of guilt around for no reason.'

'How do you know that?' I swallowed my wine to keep my throat from clogging up with more tears.

'I pay attention.'

I nodded. 'Fair enough. So tell me about your ex lover John.'

'He was an asshole. The end.'

A huge laugh burst out of me like steam shooting out of a pressure valve. 'Oh my God.'

'I know! I do not deserve an asshole.'

'No. You don't.'

'I deserve someone like you,' he said.

'What if I'm an asshole,' I asked, seriously worried about it in that moment of time.

'Nah.' He waved his good hand at me, stabbed a piece of Romaine lettuce and ate with gusto. I noticed he did everything with gusto, eating, talking, laughing, fucking. 'You're a good guy. You're a really good guy.'

'How do you know?'

'I pay attention.' He winked at me, and stupidly, it made my cock hard. It made me happy and it made me want to laugh, that one little wink. 'Besides, I had an acupuncturist right after I broke this ...'

'Right after *he* broke it,' I corrected.

'Right, right. Anyway, I told the guy that with the injury and the violence and the healing and the worry, I felt like I was going crazy. Was I crazy?'

'And?'

'And he said that crazy people did not worry that they were crazy. They thought *everyone else* was crazy. And I'll take that one step further and say that assholes do not worry they are assholes. They think everyone else is an asshole.'

'I think you're perfect,' I blurted before I could stop

181

myself. Before I could let embarrassment and worry override my mouth and my true feelings.

'Ditto, kid.'

Now that made me laugh. Younger than me in all ways and he was calling me kid. But when I looked into his eyes, I found a wisdom there that said maybe inside, Giovanni was older than me.

We made it to the parking lot. Or I should say, *I* made it to the parking lot before I had to have him again. It was as sudden as fainting, the overwhelming urge to have my mouth on him.

I pushed him into my SUV and he saw it in my eyes because he said, 'Oh, Mr Nacht. Here? You are so dirty.'

'I am dirty. I am dirty and horny and you smell like my shampoo which for some reason is making me even crazier to get a hold of you.' I tugged his belt buckle and his eyelids drifted shut for a moment. I struggled into the back seat with him, thanking the powers that be that I decided on a spur of the moment decision to get the tinted windows after all, and yanked the door shut behind me.

'Oh, Mr Nacht. It's so dark in here.' I could hear him grinning in the shadowy cocoon of my backseat. Only a few bold splashes of streetlamp illumination streaked the interior of my vehicle.

'Don't be afraid of the dark,' I chuckled, sounding very much like a dirty old man to my own ears. 'I'll protect you.'

Giovanni snickered, but I felt the hard length of his cock under my hand. I pushed my free hand to his chest to feel the steady gallop of his heart in his chest. I loved him. I knew that already. I wasn't fighting it; I just wasn't ready to say it aloud just yet.

'I feel the same way,' he said, and I jerked as if caught stealing.

'Get out of my head, devil boy,' I said.

'Suck my dick,' he said, with a humour so encompassing, I smiled so big it hurt my face.

'I think I shall.' Then I moved past my unspoken feeling and tugged his jeans low on his hips. He was an inverted shadow in the dark, just pale flashes of perfect smooth flesh. An overexposed negative of whiteness and light. He moved like a ghost and I pushed my lips to one jutting hipbone, simply feeling the warmth of him with my mouth.

'Oh my God, you can't just sit there with your mouth on me.' He breathed out the words like a short prayer.

I smiled in the dark and moved my lips so they were on the warm, soft skin above his pubic hair. Above the jutting ready cock that was brushing along my chin. 'Sure I can. See. I like to feel your heartbeat through your skin.'

He growled and I tried not to laugh so he could hear me.

'You're trying to kill me, Nacht,' he said.

'Never. But I wouldn't mind hearing you beg.'

I held his thin legs under my hands and pinned him flat under me, breathing in the dark, sensual scent of him. He bonked me lightly on the head with his cast and I pressed my lips more securely to his hot flesh. He sighed.

'That's not begging,' I said.

'Please, Charlie? Please. Oh God, please. Please suck my dick.' He was smiling but there was an urgent seriousness in his voice too. It turned me on and made me cave all at once.

'Since you asked me nicely.' I licked the tip of him and his hips arched up like I'd electrocuted him. I sucked him deeper and he shuddered under me, his body feverish and moving like a wave.

I remembered what it felt like to slide into him. The tight wet all-encompassing feel of him. I wanted to kiss him, even though my mouth was full of him. He made me wish for two mouths, two tongues, more time, more kissing. More of him. All of him.

'Oh, you are way too good at that.' His hand tangled in my hair and he yanked short hunks so that pain sparkled over my scalp. My dick got hard from the flash of pain and I wondered if I could fuck him right here. But then I remembered that I wanted my mouth on him. I wanted to taste his skin and his come, feel him lose his control and spill into my mouth.

'I try.' I sucked his balls so that he groaned and when I pushed a finger deep into his ass, he said, 'Jesus Christ.'

'Charlie will do just fine,' I teased and added a second finger and nudging that magical spot in his body that had him banging his cast on the back of the seat like he was beating a war drum.

'I might actually address you as Jesus if you … fuck … because me being able to hold on for two more seconds would be a god damn miracle.'

'Yeah?' I pressed a third finger into him and flexed. My tongue lapped at him, tasting the salt of his skin.

'Yeah, fuck. Here we go, Jesus.'

It struck me as so funny I started to laugh and he filled my mouth with his release. My mouth full of him and laughter and his come.

He put his hands on the back of my head and I rested my forehead to his pelvis. I kissed his softening cock and then his hips, his belly, his side. 'God that tickles,' he yelped.

'Will you come home with me?' I asked.

There was a silence and he went still. In fluorescent-splashed darkness he touched my face. 'Of course. Why do you sound so … serious?'

I shrugged, laying my head on his belly. I listened to the rush of blood in my head and the steady beat of his pulse. 'I don't know when I'll have the house to myself again. No baby.'

'Are you worried that I'll mind that you have Annabel, Charlie?'

I thought about it. Let my pulse jack rabbit up with anxiety and then I spilled my guts. One sentence. Dead honest. 'I'm fucking praying that you don't, Giovanni.'

'Do you pray often?'

'Never,' I said.

184

'I truly could have bought you dessert. I can afford it.' I watched him move, fast and sure like a serpent, through my small bright kitchen.

'What would be the fun in that? Plus, this way I get to show off my mad skills in the kitchen and you can truly appreciate what a catch I am.' He stopped and smiled at me, showing a flash of white teeth and a hint of pink tongue. My internal organs turned to lava and my heart did a startled stutter-step at the ferocity of my lust.

'I don't need you to convince me of that,' I said. My tongue felt a bit too big and I nipped the end to sharpen my focus.

'Well, it's still nice to make it clear. I am a total catch.' He dipped a red, swollen strawberry in chocolate and then set it on a piece of wax paper. My stomach rumbled. How could I be hungry?

'I can see that. Oranges?'

'Clementines,' he said. 'Seedless and so sweet they're like candy. Dip them in chocolate and they're the food equivalent of an orgasm.'

'You don't say?' The word orgasm acted like a string, pulling me toward him, tempting me to touch him. I pushed up behind him, my chest flush to his narrow back. I was bulky compared to Giovanni and yet, so often, he made me feel small and safe.

'I do say, lover. I do say.' He set the segment on the wax paper, acting as if I weren't resting my hard-on to the curve of his ass. My heartbeat banged against his shoulder blade and Giovanni said 'You're warm. I like it.'

'You're warm, too.' I pushed my hand down the front of his jeans, to find his cock hard already. I wrapped my hand around him, watching him dip another strawberry with his shaking hand. His cast sat on the counter but he drummed the naked fingers that poked from inside. I felt a bubble of rage in my belly every time I saw that injured appendage.

'And I also like it,' I said.

I worked his buckle and his button, pulling down his stubborn jeans, my lips pressed the place on his throat where his pulse beat with arousal. 'Don't distract me, Charles,' he breathed. I heard the catch in his voice and smiled.

I pushed my hips to his ass and pinned him even harder to the red counter. 'Sorry. I won't.' But I wasn't sorry and I was very much lying.

I traced the fine hair up the back of his neck with the tip of my tongue and he shivered in my arms like it was cold. But the house was a nice even temperature and the night was mild. I laughed, kissing him up one side of his throat only to kiss back down the other. His heavy blanket of dark hair rested in my palm like a heavy leash.

'That is very distracting,' he sighed. He dropped another segment of Clementine and snickered. 'Damn.'

'Ooops. Mistakes don't count.' I nabbed the fruit and popped it in my mouth.

He wiggled, fought me, turned so we were face to face. 'You weren't supposed to eat that.'

'Sorry.'

'No you're not.'

I pressed my forehead to his. 'No. I'm not.'

'Was it good?'

'It was. I'll prove it.' And I kissed him. I pushed my lips to his full lips and wormed my tongue into the warmth of his mouth.

'It is good,' he said.

'Yes. Sweet and a little bitter with the chocolate.' I yanked his zipper down and pushed him back on the counter.

'The fruit!' he said, but he sounded unconvincing.

'Oh my. The fruit.' I moved the fruit with one hand while the other kept after his jeans.

When I had him bare, I pressed my lips to his nipple, capturing one rose coloured disc of flesh between my teeth until he said, 'Christ, Charlie, you're killing me.' My hand jacked him up and down, up and down, slow and steady. A mesmerising rhythm like a metronome.

'Not trying to kill you. But I do want to keep you right ... there ...' I rubbed my thumb over the weeping slit at the tip of his dick and when Giovanni exhaled he almost sounded like he was crying.

'I'm right there.'

'Are there more?' I asked, patting him down.

'There are. Lubricated for your pleasure.' He reached past my probing hands and dipped his fingers into a pocket. 'Here you go, sir.'

'I like when you call me sir.'

'I like when you call *me* sir,' he countered. 'But right now I'd just like it if you'd ...'

'If I'd ...?'

Giovanni leaned forward and captured my bottom lip in his perfect sharp teeth. He nipped me hard enough to send a zing of pain through my abdomen and straight into my cock. I watched his dark eyes even though his face was pressed right up to mine.

'Fuck me,' he breathed.

'I figured you'd want to fuck me.'

'Soon.'

'You like to be ...'

'I have no preference. But I like you in me. You. For some reason when it comes to you, I like that you're entering my body.'

It seemed so intimate when he said it that way. I was no fool, I knew what fucking was, but God, sometimes we forget to think of it that way. We forget that we are either entering or being entered. Sometimes both. And that is as intimate as you can get, letting another person in your body.

I put my hand in that hair of his, fisting hunks of it and then wrapping my fingers around his beautiful face. I kissed him. 'God, fuck ... Jesus, Gi. I like that too. Don't laugh at

187

me. You've crossed my wires, man. I feel almost drunk on you. Giddy. Don't laugh at me,' I said again, a sharp splinter of fear stabbing my gut.

'Why would I laugh at you? I feel the same way. I do.' He kissed me back like we would simply disappear if we stopped. His cast rested on my hips, his free hand roamed my back, pulling me in over and over again like I was trying to get away, but I wasn't.

'Good.'

'Now about that fucking ...'

Chapter Six

IT WAS EASY – SO fucking easy, even after so long – to push him back on the counter. His hair tumbled all round his head and over the edge of the island. I thought about walking to the other side of the kitchen island and pushing my cock into that perfect mouth again, but I shook my head to keep myself in check.

'What are you waiting for?'

'Just thinking very bad things,' I said. His knees bent high when I pushed his legs. I kissed along the swell of his bottom, ringing his ass with the tip of my tongue until his cock stood true like a flesh and blood divining rod. I swooped down to suck him in deep and then pushed past the tight ring of anus into the heated pressure inside of him. I held his knees high, watching his face. Watching his cock.

He put his unsheathed hand on top of mine, his head swivelling back and forth, back and forth like he was saying no in the slowest possible way. 'Put your hand on your dick,' I said. I wanted to watch him jack off. I wanted to see the tan of his hand against the pale flesh of his prick.

'Patience.' His fingers pressed to the back of mine, an inverted squeeze of my hand as I slipped in and out of him.

I grunted. Patience, my ass.

I held his legs wide, his knees high, fucking him in slow measured strokes so that I didn't lose it right there.

Giovanni opened his big brown eyes and watched me.

'What?' I touched his cock, stroking him with the tips of my fingers and then loosely cupped fist. He sighed, his body shuddering under me.

'I like watching you. You're beautiful.' He grinned and my body went taut, ready to surrender, ready to shoot. I inhaled deeply. Shook my head.

'Um, I think it's you who's beautiful. Look at you,' I said.

'Look at you.'

'Look at me holding your dick,' I laughed. 'Now you. I want to see. I've got about 30 seconds left in me.' Honesty was the best policy in life and in orgasms.

'Fine, fine. Impatient much?'

'Always.'

'Why this?' His long fingers wrapped around his hard length and electricity zipped up my spine, the fine hairs on my arms waving with the current.

'I like it. It's sexy. And it's sexier because it's you. You have the most amazing hands. And cock. Body ...' I chuckled, feeling pleased and silly in the same pulse beat.

His lashes dipped before he fought to keep his eyes wide. 'I'm almost done for. You fucking me is one thing. You fucking me face-to-face so I can watch you ... cruel.'

'Cruel? Why's that?' I cupped his ass, tilting him just so and rocked into him with sweet short bursts.

'Because it's so god damn hot I don't last long.'

'On three,' I joked, but I smacked his ass cheek with my thrust and he groaned.

'One ...' Giovanni's hand flew and I realised we were doing it. We were counting down our fucking to our coming. A celebration with semen.

That made me laugh, the fucked up way my mind worked, and I said on a strangled tone, 'Two.'

'Charlie, I'm done, baby.' He said it softly and then, 'Three.' I watched his come coat his hand. Watched the pearlescent flow cover his elegant fingers and it was only when I heard myself cry out that I realised I'd tipped into my own orgasm right along with him.

'Come to my bed with me. I want to hold you.'

'But my fruit.'

'Breakfast,' I said and gathered him up off the counter. I kissed his cheek, his nose, his lips until he obeyed.

It was the middle of the night when he took me. I woke to find him stroking my back. His fingers trailing down the backs of my thighs and tickling the backs of my knees.

'What're you doing?' My brain struggled to surface from the dark murk of sleep.

He kissed my ear. 'Touching you. Getting you hard. Then I plan to fuck you.'

'Oh you do?' I put a challenge in my tone but my cock went stone hard at nothing more than his whispered words.

'I do. Do you plan to let me?'

I hitched in a breath as his lips touched my shoulder and his cool fingers closed over me. 'I could be persuaded.'

Giovanni's tongue trailed up the back of my arm and goose bumps erupted on my skin. The room was black but for the green digital numbers on my clock. 'It's difficult, I'm sure, to give in to me. To submit to being fucked. When you've been through so much.'

My throat narrowed and in my mind's eye I saw that fucking cast. Here he was talking about all I'd been through while sporting a broken arm and a recently broken heart. I shook my head, but my eyes stung. My body wanted to cry. My mind wanted to stop my body.

'I'll submit to you. I'll receive you because it's you. And you, Giovanni, are different. And *you* have been through so much.'

'We'll call it a draw, then. So, will you let me in, Charlie? Will you take me on?' His fingers ringed my ass and my body warmed to his touch. My belly felt full of fire and a humming energy of need.

I pushed my ass up to answer him, opening myself just enough that his finger could penetrate. Then his mouth was everywhere and he was spreading me, opening me up, laying me bare under him. It felt like more than my body, it felt as if my soul was bare to Giovanni. His skin was warm and the lube was cool and I lay sprawled as if boneless while he tenderly took me closer and closer to where we were going.

When he thrust into me, that sharp sparkle bite of penetration sounded in my gut and I felt the tears then. Not because he'd hurt me, not because I'd had a long dry spell, but basically because I was letting someone into my life. And my instincts – as fucked up and far off as they could be at times – told me loud and clear that he was good. Giovanni was good and my life was about to get better. If I let it.

I came with a rush of heat and more tears and heard him say, 'Sweetheart,' as he followed suit. Then it was small, lithe Giovanni Rustici gathering me to him and petting my hair as I fell back into a peaceful slumber.

I hadn't slept that well in months.

Until about 5.45 a.m. when the phone rang.

At first I thought it was the cell and I reached on the floor for my jeans but I heard Giovanni speak and realised it was the bedside phone. The portable rested on the nightstand on the side of the bed he was currently occupying.

'Hold on a minute. I'm pretty sure he's awake.' Then to me he said, 'Sorry. I just grabbed it without thinking. I woke up, heard a phone and reached for it.'

I had no qualm with him answering; I simply wondered who was calling me. He answered my unspoken question.

'It's your mom, Charlie. About the baby.'

My heart fell to my feet and I gasped for air that a moment before I'd had plenty of. 'Mom … Ma … what's wrong? Is Annabel …?'

'It's Mariah, Charlie,' she whispered into the phone. 'She's here.'

I blinked, sitting up and trying to get my balance. Lack of sleep and fear had done a number on my equilibrium and for a few seconds the room kept moving even when I had stopped. 'Oh. That's OK. She …'

'She wants to take the baby, Charlie. She wants to take her. She says she has a court order.'

My stomach went cold. I felt like I'd be sick. 'She has a lot of law in her family, Ma and … where has she been? Why now? What the fuck,' I said. My voice wasn't mine. It was some strangled petrified replica.

Giovanni's hand rested on my back, a warm, reassuring presence. I wanted to fall backwards into his hand and disappear. Surround myself with the satisfying, soothing weight of his touch and simply wink out like a dying star.

'Just come, Charlie,' my mother said. I heard Annabel in the background and then the voice of my once best friend, Mariah. The sound of her voice broke my heart. The fact that once it was a voice I spoke to every day, a staple in my life. And that now that voice signalled anxiety to me. That she was here after being gone, after being not well, to take my daughter. To take away the unexpected joy, pleasure, responsibility I never thought I'd have and often felt I couldn't handle, but couldn't seem to stop wanting.

'I'll be there. Don't worry. Don't let her leave,' I said and pushed the off button. 'I have to go,' I said, my voice hitching. Giovanni's lips pressed my back where his hand had been.

'Can I come with you?'

'Would you?' I asked, semi-amazed that he'd want to put himself in the middle of this shit storm.

'Try and stop me, Charlie.' We both stood, pulled on our jeans, tried to wake up. It was like stumbling out of a fog into a fire. Both of them disorienting, neither of them comfortable.

'Jesus fucking Christ. Why? Why now? Why at all?' I pushed my feet into slip-on sneakers and put my wallet in my pocket. 'She wanted nothing to do with the baby. Nothing. She would forget to feed her, Giovanni! Feed her!'

193

He nodded, lacing up his high tops. His hair was a mass of tangles and bed head and he'd never looked more gorgeous to me. 'I hear you. My sister had post partum depression with her second and third babies. There were days she insisted we take her to the local psych hospital. And there were days that I sort of agreed with her. But she got meds and help and finally it did pass and she loves her kids. More than most I think.'

'Great. So now Mariah's back and plans to become mother of the year and take my fucking kid,' I roared. I didn't think. I lashed out, punching the wall above my night stand. The pain jarred up through my hand, into my elbow, rocketing through my fingers so all the air died in my lungs. 'Fuck,' I said and dropped my bloody knuckles to my side.

'You OK?' He kept his voice soft and kissed my shoulder.

'No.'

'Of course not. Who would be! We'll figure it out.'

'I hope so. Sometimes I wonder if I do want Annabel, but I know I do. Deep down I know I do. And right now, there is zero fucking doubt I do. The thought of losing her is …' I flexed my hand and winced.

He kissed me again. 'You're not going to lose her. We'll figure it out. This was your best friend. This is your kid. It will be fine.'

'Promise me.' Completely irrational, but I just wanted him to say it to me. I wanted someone to say it to me. Even if it was a lie.

'Promise. Now let's get going.' Around the edges of my window shades the sky was purpling, preparing for dawn. Little slices of light crept into my room and I wanted more than anything in the world to crawl back into my bed, pull Giovanni in with me and cover us over with a mountain of blankets. I wanted this all to go away and be fine. Be good. Be right.

Chapter Seven

'I DON'T KNOW WHAT she's saying, Charlie. I don't know what she means. She insists she's ready to be a mother. That she wants to take Annabel to California.' My mother twisted her hands in on each other and I felt like doing the same. Instead, I patted her shoulder to show her it was fine. Even if it wasn't.

'We'll get it worked out, Ma. Mariah would never take the baby from us.' Would she?

'The baby's with her. And you ...' She turned to Giovanni and I held my breath. Where was this going? She got to him in three big steps and hugged him. 'I wish we were meeting under better circumstances.'

'Me, too, Mrs Nacht.'

'Please. It's Ma. Or Marie.'

'Ma it is.'

'Good boy,' she said and patted him.

I'd have been amused were I not so half-crazed with worry.

'Jesus, Charles,' my father said, walking in the room. He held a tray of coffee mugs and wore his favourite grey sweatpants that were more holes than pants. 'What the fuck is going on?'

'Joe!' My mother shook her head but took a cup of coffee and began to doctor it with raw sugar and heavy cream. She handed it to Giovanni without asking him how he liked it.

'Sorry, Mamma. Sorry.' My father shook his head, his jaw set in that way that signifies true fretting.

'Dad. What will I …?' I shook my head, tears working me up. I swallowed hard and accepted a cup of equally doctored coffee from my mother. Giovanni sipped his and watched us.

'You'll do fine. We'll get a lawyer if need be. A good one. Phil Hansen's boy, Duke, is a lawyer. I don't believe her anyway, Charlie. Taking that baby. You've been all that baby's had. You and this family. I don't know what the fu …'

'Joseph.'

'Sorry. Sorry.' But his face said he wasn't.

Annabel cried and I heard Mariah cooing to her. To no avail. The baby continued to wail. 'When's the last time she ate, Ma?'

'She's due,' my mother said.

I grabbed a bottle, nuked it, shook it vigorously and then tested it. 'I'll be back.' They all watched me walk out as if I were going off to war. I felt like I was.

'Hey, baby girl.' I addressed the baby first. When her big blue eyes found me, she lit up. The tears stopped and she angled her chubby body and thrust out her pudgy hands and flexed her fingers to me. My heart broke. My daughter clearly wanted me and I had to just stand there. I didn't want to provoke Mariah if she was in a delicate place. And she looked to be.

'Charlie,' Mariah said, but it sounded more like a sigh than a word.

'Hey, Mar. You OK?'

Shadows under her eyes made the rest of her face look super pale. Her lips were chapped and chewed. She had a nervous habit of gnawing her bottom lip when she worried. A small split in her lip looked red and painful. I wanted to hug her. Then I wanted to take my baby before I lost my mind.

'Just tired. I drove. It was a long drive.'

'I imagine so. Here you go, baby girl.' I handed Annabel

her bottle and her fingers touched mine. She cried out for a second, demanding that I take her but then her hunger won and she popped the bottle in her mouth and started to drink. But her eyes never left us, as if she didn't trust me to leave her sight.

I felt like I'd abandoned my daughter by having my mother take her for the night.

'I tried your house, but you weren't home. I swung by here earlier, saw your ma with the baby. But I got scared so I went home …'

'And then you came back because?' I held my finger out and Annabel took it. But I made no move to actually take her from Mariah.

'Because I can be a good mother, Charlie.' It was almost a plea.

'No doubt. I never thought you couldn't.'

'Yes, you did. You all did. I know it and so do you. Talking, always, about how poor, poor Annabel has no mother because hers is fucking crazy. And poor, poor Charlie was just trying to help Mariah out and now he's stuck with a baby he didn't even want. You're gay for fuck's sake!' She said it as if it was a new discovery.

I shook my head, squeezed Annabel's soft pink fingers. 'I'm not stuck. And no one is bad-mouthing you, Mar. I think you're …'

'Nuts?' She nearly spat the word out.

'Overreacting a bit. Worrying about nothing. No one has ever doubted you'd be a good mother once you got yourself together. What happened wasn't your fault. It was a chemical issue. Sadly, babe, it happens every day.'

I heard a rustling by the door and knew my mother well enough to know that she had planted herself on the other side of that archway and was listening to every word we said. I also knew Marie Nacht well enough to know that she had Giovanni in a death grip and he was with her. No doubt the murmuring I heard was my father on the phone. Logical,

197

practical, calm and ever-ready. He would have taken it upon himself to get this all worked out.

'Not to me. I had no idea that …'

'Of course not. No one thought that you did anything wrong. We just wanted what was best for you. For Annabel.'

'My mother said there's talk all around town.'

The reason my mother was Mariah's surrogate mother was because Mariah's actual mother was a fucking nut who liked to stir the pot. I tried not to roll my eyes or cuss out her mom. Bad move.

'The only talk about town has been people asking after you and hoping you're OK. And saying what a beautiful daughter you have. *We have*,' I amended quickly.

'I have the papers Charlie. I do. My mom helped out.'

Fucking Sandra Bennett, meddler extraordinaire.

'Your mother has had zero to do with this baby.' I sighed. My anger was just under the surface, but exhaustion and a crushing sadness won out. 'Why would she care if you have her?'

'She said she saw Annabel all the time,' Mariah said, her mouth opening and closing in shock.

'She lied. She doesn't want me to have the baby because I'm gay. She doesn't want the baby because the baby is out of wedlock and came from the union of you and a gay man. A fag,' I said.

'My mother …'

'Is a hateful cow who would rather put you in a position you can't handle right now, physically, mentally or emotionally, put our child at risk and make people who *have not been talking* start talking.' I could hear my voice rising, but felt powerless to stop it.

She blinked at me, her big blue eyes, so much like my daughter's, filled quickly with tears. She turned some, holding the baby as if she were a weapon. 'You do think I'd be a bad mother. That I *am* a bad mother. It's all perfectly legal, Charlie. I have the papers.'

Sadly, I didn't doubt her.

My father stuck his head in. 'Charlie. The cops are here. Let's get this straightened out.'

I could see where this was going and it was nowhere good.

'Let's go.' Mariah followed me slowly. And Annabel started to cry. Again.

I went to school with Mickey Marsh. We'd always been friends. He was one of the first people I came out to and would be the last person to care about labels. He shook his head, eyeing the papers as Mariah tried to soothe a shrieking Annabel with a pacifier. Annabel loathed pacifiers. The screaming was breaking my spirit and giving me a headache. Giovanni came up, touched my back. I could almost read him perfectly, wondering maybe if holding my hand was too much. Trying to gauge who knew what about me and was it cool to comfort me with affection. Always a minefield for us freshly-dating gay folk. I cut him off at the pass by taking his thin, warm hand and squeezing it.

'Everything looks kosher, Charlie. I wish I could say otherwise. I've put in a request that she not leave the state until you can go before a judge and whatnot. But that's also, sort of casual. Technically speaking, she can leave if she wants.'

I shivered, even though I wasn't cold. 'What did she say?'

'Luckily she agreed. Said she'd be staying with her mom for a few days while she decides if she's relocating or staying put.'

My heart leapt at the hope that she'd stay put.

'Thanks, Mick.'

'Hey, anything I can do to help, I'm there. I can make a few calls tomorrow if you want. It's my day off.'

I fished out my business card and handed it over. 'That

would be a god send. Thanks, man.'

'No problem.'

I watched Mariah try to bounce the daughter she barely knew. I watched her try to sooth and pacify and calm. And I watched the frustration of being unable to do so stain her pretty face. I wanted to take the baby and just rock her the way she liked, sing her some Zeppelin and let her brush her little fingers in my hair – which always worked the best. Instead, I had to watch.

'At least she's not leaving,' I said to Giovanni. As if it were really something. My mother turned, tears running down her face and hugged my dad. My dad looked on the verge of tears which simply meant his handsome face went more stoic and static and regal than ever.

'It's something,' Giovanni said. 'For now.'

'I didn't want kids anyway,' I said.

'Charlie ...'

'No, I didn't. It's fine,' I said. The pain of distancing myself was a bite on already raw skin, but I'd be fucked if I would just watch it all happen and crumble like dried mortar. I had to not care. I had to push it away.

'Charlie.' He sighed again.

'Let's go. I'm gonna say goodbye to my folks and then we'll go.

'What about ...'

'The baby? What am I gonna do? Stand here and watch her scream and cry and just fucking stand here? Don't you think she's wondering why Daddy isn't coming to get her? To help her? To save her? Because he can't, he's failed. So let's just fucking go.'

I stalked over to my parents and waved off their words. I kissed my mother – now sobbing – took my dad's hug and left. The sound of Annabel shrieking followed me for miles after we left. I knew it wasn't really there. Just an echo bouncing around inside my brain. Of my failure.

Chapter Eight

GIOVANNI WAS A WISE man. He said nothing on the drive home. His only sign that he was paying attention was reaching out to brush his fingertips over the back of my hand as I white-knuckled the steering wheel. I cranked the radio and pretended it was all fine.

In the house, I made another pot of coffee, scrambled eggs, bacon, toast. All the movement helped settle me. I kept thinking I needed to make the baby's cereal. To cut her some soft fruit. To make her a bottle. She only got a few a day now, but she still loved them so.

Then reality would swoop in and sicken my stomach and blacken my mood.

After watching me inhale my eggs and simply picking at his Giovanni said, 'Charlie, you're going to have a stroke if you don't let it out.'

'There's nothing to let out.'

'Bullshit.'

'Aren't you supposed to be at work?' I had texted my crew that I was out for a few days on the way to my parents. But Giovanni had a job, too.

'I called in. Family emergency.'

I laughed. It wasn't really a nice laugh. 'Family?'

He shrugged. 'I have none, and in just a few days ...'

I waited, staring straight at him, giving him no out on this one. I felt enraged, petulant and helpless. The feeling of total frustration was so all-encompassing, I nearly felt like it was tangible.

'You guys have become family,' he finished softly, almost looking ashamed.

'That's so irrational.' Even as I said it, feelings inside of me matched his like a mirror's reflection. But I was too full of anger to acknowledge the resonating emotions. 'We're not your family. You don't want this to be your family.' I stood so fast my chair rocked back, but it didn't tip. 'This dysfunctional shit-box is not what you want to call home.'

'Then you've never seen the dysfunctional shit-box *I* came from. Makes this one look like the Taj Mahal.' He grinned and my normal flutter of emotions was stagnant and black. Even he could not cheer me out of this.

'No.' I said, moving fast.

He moved fast too, standing in a blur and grabbing my arm. 'Hey, you don't get to say no. I feel what I feel.'

'No,' I said again.

'Yes,' Giovanni squeezed my arm.

'Let go,' I said.

He squeezed again. Said nothing.

'Let. Go. Or I'll help you let go.' I heard the menace in my own voice. Felt the swift swell of rage and was powerless to stop it.

'No. You don't get to tell me I don't love you,' he breathed.

My arm rose up as if on its own. A man possessed with fear and black, black rage. I took a swing and at the very last second my eyes caught the gaudy white flash of his cast. The already broken arm, the ex, the anger I felt toward that cowardly partner, all of it rushed through me like dirty water breaking a dam and I moved at the last instant. Not hitting him, managing to come all the way around on the downward stroke and punch myself in the thigh.

And then I was crying. Crying like the world was ending because it felt like it was and Giovanni was the one holding me together.

'Jesus, I'm no better than John.' I nodded even as he

shook his head and smoothed my hair back.

'Do not even go there. This was a bizarre circumstance.'

'I almost hit you.' My hand clutched him just above the knees and I felt his pulse jump near the inside of his knee.

'I pushed you.'

'No excuse.'

'Sure it was. Babe, we're still men. We piss each other off.' He pushed my chin up so I had to look at him, his smile made some soft part of me swell like it would burst and rip apart. I loved him. I knew it.

'But ...' I shook my head. I would never have forgiven myself had I hurt him in anger. He'd made a joke here and there about pain and pleasure in bed, but never in anger. Raising my hand to Giovanni – still with his arm sheathed in a cast, no less – would be the most cowardly thing I could imagine.

He wiggled a little until I let loose my grip and then he dropped to his knees so we were pretty much eye to eye. Two men, breathing hard, kneeling on the carpet in the middle of one of my biggest nightmares. Giovanni touched my jaw, ran his fingers down my throat and I felt duelling emotions. I wanted to kiss him and be happy, I wanted to cry and be vulnerable. My friend had taken my daughter. And I didn't know if she was being cared for. I could only pray.

'But nothing. It will all work out. OK?'

I nodded.

'I promise,' he said.

'You can't.' I touched his full bottom lip, pushing the pad of my finger to the flesh so it plumped out with the pressure. I slid my finger back just a bit until Giovanni opened his mouth and licked the tip of my finger slowly with his wet, pink tongue.

'I can. I promise. We'll get it worked out. Even if on the one-in-a-million chance she does take the baby to California, we'll pack up and move.'

'Oh, we will, will we?' I laughed but my chest swelled

with emotion for this man.

'We will. We will go out there and … pick fruit! Or fish. Or clean boats. I learned how to do that. You dive and scrape the barnacles from the hulls. Hey, there's a million things one strapping and one wannabe-strapping guy can do in California.'

'You're strapping,' I said. I palmed the front of his jeans, feeling the bulge of his arousal under the light cup of my hand. 'I want you. Please say you want me.' I felt so naked and fragile – like I had my neck bared to a blade and was just waiting to see my fate.

'Silly boy.' His lips pressed to mine and I felt the tickle of his eyelashes brush the tops of my cheeks. He had impossibly long eyelashes. Gorgeous, dark lashes that most of the women I knew would mortgage their house to acquire. 'I always want you. Not one breath has passed since we met that I didn't.' His hand slid the length of my jean zipper and my cock twitched with more life though I was already hard and ready.

'Lay back,' I said.

'*You* lay back.' He grinned.

A war. We both wanted to be the giver. How sweet of us. Another slow flex of my heart. A feeling I barely recognised as love. 'You lay back and I'll be on top.'

'Oh, baby.'

'Smart ass,' I said but then we were tugging our clothes. Zippers and rustling, flexing of fabric and discarding of belts.

I pushed him back and kissed his ankles. The fine chocolate hair that curled against his pale skin was the sexiest thing I'd ever seen. The scar above his right knee cap and a birth mark on his opposite knee cap.

'Another stab wound from a past life?' I asked, licking it.

'What can I say? I must have pissed a lot of people off.'

I kissed the soft, soft skin of his inner thighs and took my time, pushing my lips to the inside of his leg with barely any

204

pressure so that he whimpered. Then I pressed my teeth to his flesh so he hissed.

'God, you are fucking with me,' Giovanni gasped.

'I'm savouring you.' And I was. I could not bury myself in my frustration or rage. I felt those feelings but I couldn't let them pull me under. I had to focus on not falling to pieces. Doing that would not help me or Annabel and letting myself feel my love for Giovanni made me feel stronger.

'Come up here. Spin around,' he begged.

'In a second.' I nibbled the tip of his cock and he jumped like a fish on a wire. It made me laugh for a second.

'Jesus, Charlie. Please.'

'Hold on,' I said. I licked the back of his cock and watched his thighs go tense like he was trying to brace himself for some invisible impact.

I took him deep in my throat, feeling him grow longer and harder with each wet lick I administered. Finally, he pushed his fingers in my hair and yanked so hard my eyes filled with water.

'Look, spin around and let me at you or I swear I'll come right here and now and it'll all be over.'

I pushed my nose to his hips, nibbled his skin, kissed the side of his thigh and said 'Ooooooh, big threats.' My fist moved lazily up and down his shaft as he tried so very hard to not react or arch up to meet my stroking.

'I mean it, Charlie.'

'Fine,' I said and swung around, my cock dangling over his open mouth. I looked down the length of my body at him, my fingertips still stroking the slit of his penis. I grinned and he grinned back.

'Poor you. Fucking a guy who wants to make you come.'

'Boo hoo, me,' I laughed. I had to let myself get lost in this for a bit. I had to push my pain away and I embraced my small laughters like they could save me.

'Indeed.'

For those moments it obliterated all the pain. Every

gentle thrust of my hips that forced my dick lower in his throat. Ever gentle suck I gave his hard member. Every sigh, kiss, pinch, spank and moan blotted out the worry and the anxiety. It didn't make it gone, it just pushed it from the forefront of my mind and I was lost in the emotions that all tumbled over each other to be felt when I was with Giovanni.

I came with a long low cry that was half sadness, half joy. The sounds I made, the way my mouth worked on him as I sounded off my orgasm all served to tip my brand new lover over the edge. His trim hips shot up and he pushed himself up and deep, filling my throat so I gagged a bit and that made me laugh. He came with me laughing, lapping at him, trying to keep up with the flood of salty liquid he spilled out.

'Laughing is so rude,' he snorted.

'Not really. I think you gave me a fat lip is all. And I almost died.' I collapsed on him, pressing my cheek to his hairy thigh, my legs a wide V beneath his chin. 'Near death experience,' I sighed.

'Urph. You are crushing me, you big oaf.' But his fingertips tickled my balls and though my cock didn't really respond, my heart did and I wanted him all over again. I had a feeling I would just continue to want Giovanni the way I wanted air – continuously and in copious amounts.

'You love it.' But I moved, raising my lower body just enough so that I wasn't crushing the air out of his lungs.

'I do. I really do.' He ran his palms up and down the back of my thighs and I listened intently to the sound of his heartbeat slamming through his body.

'Take a nap,' he said when I yawned.

'I'm not tired.'

'You're lying.'

I yawned again and rolled off him, I turned and gathered him in my arms so I spooned his back. My cock to the seam of his ass, my hands criss-crossed over his chest so I could feel his heart's rhythm. 'Not too much. Not too tired,' I lied.

'Sleep a bit. Just sleep on the sofa and I'll potter. I'll do some laundry or dust or read a book.'

'You sound so domestic,' I said. But my eyes did feel heavy. Lack of sleep, sex, worry, fear … it was all a perfect storm that equalled exhaustion.

'I can be very domestic.'

'I believe you.' I pressed myself to his back and soaked in the feel of our closeness. Our intimacy. God, how I had missed holding someone. Being held. Fucking and wanting and aching for another person. It was staggering and intense and my chest felt heavy with the crush of my feelings. I almost felt too fragile to breathe but in the same moment I felt invincible.

'Take a nap and I'll figure dinner for us. How's that?'

'It's barely lunch time.'

'So it can be a nice slow-cooked dinner.'

'My stomach is growling.'

'Fine, fine. I'll make us a snack and then you'll rest?'

'A hot guy making me food and insisting I nap so he can make me more food?' I kissed the back of his neck and watched his skin erupt in a fine sheen of bumps. 'Where do I sign up?'

Chapter Nine

I KEPT MY WORD. He made salami and white bean bruschetta with fresh greens he yanked out of my "garden". Garden is a loose translation of the mess of what I assumed to be weeds out back left by the previous owner. Apparently, there was something edible back there.

I polished off my plate, eyed his and smirked when he covered his only half empty plate with his casted arm. 'Back off, Jack.'

I sighed, letting the pain in my gut from worry mingle with the happiness in my heart from Giovanni. Why couldn't it all be happy? And would I ever get there? Just happy? Content? No angst or worry or fighting? The thought made me tired.

I tried to stifle a yawn and my jaw popped from the tension.

'Stop fighting it and go lie down,' he said.

'What about you? Aren't you tired?'

'Number one, I require very little sleep for some reason. Truly, I think I have some attention disorder or whatnot. Or just a shit ton of energy. Number two, if I go up there with you – I'm no fool and neither are you – we both know what's going to happen.'

I took his hand, ran my thumb along the small slope of his palm. 'We'll sleep the sleep of the innocent,' I attempted with a straight face.

'No. We'll fuck the fuck of the bunnies is more like it.'

I put my head down to hide my smile, but let my

shoulders relax in defeat. 'Fine, fine. I'll go sleep like a pussy and you can scrounge for what to feed me for dinner.'

Giovanni leaned in and kissed my lips softly. A familiar gesture that twisted my heart in my chest. 'Exactly. Except for the pussy part. You'll go sleep like a man who has a lot to do in the evening to come.'

'Oh yeah? What do I have to do?' I ran a hand through my hair realising I still desperately needed that cut and that I was so tired even the roots of my hair ached for rest.

'Me,' he said and kissed the tips of my fingers.

There was something wholly satisfying in hearing Giovanni pottering around in my kitchen while I dozed. The dull thunk of him opening and shutting cabinets. The rattle of dishes and the low hum of the dishwasher being run. The smells made my stomach rumble every time I surged up from sleep long enough to wonder why I was sleeping during the day and why someone was cooking in my kitchen. I would surface long enough to remember that my daughter had been taken and maybe for good and then I would feel the mixed emotions of dread and contentment at knowing the man on the floor below was caring for me.

'Fucked up, is what it is,' I mumbled and rolled to my side.

On the nightstand was a picture of Annabel at one month old. She grinned her toothless wet grin and looked like an angel. In the photo she wore my all time favourite Annabel outfit. Yellow diaper cover with a duck's face on it and a yellow and white striped shirt. Her feet were sheathed in bright orange booties that looked liked webbed duck feet and she looked like a little ball of sunshine. My throat narrowed so swiftly I could barely swallow and since I was alone, I let the tears come. My father had told me upon Annabel's birth that nothing would lift me up and break my heart at the same time as having a child.

I hadn't believed him. Then again, I've never been too swift on the emotional front. I had to live it to know it. To believe it. And here I was missing her as if one of my fingers had been removed from my hand. My life felt more complete with the arrival of Giovanni and now, suddenly, less complete with the absence of the baby.

'Daddy will figure this out,' I told the picture.

Somehow I dozed back off.

'Sleeping beauty, it's been three hours.' Cool finger tickled through my hair and stroked my forehead. 'Thought you might want a wake-up call.' Warm lips pressed to my cheek.

I grabbed him and tugged him down into the bed with me. Snuggling him to me like the world's biggest teddy bear, I kissed him hard despite what I knew was sleepy breath. 'I do. Bend over and we'll talk about me getting up,' I laughed.

'Later,' he said, giving me a half-hearted punch but a full-throated laugh. 'For now, you have to get up, call your mom and eat my food and then we need to talk.'

Lancets of fear shot through me and I opened my eyes fully. 'Talk? As in, "it's not you, it's me", kind of talk? As in, "see ya, big boy", talk?'

'Jesus pleesus. No, not that at all. I just found you; you think I'd give you up?'

I blew out the breath that I'd held captured in my lungs and said, 'Then what?'

'I wanted to talk to you about going away for a few days is all. It's fall. I was thinking a trip to the lake. To see the leaves and drink wine and hike and wear sweaters and jeans and look like a swanky ad for fine men's clothing.'

A bark of laughter burst out of me. 'Yeah, I'm the men's model type.'

'I've got news for you, boyfriend. You're not hard to look at.'

'Yeah?' I rolled fast, rolled on top of him, pressing my hard cock to his hardening cock. My hip bones banged his, our bellies pressed together. His heart beat in counter time to mine. 'Not hard to look at. You sure? Should I strip for you so we can confirm?'

His dark pupils had gone so wide it ate up most of the coffee coloured iris. He looked tempted and drugged and sexy as hell, but he leaned up to me, a lock of dark hair slashing across his pale cheek, and kissed me. 'God, stop tempting me. Later. Come call Marie. Eat my food. Talk to me.'

I pushed his arms high. My left hand trapping the rough cast, my right his slender wrist. I pinned him there just for an instant, exerting my power because I needed to and I knew with him it was safe. I kissed him hard until he parted his silken lips and let me thrust my tongue into his mouth. Giovanni let my tongue bully his until I had to fight just to draw a breath.

'Fine,' I said, pulling back fast before I lost my control. 'Later.'

'That seals it.' He sat up on the bed, putting a hand over his eyes, his cast over his heart.

'What?'

'You are trying to kill me.'

'I think I was trying to fuck you.'

'But I'm dying of want over here.'

'We'll fix that.' I cocked my eyebrow at him, parroting his own words back to him. 'Later.'

'My God. You made me meat. I might weep.' Giovanni had made a gorgeous roast with all the trimmings. Potatoes, carrots, onions, red gravy and meat gravy. He'd whipped out some stewed tomatoes and an olive tray and even dessert. 'Is it? Say it's true.' I pointed to the cake.

'Flourless chocolate cake. Coffee's perking.' He looked so proud I thought he might pop.

My mother had told me she'd spoken to Mariah and Annabel and that I should call after dinner to speak to the baby. Speaking to the baby might turn me to dust – I feared

211

it – but Annabel hearing my voice might be best for her and that was all that really mattered.

But for now we'd eat.

'Marry me,' I said, plunking down in the chair. Then the room grew silent and he cocked his head, studying me. I reached up, pushed my finger up through one of the spiral ringlets of dark hair that sprang up whenever his hair got damp. The humidity of the kitchen and all the cooking had caused a few to spring up.

'Don't tease me,' Giovanni said softly. He sat across from me, lit a candle with a lighter.

'I have matches.' I nodded to the sideboard.

Giovanni wrinkled his nose. 'The sulphur fumes make your food taste weird. Or maybe it's just me. Either way, the lighter causes zero fumes.'

I shrugged, holding my plate up for him to load me up. And he did. Giovanni served his gorgeous meal with all the pride of a new pappa. 'More?'

'Load me up until I can't keep my arms up,' I said. 'Tomorrow I figure I'll get up and run. Haven't been able to since the baby because I had no one to watch her. I can get up and do six or seven miles.'

He looked surprised.

'Or whatever my old out of shape body can handle.'

'You are so out of shape. You are downright soft around the middle.'

I looked down while he chuckled. 'Tell me you're kidding.'

'Sweetheart, I'm kidding. Of course I'm kidding. Do you own a mirror, babe?'

I shook off the compliment. I wasn't in a place to hear I was good in any way, not even the looks department. 'So the lake, huh?'

'Yep. My folks have a little place. I called my mom, gave her a very brief rundown and she said it's empty and all ours. It's only two rooms. A main room with kitchen combined and a small bedroom. And a loft that is an extra room in a pinch, but I figured you won't mind sharing with me.'

I nodded. 'Not at all. Not even a little, you smart ass.'

That made him shut his eyes and smile. I loved seeing him smile. I loved seeing him comfortable with me, the joking, the ease with which we'd seemed to click together like two pieces of one machine.

'It's small and it's humble, but it's also right on the lake and it's free.'

'Free! My favourite.' I held my plate up and he blinked at me.

'Wow. Um … were you hungry?'

'Yep and I still am.'

'But the cake.'

'I'll eat the cake.'

'Really?' His brown eyes looked suspicious.

'It's cake. Trust me. I'm eating it. Now hit me food tender. Give me more.'

I ate a whole second plate. The pit of worry in my belly refused to fill, but my body did. I ate until I was more satisfied than I'd been in ages. Then I ate cake. Then I kissed Giovanni and said 'How about an after dinner shower?'

'Do I smell?' He kissed my shoulder. My body seemed to ripple with my arousal.

'No, but let's wash all that flour and sugar and stuff off you.'

'There was no flour.'

'Whatever,' I sighed. 'A technicality.'

'True. Nothing but a technicality.'

'Then when our shower's done we can settle on our itinerary.'

'Oh, aren't you the world traveller?' His fingers slipped inside my jeans and he stroked me with gentle touches until my body responded to him with an urgency I couldn't' remember feeling.

'I've always wanted to use that word, to be honest.' I hummed to a tune only I could hear and pressed myself into his hand.

Giovanni bit my lower lip and the burst of pain shot through me, stoking my pleasure. I wanted to feel his teeth on me. I wanted to pin him to the shower wall and let the water beat away my muscle pain and have Giovanni help erase my emotional pain.

'You used it well. I just need some stuff from my place and then we can go. Whenever you want. Whatever you want.'

'Tonight? You up for a drive tonight?' I pushed my hands into his hair, wound the long strands around my fists and tugged so he gasped, his lips against my throat.

'Whatever you want,' he said again.

'Come upstairs.'

Chapter Ten

IT WAS ONLY SEVEN in the evening. The day was flying by
and taking for ever, an oxymoron of hours. If we got on the
road, getting to Dalper Lake would take about three hours
max. I'd only been there once or twice, but the lake and the
surrounding land was the stuff travel brochures were made
of. I was eager to get up there with Giovanni. If I was going
to feel helpless and frustrated, it might as well be in a
gorgeous place with a gorgeous boy.

'I only need some jeans and some shirts. And my
cologne. Some shampoo. A sweater, it gets really cold there
at night. It can be a bazillion degrees during the day but at
night it drops and you need to snuggle. It's nice. Did you
remember a sweater? Should I throw one in for you?'

I laughed, grabbing his good hand. 'God, you are talking
a mile a minute. Are you nervous? And yes, I did remember
a sweater.'

He winced for a second and I wondered if I'd hurt him,
but then he said, 'It's John. He should be at work, but
I'm ... nervous is a good word,' he said.

I bit my lip. I had a whole string of expletives lined up
behind my tightly sealed lips, but throwing them out would
only serve to upset Giovanni and that was the last thing I
wanted. 'I'm sure he's at work. And I'm here if you ...' I
searched for a way to say it without sounding all beefcake
macho bullshit. 'If you need me, I'm here. You say the word
and I'll put my rusty two cents in.'

He laughed at that, leaned in and kissed my cheek.

'Stubbly. Niiiiiiice,' he whispered in my ear, his mouth pressed to the lobe. It made my shoulders jerk inadvertently and my whole belly rolled in on itself, a warm wave of lust filling my core.

'Careful, or I'll pull this car over.'

'Oh, Daddy,' he said and batted his lashes.

I sighed. 'I said it once, I'll say it again ... smart. Ass.'

'Right up here. Make a left and then a right on the first street you see. We're number three.'

My hackles went up at the *we're,* but I did as instructed, seeing him get more and more uptight as the houses flew by. I parked my car in front of number three and stared at it hard as if eyeing it up would reveal the secrets of the relationship that had inhabited inside. How had this guy hurt Giovanni to the point of breaking a bone and then stepped past him to leave the house?

Then I remembered my half-assed swing at Giovanni and my cheeks burned.

'You're nothing like him,' Giovanni said. 'Stop it.'

'Stop reading my mind, devil boy.' But I smiled. 'You want me to wait here or come in?'

I was torn. I wanted to go in and see and yeah, snoop. I also wanted to go in so I'd be with him in case anything happened. I did not want to go in because irrationally, I did not want to see evidence of a life before me. Giovanni meant so much to me, so fast, the thought that he'd been with someone else so recently was a startling thought.

'Come in?'

'Sure thing. Whatever you want.'

Number three, Secular Drive was a small blue bungalow with a squat whitewashed porch. The door was painted yellow and that made me smile. Something told me Giovanni had chosen that colour. He caught me grinning.

'They say yellow front doors are the most welcoming.'

'I see.' I cocked an eyebrow at him.

'Oh hush up and follow me. This shouldn't take long. I'll

216

figure out the nightmare of getting all my stuff later. Once I've figured out the nightmare of where I'm going.' He rolled his eyes and unlocked the door.

'You can stay with me,' I blurted. It was an impulse but I felt no impetus to take it back.

'Stop.' He opened a closet door just inside the foyer and grabbed a big black duffle bag off a hook. When he turned, I pushed up against him, crowding him back to press against the closet door.

'I'm not kidding. You can come live with me.'

'But you have a kid and ...'

'No I don't.'

'You will, Charlie. You will. We'll get it all worked out and Annabel will come home.'

I shrugged: 'So, I have a kid. We'll get it worked out. She won't be the first kid to have two dads who love her and dote on her and want to beat up her boyfriends.'

He smiled at me, but his eyes welled. 'Charlie ...'

'Come live with me.' I kissed him again.

'Later. OK? We'll talk later. Right now, I want to get in and get out. I feel like I can't breathe in here.'

I was mildly hurt, but I understood. It had all happened in the blink of an eye with us. Plus, it was unfair to ask him to think straight in a place he felt insecure. 'Let's do it then. What can I do?' I stepped back, eyeing the living room with its rich jewel tone furniture, the dark wheat coloured walls and the gorgeous sconces. I'd lay money that Giovanni had decorated the small house.

'Come with me. I'm trying to think of what I need while I'm here. But the mojo of this house,' he flung his hands around, one – elegant with long, tapering fingers, the other – cumbersome with plaster and broken bones. 'It's sucking my brain out.'

I followed him into a bedroom done in aubergine, butter yellow and white. Aubergine is an eggplant colour for you blockheads like me. I only knew its name because of my mother's bedspread.

I held the duffle while Giovanni tossed. He threw a leather envelope of papers from his nightstand in first. A wooden box with the eye of Horus inlaid on it.

'That's my passport, birth certificate, social security card, yada yada.'

I nodded. 'Boots?'

He turned, made a noise like a startled bird. 'Oh, my lovely boots.' He tossed them in next.

'Nice,' I said, grinning.

'Italian,' he said. Then he was off and mumbling to himself. 'Jeans, sweater, pyjamas, skivvies, flannel, slippers, tennis shoes, lube.' He said it all as he dropped it in and the bag got heavier and heavier.

'Take the lube out,' I said.

He turned and stared, his big brown eyes growing bigger still. 'Why?'

'We'll get new. I don't want that shit. Leave it here. With your old life.'

He didn't say a word, simply reached in and plucked the bottle out of the duffle and tossed it in the trash can by the door.

'What else?'

'Well, if we're getting lube then we must be stopping so I can get a new toothbrush and all that jazz on the road. Right now it's at my sister's. I've been using yours.'

'You know, anyone else and that would totally gross me the fuck out,' I snorted.

'I'm flattered.'

'Coat?' I asked.

'Down in the foyer closet. I guess I'm good. I got important documents and papers. Essentials for cabin living. The linens and dishes and stuff are stocked on the property year round. We're good to go.'

'Good to know,' said a voice. 'Go where?'

'John,' Giovanni breathed.

I turned, clutching the bag, refusing to give into the rage now bubbling just below the surface of my skin.

'And who's this?' John asked, not acknowledging Giovanni's surprise.

'This is …'

'Charlie,' I said. I pinched the fabric of the bag in between my fingers to keep from dropping the tote and hitting this clown.

'Charlie. You the new one?'

I didn't say a word. Just eyed him up. He was about my size, a bit bulkier, dark hair and sharp green eyes like shards of glass. His bulk was intimidating and he carried himself in a malicious manner. I didn't get it. What had Giovanni seen in him, but when it comes to love and jeans we all have bad taste at some point or other.

'Let's go,' I said to Giovanni.

He moved in a quick jerky walk that made me think of shock victims. 'It's OK,' I said to him as he moved.

'Really? Is it OK? You break into my house …'

That broke Giovanni's fugue. He wheeled around, long hair flying. 'Your house? Please. And I still have my key. How did you even know I was here?'

'Finnigan down the street called. I told him if he saw you there was a reward for letting me know on my cell if I was at work. I bounce at a bar,' John said to me.

'Shocking. I'd have pegged you for a florist.'

He frowned and took a step toward me while a bubble of hysterical laughter rose up and popped out of Giovanni's mouth. He clamped a hand over his lips and headed out of the room. 'That Finnigan always was a fucker,' he said behind his hand.

'I told him there was a reward because I liked the idea of putting a price on your head,' John said, his lip twisting up a cruel scowl. Oddly, I would have been attracted to him under different circumstances. But I was more evenly matched for him physically. Emotionally, too, since I seemed to have a wider streak of malice than Giovanni did.

'John …' Giovanni started.

John took an aggressive step toward the man who currently owned my heart and I dropped the luggage. 'Don't,' was all I said.

But he did. He reached for Giovanni and Giovanni flinched. That was all it took. My arm shot out before my brain engaged and I clocked John with a sharp right jab. His head rocked back, his cheek split wide and dark red, nearly black, blood immediately welled to the surface of his rough tan skin.

'Motherfucker.'

'No thanks, I prefer boys,' I said, and there was my own burble of hysterical laughter.

Giovanni grabbed his bag and beat feet to the steps. 'Go on,' I called. Me. I stood and waiting for my new friend to recover.

'Not quite done with me?' he growled, standing straight. He brushed the bead of blood away as if swatting away a gnat.

'Not quite.'

'You think you're his saviour.' His smile was cruel, his voice dark.

'I'm no one's saviour, but I'll sure as shit give it a shot. I'd like to be. He deserves it. Now I want you to go in your room, sit tight. We'll leave and then you're free to do whatever you like. You know, like get bent.' I tried to cut myself off before that final sentence, but anger and a big mouth wouldn't let me.

'He's a bitch. He's a nag and a sniveller and a little cunt.'

'Oh see …' My right arm shot out again and I heard a satisfying crunch as my knuckles brushed the bridge of his nose. It might be my knuckles I heard, but I just didn't care. The level of pain in my hand told me I'd been right. When he started bellowing I knew for sure. I'd broken his nose.

'My dose,' he said, and clamped a hand over his face.

But his predatory green eyes narrowed. This man was a brawler. He wouldn't be stopped by the likes of a broken nose. He'd want more.

'Poor, poor ugly nose,' I sighed. I took a step forward and he took a step back. 'Go sit down.' I hoped he would because I was suddenly and completely fixated on kicking his bully ass down the steps like he had my Giovanni.

But his pride got in the way, stuck its bullheaded foot in and tripped him up, because John's eyes narrowed and he took a stagger-step toward me. At the last second, I stepped back, almost pressing my back to the hallway wall and I planted a foot gently at the small of his back. Just enough for him to lean forward to keep his balance. I caught his meaty forearms up and pinned his wrists behind his back and levered him forward to keep him off balance. 'Here's where we do the old bouncer's waltz,' I growled. 'You should be familiar with this.'

I hustled him forward as he bellowed like a felled bovine. At the top of the steps I allowed myself to pause and savour my victory of besting him physically.

'Dude,' he said. I could tell by his voice that was the biggest plea I would get from him. He'd rather get tossed down the stairwell than beg.

I could empathise. But I refused to have mercy on him.

'Dude, indeed. And away we go …' But then Giovanni's frightened face stared up at me from the bottom. He shook his head and his long lazy curls swayed. His big dark eyes looked sad.

'Charlie, don't,' he said. So softly I barely heard him but I read his lips and his expression.

I kept turning as I shoved, using my momentum to angle myself back toward the bedroom door. I tossed John through the open door and he hit the wall and bounced onto the bed. 'Get up and I don't care what he says to me. I'll break you,' I said, levelling a finger at him.

He gave me one short nod, his nose finally ceasing to

221

drip crimson. I hit the steps and stomped down, using my weight to show my anger. I'd stopped because I loved Giovanni. But I didn't have to be happy about it.

'Got your shit?' I growled.

Giovanni smiled at me. It was one of those half smiles, where his lip curled up like Elvis and he looked tentatively pleased with himself.

'Yeah, I have it.'

'Good, let's go before I change my mind. I don't like that guy.'

'You don't say.'

'Don't. Not now,' I said, my voice full of warning. 'You have no idea how badly I wanted to …' I let my words trail off.

'Yeah, I think I do. And I appreciate it, but I can't let you carry that around. That would have been more about all of it. Mariah, Annabel, your situation, my cast, us … it wouldn't have been pure rage,' he said. 'If that makes sense.'

It did. I would have been punishing John not only for abusing Giovanni, but for all of it. And though he deserved pain, he did not deserve to pay for sins that were not his own. I gave a short nod and a grunt and pushed the front door open with stiff arms. I really wanted to rip it off its hinges and hit someone with it. Instead I rushed out into the cool night air. The navy sky was full of tiny freckles of white starlight. The moon was a slice of silver in the sky. I turned to see where Giovanni was and he was right behind me.

He leaned in, touched my face and kissed me. 'I love you,' he said. 'I hope that helps instead of making it worse. But I needed you to know. I love you.'

My gut tingled and my chest ached. I hung my head. 'Jesus,' I sighed.

Chapter Eleven

'SEE,' HE SAID, PUSHING his fingertip to my lower lip. 'Not exactly the response I was hoping for.'

I pushed the gym bag out of his hand so it hit the dirt between our feet. I shoved my hands into his unruly mess of hair and hauled him forward. I didn't care who saw. The caveman upstairs, the old neighbour lady who didn't know Giovanni was gay, the ice cream man or the local priest. It. Did. Not. Matter. I kissed him so hard my lips ached. 'I love you too, you ass. I said that because ... you startled me and I felt sucker punched and happy and a little sick.'

'I make you sick!'

I kissed him again, pinching his neck gently so he hissed and my cock went hard. One more pinch and I said, my lips pressed firmly to his, 'Behave. Sick in a good way. Giddy sick. Roller coaster sick. Excited sick. The sick that makes you feel like your stomach has dropped. I love you. I fucking love you. And I thought I wasn't supposed to. That it doesn't make sense or it's too soon or I shouldn't or ...'

'Or you don't deserve it?' he asked, pulling his head back to stare me down in that unsettling way of his. The stare that made me feel as if he could look right inside me, so deep and so easily that he could count all the tiny bones in my body if he so chose. Or see the stains and cracks and pits on my very soul.

'I ... Can we go? Can we do all this soul searching stuff at the cabin where at least when all is said and searched I can roll you over and fuck you?'

'Or you can be rolled over and fucked,' he said, winking. He bent and grabbed his bag but then I took it from him.

'Charlie, I can …'

'Just get in the car, will ya?'

'Yes, sir.'

'That's more like it.' I couldn't help swatting his ass as he walked by. 'Now we're talking.'

'Oh, Daddy,' he said as I shut the door.

I knew he was teasing me, but I'd make him say it for real before all was said and done.

'So what's it like to fuck a girl?' Giovanni dropped a big bottle of lube in our basket and I had to bite my lip. An older woman looked up, her mouth popping open.

'Um … shh.'

'Sorry.' Giovanni gave me a stage whisper and winked at our eavesdropper. 'What's it like to fuck a girl?'

'You've never?'

'Never.' We turned the corner into a deserted oral care aisle. 'I am a pussy virgin and proud of it.'

I shrugged and dropped my favourite toothpaste, mouth rinse and floss in our basket. 'Warm and wet and tight. It's not bad. See, it's not down below that snags me up with the ladies.

He grinned. 'It's the old grey matter? The largest sex organ, if you will. Which is saying something, because I've seen your other sex organ and it's pretty big.'

I heard the lady make a strangled noise and couldn't help myself. I found myself bent double, fists on my thighs, laughing my ass off. 'Well, thanks.'

'No problem. Soft?'

'Pardon?'

He waved a triple pack of toothbrushes at me. 'Soft OK?'

'Medium?'

'Medium it is.' He swapped them out and we headed toward the cash register. 'Thanks, Charlie.'

'For what?'

Giovanni touched my shoulder and briefly held my hand and squeezed. 'You're fucking with me, right?'

'What?' I pulled out my wallet and fished out my ATM card.

'For sticking by me. For kicking his ass. For not truly hurting him. For listening to me when I asked you to rein it in. For coming with me to the lake. For … being who you are.'

My chest shimmered with those last words and eavesdropping lady be damned, I leaned in and kissed the tip of his nose. 'You make me better.'

'Liar.'

'Giovanni?'

'Yeah?'

'You have no idea how close that prick came to being airborne. And then I'd have been ready for round two at the bottom.'

The clerk rang us up and gave me a total. I swiped my card. 'I hope it snows tonight.' He was staring at the big glass windows of the store, blotted navy by the autumn sky.

'Isn't it a bit early? It's only October.' For some reason it hit me, Halloween was coming. My Annabel was to be a candy corn this year. The costume was in my closet, her little orange booties tipped with black smiley faces. Her little white cap made to resemble the pointy end of the candy. My heart felt leaden, but I smiled at the clerk.

'It snows way early at the lake sometimes. I hope, I hope. A guy can hope.'

I hoped I had my daughter back in time for her to be a candy corn. 'Yes, a guy can hope.'

The car ate up black road and blotted out the dark with shining rings of headlight. Giovanni dozed, cradling his cast to his chest. His lips twitched like he was dreaming and couldn't decide if he should laugh or cry. I wondered if he was dreaming of John. I hoped he was dreaming of me.

I stared a moment too long and he opened his beautiful eyes and said 'Whatcha looking at?'

'The man I love.' It made me feel lighter to say it. I almost forgot my fear and my worry when I watched him. His long lashes fluttered and he fell asleep again. I had forgotten that Giovanni had had just as little sleep as I had and had been up just as early. But while he'd insisted I nap and sleep off the staggering fatigue, he had cooked me a dinner and flitted about. Now the need to crash had caught up with him and I faced the flat stretch of road with nothing but the sound of tires on tar. I didn't want to disturb him with the radio.

'Wake me when it starts to get windy and twisty,' he said.

'What?'

'The road.'

'Mm-kay.'

'Promise?'

'But what if you look all snug and sweet?' I asked.

'Tough shit. Wake me. I love it – this area, the lake, the way it looks at night.' He shivered, pulling his big cream coloured sweater snug around him. 'I want to be awake.'

'OK,' I agreed but he was already snoring lightly before I got the whole word out.

A deer darted out just as the roads were getting windy. I stomped the brake and felt my heart rocket like a race horse. 'Jesus fucking Christ,' I hissed.

'Careful, it's mating season. Like most of the animal kingdom they turn butt ugly stupid when fucking comes into play.'

I messed up his hair, waiting for my pulse to calm back down. The road was deserted and we sat for an instant before I straightened out the car to soldier on. 'Thank God we're alone tonight. I'm sure that would have caused a doozy of an accident. I've had enough unforeseen events in my life lately.'

'What about me? I was unforeseen.'

'You were a surprise. There's a difference.'

'Not really. It's your perspective. The body does not know the difference between excitement and fear. Only the mind.' He tapped his finger to his temple. Before I could tell him my head was empty, he said, 'Look, it's snowing. When we get there, you'll build me a fire.'

'I can do that.'

'And we'll unpack.'

I turned another sharp turn and my headlights bounced off the reflective markers, flashing back in my eyes. 'Done and done.'

'And I'll make us a snack.' His hand rested on my thigh and I felt a companionship and ease I could not remember feeling. My heart wished for an instant that Annabel was in the backseat, thusly making us a family. What a beautiful family we would have been.

'I'm there.'

'And then …' That hand slid higher. 'Then, you'll fuck me.'

'You don't have to ask me twice.'

The cabin was waiting for us--short and squat and made of golden wood. The front porch sported four rocking chairs and the door was painted red. Giovanni pulled open the screen door and I dropped our bags at the *Welcome* mat.

'Here we go. Paradise. OK …OK, not paradise. But free and away and there's a lake and snow.'

'I'm already on board, babe. Open the door.'

The inside was one huge swooping room. A living area in front of a fire place, a small flat screen with an entertainment centre, a kitchen counter with four tall stools that looked into a small kitchen. A one-ass-kitchen as my mother would have called it.

There was a bathroom at the end of a short hall and a doorway I could only assume to be the main bedroom. Above the kitchen was the loft area he'd mentioned.

'What's up there?'

'A futon, some bean bag chairs, another TV and a nightstand. Not much. Why?'

'Can we sleep up there?'

He cocked his head and eyed me. 'Sure ... but why?'

I didn't want to admit it to him but forced myself to. I had to trust him. In for a penny in for a pound. 'I feel a bit stalked. After the John thing. I almost feel like we're prey. They've taken my daughter, your ex tried to be all caveman. I'd feel safer up there.' I said it fast like ripping off a verbal bandage.

He shook his head and kissed me. 'Of course. And look.' Giovanni pointed and my eyes followed his finger.

Even with the loft was a huge half moon window set over the front door. Through it was clearly visible a flurry of snow flakes, a serene image if I ever saw one.

'We can so totally lay up there naked and watch it snow.'

He kissed me on the back of the neck and I trembled. 'I like the way you think.'

I turned and grabbed him up in my arms, pulled him to me. 'I like the way you look and smell and ...' I pressed his hips to mine so he could feel the hard line of my arousal. How much I wanted him again. 'Feel.'

'Make me a fire.'

'Make me a snack.'

'Deal,' he said.

'Sealed with a kiss.' I kissed him, shoving my fingers up under his sweater and tracing his flat belly. I tweaked his nipples with small pinches and rubbed my hands along the ladder rungs of his ribs until he pushed me back and said, 'No cheating. God, you are *so* distracting me.'

228

Chapter Twelve

I MADE HIM A fire, something I'd only done once in my life. I miraculously managed to open the flue before getting it going. Giovanni made us an omelette. We'd stopped for fresh eggs, milk and a few other essentials like coffee. The pantry was pretty well stocked for a cabin that according to him was rarely used.

'That was pretty damn good,' I said. I put my stockinged feet up on the rough wood coffee table, feeling oddly at home and just a touch out of place.

'Thank you, thank you. I try. Sorry I had nothing sweet to offer.'

'I think you do.' I put my arm around him, a cheesy re-enactment of a million ham-handed high school efforts to cop a feel. 'I think *you're* pretty sweet.'

Giovanni snorted. 'God. That was awful.'

'Tell me about it. But it's true.' I tugged him in, kissed him until he parted his lips and let my tongue push past the plump barrier of his tongue. He kissed me back so fiercely my cock sprang to life just from that single wet, warm touch.

'What do you want?'

The question seemed to hold weight. More than, what do you want right now? More like, what do you want ...? Period.

'You.' It was true on all fronts.

'Here I am.'

'Do you trust me?' I remembered my mission to make

him say "Daddy" for real. Not in a joking way but in a moment of total surrender.

'Of course.'

'Take your clothes off. Lay in front of the coffee table.'

The huge glass windows were dotted with melting snow. I didn't see curtains. He caught me looking, even as he stood and yanked his sweater over his head. 'No one's for a mile or so. There's no curtains. But I don't care, Charlie. I really don't.'

He turned his back to me and dropped his jeans, his boxers. Then he stepped free and lay on the rug in front of the table. I took off my belt, sliding it slowly from each loop as I stared down at him. Giovanni tried to smile, licked his lips, shifted nervously.

'Scared?'

'A little.'

'Why?' When my belt was out, I looped it loosely and set it on the table. I knelt and waited, looking him in the eye, not letting my gaze waver.

Giovanni swallowed hard and his Adam's apple bobbed. I leaned forward and licked him there and then sat back on my heels, continuing my silent attendance.

'I'm not sure what you're going to do to me.' His voice broke on that last part and I felt almost cruel. Almost.

'But you trust me?'

'Beyond measure.'

My chest ached at his honesty. Somewhere around my solar plexus a pulsing need had taken root. I wanted to weep and laugh and kiss and fuck and curl against him and lose myself from all the bullshit of Mariah coming back. I wanted to pour all of my frustration out and soak in nothing but my want for this man. So I did.

There was nothing I could do about Mariah right now. But I could show Giovanni what his love and trust meant to me. That I deserved it. That I would do right by him. 'Put your arms up above you head.'

230

He raised them up, the movement pulling his pale skin taut over his ribs. The small hairs in his armpits were wavy like his hair and I pushed my fingers through them gently. Giovanni danced under me, snickering. 'That tickles more than I can stand.'

'Don't move,' I whispered and despite his statement he stilled. 'Now scoot up.'

I had him shimmy up until his elbows were level with one squat, thick leg of the coffee table. 'Bend your arms and cross them.' His forearms ran the height of the leg and I belted him to the table leg at the joint of his elbow. 'It's a bit harder because of that fucking cast. When do you get it off? It's nothing but a dirty reminder of that asshole.'

'Two weeks.'

'Good. Now is that too tight? Should be tight enough to keep you there, but not tight enough to restrict blood flow.'

'It's good.' His big brown eyes were huge, there was real fear there. Had John ever tied him up? Had he been cruel when he had?

'Done this before?'

'Yes.'

'Him?'

'No.'

'Someone else then. Was he good to you?'

'Fair. A bit oblivious.'

'Hmm.' I didn't say anything else. I dipped my head and sucked one flat nipple into my mouth. My tongue ran every bump and flat of skin, my hand stroked his silken hair and I sifted it through my fingers like bits of corn silk. 'You're beautiful.'

'Stop.'

'You stop. You are. And we're not going to do anything funky tonight. No spanking or punishment or any of that. Just a nice pretty boy tied to a big utilitarian coffee table for me to enjoy at my leisure.'

He shivered under me and I kissed the place over his

heart, feeling his wonderful heart beating wildly under my lips.

'Shh.' I dropped tiny kisses along the flat of his belly, licking his sides so he jumped under me but tried valiantly not to. Wrapping his cock in a loose fist, I gently stroked his shaft so he exhaled like he was deflating. I smiled, pushing my tongue to the jut of one hipbone and then the other. I kissed a circle around his dick, kissing everywhere on his pelvis but where I knew he was praying for me to go.

'Charlie ...'

'Daddy,' I said and grinned so hard I almost choked. 'And see now, you talked. So you have to wait just a little longer ...' I pushed his thighs wide and dropped slow wet kisses on his inner thighs, way up high where his leg creased. Where he smelled most Giovanni-ish. Smoky, spicy, leather and cotton and denim. I could leave my face buried at the junction of his leg and his crotch all day long, but he was nearly weeping. So I kissed down to his knee, dragging it out, making him squirm. My fist did another slow, torturous drag up his shaft and his trim hips shot up and he gasped. I thumbed the dot of pre-come on his tips and said, 'Say it.'

'Please ... Charlie.' I could hear the defiance in his voice. I could hear the amusement too. But I could *also* hear the near desperation.

I tsked at him. 'Such a shame you couldn't be a good boy.' I kissed his belly button, stuck the tip of my tongue into the shallow divot. I knew my hot breath feathered across his belly and I glanced up to see him staring me down.

'Jesus Christ.'

'Just Charlie Nacht. Or ...' I chuckled. 'Daddy to you.'

'I've never called anyone that. Not for real.' He frowned. 'It's kind of creepy strange dirty, Charlie.' Even as he explained in a breathy rush, he rocked his hips up to try and get my mouth where he wanted it.

'I agree. And I'd never ask anyone to call me that. But you.' I licked his ribcage and his body trembled like he was sick. Sick with me. With want. 'I want you to call me that, Giovanni. Just once. I want you to mean it. No matter how creepy strange dirty it is.'

I was telling the truth. I don't know why I wanted it, but I did. And it was OK to tell him, and somehow that was key.

'I'll try.'

'I'll make you.'

He snorted.

'I'll coax it out of you,' I went on. I licked just his balls. And just for an instant, just with the very tip of my tongue, which I made rigid.

'Oh sweet merciful Lord,' Giovanni said.

'Nah, just Daddy will do.'

My lips returned to every bit of skin on him but his cock. I sucked and licked and painted him with lavish laps of my tongue. I touched and stroked and patted until he tossed like a dying man and finally, when I thought I would crack before him, Giovanni said, 'OH fuck, fuck, fuck, do it. Suck my cock, Daddy.'

And the word rolled off his tongue as easily as the word love had and I sucked him deep before he even finished his exhale. I took his cock as deep as I could, impaling myself with him, sucking deep greedy breaths through my nose. Oxygen that had been steeped in the heady scent of aroused man. I sucked him and oxygen into me in equal measure until I was light headed with air and with him.

My fingers pushed deep into him, pressing the small knot of flesh that made him almost weep. His toes gripped nothing, his legs trembled, he tested his belt bond with great strength so the table jittered across the hardwood floor and jumbled the edge of the rug up as it went.

I watched his face as he got closer and closer. He looked like a painting by a master. A piece of art. A great and gorgeous angel fallen to earth. I watched him until he said,

'Don't, don't, don't. Fuck me. Fuckmefuckme-fuckmefuckme ...'

The chant wormed its way into my head and I hurried, a rush of hands and intentions. I moved fast and found myself pushing into him before I even realised I had reached my goal. His cock in my hand, his eyes pinned to mine, mine pinned to him, I pushed his knees high and watched his bound hands tangle with each other. One of them mostly swallowed in his cast that I wished so badly was gone already.

I rocked into him, watching the waterfall of his hair sway with each thrust and when I was right there, right fucking there, I said, 'You are so perfect.'

'Back atcha.'

I barked out a laugh at his crooked grin and spilled out my orgasm, working his cock faster and faster until he was giving me his own.

After a moment, I pushed my face to his belly, felt his heartbeat slamming his warm skin up under my cheek. 'Unbuckle me. I want to hold you.'

So I did. We climbed into the loft and bedded down on an old black futon with a wooden base. Curled around each other like two warm animals, we listened to the quiet of the lake.

'It's raining now,' I said. 'Sorry.'

Giovanni pushed himself back against me, his ass cradling my front. His back pressed to my chest. His soft hair tickled my cheek. 'It's OK. I like rain.'

We fell asleep that way. Autumn rain and some secretive thing bounding across the roof over our heads.

Chapter Thirteen

IT WAS OUR THIRD day at the cabin. The air had turned cool for what I thought was for good. Maybe not back in the city, but out here. I'd called Annabel every night, listening to her cry and coo and sigh into the phone. It broke my heart but until we got this situation sorted I wanted her to hear my voice.

Every time we spoke Mariah sounded more desperate and her mother more angry. She wanted Mariah to be something she wasn't. A cookie cutter TV mother who had no issues. Mariah had suffered the ultimate defeat, having a baby she desperately wanted and then finding she couldn't deal.

'You tell him that you have every right to take that baby back to California. I don't know why you're sticking around here. And what kind of father runs off to have sex with another man in the woods when his child has been taken? Oh, I really believe he wants to have that baby back.'

Her voice was venomous and I quivered with rage. Giovanni stroked my back and Mariah sighed into the phone. 'Do I need to relay any of that to you, Charlie?'

'Um ... no. I had to go Mar. I had to. Being there, being at home and unable to do anything ... I had to.'

Mrs Bennett had nailed my worries and my fears on the head with her vindictive hammer. I did worry what anyone would say about me going away. But doing something rash because I was in the close vicinity seemed more dangerous to me.

'I know that. Don't worry. I know.' I could see her in my

mind's eye. Sad, thin, pale and defeated. I did not believe for even a moment that Mariah was better or more in control of her life. I did not believe that she would be a better mother to Annabel now. I thought the whole thing was orchestrated by her great venomous mother, who in my mind's eye was some Cthulu-esque creature with tentacles and sharp claws. She was more intent on the community at large knowing that Mariah was now a proper mother and had taken baby Annabel back to California – out of sight, out of mind for her, mind you – and all was right in her fake world.

It was better for Annabel to have an unstable home but folks not chattering than to leave the baby with me where she was the centre of someone's world and cherished. Yes, exhausting. Yes, unexpected. But God, so very fucking loved.

I let the silence tick off for a bit and then, 'Why are you staying here, Mar? Why haven't you beat feet back to the west coast?'

'I don't know.'

'Sure you do. We were best friends for a million years, remember? Why?'

I could literally hear her shrug. The way she made a soft noise when she did so, the small rustle of the phone to her ear. 'Can't quite seem to do that to you, Charlie.'

'Mar, listen, we are friends. You will always be my friend, no matter what. Are you OK?'

I waited, hearing more thick silence. Giovanni set a mug of tea in front of me and I wished it would magically turn into a beer. Or a scotch. When it didn't, I sipped it slowly.

'I'm fine.'

I didn't believe her. 'Mar, I love you, honey. And I'm not angry with you. I will help you if you need me.'

'It's just I …'

There was a scrape and a muffled thud and then Sandra was on the phone. 'Charles Nacht, you will leave us alone or

236

I will get a restraining order.'

'For what, Mrs Bennett? I'm not harassing anyone. I just want to talk to my daughter. A right I'm still allowed.'

I could hear Mariah crying in the background, weeping softly. My heart broke for her, for me, for the baby most of all. Giovanni pet my hair like I was some giant distressed feline. I smiled at him because I couldn't help it.

'Just go ... away,' she said and slammed the phone down.

I sat and put my head in my hands, waiting for my heart to unbreak and slow down. It did slow down, it remained broken.

'I know this is a dumb ass question, but are you OK?' He stroked my shaggy hair.

'Yes and no. The baby sounds fine, the mommy does not. This isn't her, Giovanni. This is her mom. The part-time alcoholic, full-time buttinski. She doesn't care that the town talks about her being half snookered at the chief of police's daughter's baby shower, but she does care that her daughter couldn't handle motherhood and was brave enough to say so. A DUI doesn't phase her and I guess is fine to talk about, but the fact that her daughter has a chemical imbalance and chose to give custody to a gay man is too terrible to contemplate.' I squeezed my mug so hard I feared shattering it. So I set it on the counter and stood. 'I need a hike. Want to hike?'

'Sure. I could go for a hike. We can see some leaves and burn off some steam.'

'Real life will come back soon enough. There are only so many vacation days to be had. Let's use them wisely.'

We laced up, filled water bottles and a pack with snacks and I watched Giovanni fumble with the clasp. Once again, I was reminded how badly I wanted that fucking cast off him. And when it was, I'd stroke the tender pink skin underneath. I'd lotion it for him. I'd wrap my fingers around it like a flesh bracelet when we made love. I'd kiss his fingers and

237

his palm and his wrist like it was precious.

'What you thinking?'

'Dirty things,' I said.

'That's my daddy,' he chuckled and kissed me on the jaw so that I clung to him like I was drowning.

'Don't tease me.'

'I'm not. You're the only one that I'd ever call that. But somehow now it's like a dirty little secret we share.'

'First of many, I hope.'

He cocked his head. 'You OK?'

I grinned.

'Sorry! Sorry! I know. Stupid. Ass. Question. But I mean apart from that. You're looking at me funny.'

I didn't know I was going to say it until I did. 'I'm scared.'

'We'll work it out. You'll get her back. Your folks said last night on the phone that that lawyer was …'

'Not that. About you.'

'What about me?'

'I didn't know I wanted to be a dad and then I was. So when it was taken from me, I was … I am staggered.'

'Yeah. I know.' He leaned against the counter, gorgeous and silent letting me talk.

'I didn't know I wanted to be with someone. I didn't know I wanted love. And you came along and there it was. All of a sudden. Out of nowhere. But I want it, I cling to it, and I'm afraid that …'

'You'll lose it?'

I nodded.

Giovanni grasped my arm and tugged me, an imbalanced, cockeyed effort to yank me in. Something he could have done easily two-handed. I fell into him, pushed against him. Let him soothe me.

'I'm not going anywhere,' he said, kissing me. Softly at first and then harder and harder until I buried my hands in the madness of his hair.

'No?'

'Well, I'm going on a hike with you.'

I tugged him in using his skinny hips as handles. I licked his lips, his tongue, kissed his nose so he purred.

'Then I'm going to shower with you.'

My fingers tiptoed up the zipper of his fly and I rubbed his cock but didn't push my fingers in to touch his actual flesh or there would be no hike. We'd call this an appetizer.

'And then I'm going to bed with you.'

I pinched his nipples through his flannel shirt and he yelped. I nipped his jaw and he sighed. But then he levelled that dark brown gaze my way and he touched my chin to make sure I was listening.

'But I'm not leaving.'

My heart loosened form the fearful fist it had become. 'I believe you.'

'You better.'

'Yes, sir,' I said.

'Hey, that's my line.'

'Get your boots on.'

We walked for hours and Giovanni showed me the make-out spot (where we proceeded to make out). He showed me the deserted, rundown cabin that had been part of the Underground Railroad. We traipsed through the ruins for a bit and then hiked to the top of a hill that looked down on the lake itself. A whole rush of deer took off at the sight of us and we laughed, watching their cotton white rear ends bound off like we were big bad predators instead of hiking lovers out in the fall air. We clambered over stream rocks and up muddy banks until we were filthy and dirty and soaked. Then we hiked home and showered. Giovanni got down on his dirty knees, grime and river silt running down the drain as he sucked my cock. His dark hair looped around my fist so I could see the perfect art that was his face.

Then I pushed him up against the slick tile and made him

beg me before I made him come.

It was during a late night show about a psychic, and some wine in front of the fire that the call came. The moment I heard my phone ring with my mother's ring, my stomach fell. I knew. It was bad.

'Ma?'

'Charlie, come home. Mariah's gone. She left a note. A bad, bad note. But she took the baby.'

That's all she managed, because I hung up and we tossed our bags in the car.

Chapter Fourteen

THE SPEED LIMIT WAS 45 on the main stretch of road leading to the beltway and I'd more than doubled it. It got worse on the freeway.

'Charlie, you need to slow down some or you'll kill us both.' He held his cell phone pressed to his head and then, 'Marie? It's Giovanni. Charlie wants to know ...' Then he pressed his lips together and listened. All I got were a few unh-hunhs and clicking noises.

I wanted to yell. I wanted to scream. I wanted to demand why all the noises he made sounded like something from some National Geographic documentary. Instead, I bit my tongue and waited, knowing that he'd never make me suffer. Knowing he couldn't relay any information if he couldn't hear. I tried to back off the gas a bit – managed for a moment – failed.

Finally, after what seemed like an eternity he shut the phone. 'She left a note at home saying that she couldn't do it. That it was too much to have failed as a mother twice. That she just couldn't handle it and that the baby deserved better ...'

My face went hot even as my fingers went numb. All of my wires were crossed. Surges of rage tried to drown out spikes of terror. I gnawed my lower lip so hard I tasted blood.

'Mariah's mom called your mom because she didn't want to call you. She called demanding to know if the baby and her daughter were there. That's the only reason any of us know anything. Apparently, Mrs Bennett has a bit of a jealousy thing with your mother?'

I nodded, hit my high beams, lay on the horn, darted around the guy in front of us. Giovanni clutched his heart and gasped. My heart raced. 'Sorry. Sorry.'

'Jesus fucking Christ ...'

'Sorry!' I bellowed.

'Anyway, she assumed that Mariah would run to Marie with the baby. And when she found out she hadn't ... she flipped out. Worse. If that's possible.'

I shot around a pick up truck that seemed to have the distinct mission of driving me insane. I didn't lay on the horn, though, so I hope I scored some points for that.

'Any ideas where she might be, Charlie?' He put his injured hand on my leg and patted me.

'A few.'

'You don't think she'd hurt the baby, do you?'

I couldn't even think that way or I'd crash the car, go insane or throw up. Probably all three. But I tried to stay calm. 'I don't know, Gi. Once upon a time I'd have heartily said no. But having Annabel triggered that PPD; it set an imbalance in motion. Like starting a metronome. And her mother bullying her into coming back here and putting pressure on her ...'

'Fuck.'

'Yeah, fuck.'

'I don't know what she's capable of now. For her, for the baby. I don't think she could do it. I think she'd hurt herself first, before ever hurting anyone else.'

'Why didn't she just leave the baby with her mother?'

'Would you?'

'Fuck no.'

'Neither would Mariah.'

'Where are we going?'

'Double Ridge Park.'

Hours drag by like years when you think your child is in

jeopardy. The trip from the lake to the park seemed like an eternity. Pushing the car to breakneck speeds still felt like I was driving at a crawl. The state park was very close to my parents' home and Giovanni called to check in.

'No word. No one's heard from Mariah. The cops have been called and that one who's friends with your family?'

'Mickey Marsh.'

'He's there. And the lawyer they know. This could play out …' He petered off, but I knew what the rest of that thought was.

'I just want it to turn out OK. But yes, this could sway the law in my favour. But I wanted us to work it out, Gi. This is not how I wanted any of this to go.'

'No shit. I hear you.' He leaned in and kissed my neck, inhaled deeply and kissed me again. 'Totally inappropriate right now, but I love the way you smell.'

I smiled. 'I love the way you smell too.''

'Yeah?'

'Yeah.'

'It'll be OK, Charlie.'

'From your lips …'

'I know, I know. But it will. I can feel it in my bones. The same way I knew when I sat down to eat an icy with you and your adorable little baby that it was you. You're the one.'

I turned left and the tires squealed. If I could get to Mariah … if I could get to Annabel. If I could go fast enough, far enough, good enough … maybe I could have what I wanted. What I hadn't wanted at all and now wanted most.

A family.

'Ditto. You are my one. And we are here. You OK to run?'

'Sure. Lucky there's no snow.'

'It's dark and it's shitty and I don't want you to break anything else.' I slammed the car door and he followed suit.

'I'm not a fucking princess, Charlie. I didn't break this.' He waved his cast around as I dug in the trunk for the big spotlight I kept in there for emergencies. 'It was broken for me.'

'You should have let me kick him down the steps,' I growled. I found the light, thumbed the switch and was relieved to see it jump to life.

'That's not who you are, Charlie,' he sighed.

'It's who I wanted to be at that moment in time.'

'You'd have regretted it.'

I grabbed his hand, kissed him. 'I doubt it. Now follow me and try to keep up. I think she's back at flat rock.'

I took off running and Giovanni kept right on my heels. He was lean and light and apparently could run like the wind.

Mariah was not on flat rock.

'Shit.' I kicked the edge of the outcropping, wrath burning my face like a fever. 'I thought for sure ...'

Giovanni cocked his head and put a finger to his lips. 'Hold on,' he said.

Then I heard it, too. Weeping.

'Mariah!' I called.

The weeping ceased, but then a startled cry.

'Mariah, it's me! It's Charlie. Where arc you? We're here to help you!' But my heart was trip hammering because if she was up in the hills, where she'd apparently climbed, where was Annabel?

Giovanni hurried along the flat rock, following the outcropping along its edges. He shone the beam around the perimeter and even down into the shallow water below. Just the thought of the baby being down there made my stomach cramp with sickness.

I waited to hear her and heard nothing. 'Mariah, do not do this,' I boomed. 'Do not hurt yourself. Do not hurt the baby. You are loved, honey. You just aren't cut out for this right now. And that is OK! No matter what your mother says.'

Giovanni shook his head and made the all-clear sign. The baby wasn't down here.

'It's just right now. And right now is not for ever. You still have time to be a mother. And if you can't, sweetheart, we love you anyway. And we get it. Annabel is loved. She will never hurt for attention or affection or love in any way. And as long as I'm her father, you are always welcome in her life and mine.'

I scanned the rocky hills along the edges of the rock outcropping. I saw nothing but blackness. Nothing but a giant ink stain that hid the woman who had once been my closest ally in life. The mother of my child. I scanned and I hoped and I tried to keep my voice calm even as my heart jumped in my chest from the force of my fear.

'She's not here,' Mariah said. I jumped and Giovanni sucked in a breath. She'd come closer as I spoke, my words muffling her progress.

'Jesus, Mar,' I sighed, clutching my chest. Then her words sunk in and my heart fell into my gut. 'Where is she?' I grabbed Mariah and shook her before I could control myself.

She sobbed, hung her head and my fingers went numb with fright. But then ... 'I dropped her at your house. I was going to jump. I was going to call Marie right before I did and tell her to go get the baby. Don't let my mother have the baby, Charlie. She drinks way too much. She's way too needy and righteous and tainted. Don't let her ...' Mariah dissolved into tears and I held her to my chest, feeling my soul come back into my body now that I knew the baby was fine. Unattended but fine.

'Where is she in the house?'

'In her crib. I left her there. She was sleeping. I'm sure she needs a diaper and a bottle and all that, and she's probably way pissed, but she is safe in her room.'

'Giovanni ...' I started.

But he was already dialling. I turned back to Mariah and brushed her hair out of her eyes. 'Why did you really come back?'

'My mother. She couldn't stand the talk.' She put her head down. She looked haunted and ghostly in our pale circle of bright torchlight.

'I think she fucking imagined the talk, Mar.'

She shrugged. 'Probably. She isn't all there, Charlie. I didn't even realise how much worse she'd gotten until I came home. I think she needs some help, too.'

'Speaking of help …'

'Let me go. I'll just go up and finish it and …'

'No. Mariah, listen. Let's get *you* some help. Let's get you situated.'

'I can't even mother my child,' she said.

'And I didn't want her to begin with. But life has a way of working out. And you can work out yours. You concentrate on getting you better and then you worry about the rest. You were doing the right thing. The only thing you did wrong is talk yourself out of doing what you needed.'

'Can I really be in her life even if it takes me for ever to get my head on straight?'

'Yes.'

'What if it takes me even longer?'

'Longer than for ever?'

More tears, tracking wet black lines down her pretty, tired face. 'Yes.'

'Me and Annabel aren't going anywhere, babe. When you're ready you let me know.'

'And him?' She nodded to Giovanni.

I waited a beat. Would this somehow break her? Would it be too much? But I opted for honesty. 'I love him. I want him in my life. Mine and Annabel's.'

She wiped her eyes, tried to smile. 'Good,' she said. 'It's about fucking time.'

'Charlie?'

I turned to Giovanni even as I pulled Mariah into hug her. She felt so tiny and fragile. Something Mariah had never seemed to me before. She'd always seemed bigger than life and bright like a star. I wanted her better, I wanted her whole again.

'Your mom's on her way over to the house. Shouldn't take long.'

'Thanks.' It seemed so stupid, but it was all I could say to him.

'You OK?' he asked Mariah.

'No. But I will be.'

'Good. Now can we all go back to the car and get back to civilisation? Standing out here in the wood is creeping me out. All I can envision is Bigfoot and vampires and evil elves.'

I felt the vibration of Mariah's laughter and wished I could kiss Giovanni. I teased him instead as we headed out. 'Dude … evil elves?'

'Hey, do not underestimate the elves.'

Chapter Fifteen

WE STOOD WITH OUR faces pressed to the crack of the nursery door. We'd been back in the house for a mere 24 hours and neither of us could stop staring at the baby. That night we'd dropped Mariah at the hospital on her insistence and then arrived at the house to find Mickey and my mom and dad with the baby. Annabel had clung to me like a monkey for hours and it broke my heart. But after a few hours home, she'd gone to Giovanni like she'd known him all her life.

Now, I pressed my lips to the soft lobe of his ear and said 'You are totally bogarting the baby, man.'

He turned in the loose circle of my arms and rose on his toes to kiss me. 'Hey, we're bonding, the two of us. Don't be greedy.'

I grinned. 'I guess I can be generous. We'll have a long time to work it all out, yeah?' I tugged him forward by his belt loops and turned the soft gentle kiss into a deep wet one. His mouth tasted like the vanilla pecan ice cream we'd had for dessert.

'Yeah. If you let me, I'll stay till I wear out my welcome.' He touched my cock. Just for an instant. Through my jeans. Just enough to make my teeth ache with want and my chest go warm with affection.

'That should be oh … never.'

'Sounds like it'll all be worked out.' He pressed his forehead to my shoulder and I let my fingers trip through his long soft hair. I could feel his heartbeat pounding my bicep.

'Sounds like this stunt and her mother's total drunken arrival should seal permanent custody for you. Thank God.' He blew out a sigh.

'But I'll never keep Mariah out of the baby's life,' I said gently.

'I'd never expect you to,' he said. 'A baby should have her father *and* her mother.'

'And her Giovanni,' I said.

He snorted and I smiled, tipped his chin up and kissed him again. 'Does it bother you?' he asked.

'Does what bother me?'

His big brown eyes looked liquid with concern. I wanted to kiss away whatever was worrying him.

'How fast it happened. Me and you? And the drama around it. Do you worry it will...poof?' He made an explosion motion with his good hand.

I took that wandering hand and pressed it to my chest so he could feel my rapidly beating heart. 'No. It doesn't worry me and I don't think it will ever poof.' I turned him back to face the crack in the door and a beautiful sleeping Annabel. 'See that baby?'

'Yeah.'

'I didn't want her. I mean, not as mine to keep. I had sex with my female friend as a favour to knock her up so she could have a baby. And what happened?'

'You became a full-time single dad,' he snickered.

'Right. Totally out of the blue. Unexpected. Completely out of left field.'

'And?'

'And so were you. Out of the blue, out of left field, unexpected. I've never in my life hooked up via open car window and icies with my daughter in the back seat.'

'No? Seems the way to go to me.' I could feel the vibration of his laughter. Pushing his hair to the side, I dropped a kiss on his neck. Giovanni moaned and I slid my hands up his chest, stroked his nipples through his shirt.

249

'Smart ass.'

'Yes, Daddy.'

It was my turn to moan. Somehow that had become our secret word. I heard it and it turned me on. 'My point is …'

Giovanni reached back and gripped the side of my thigh with his hand. He pushed his ass back to my burgeoning hard-on and said, 'Tell me.'

'Some of the best things in my life have been things I didn't see coming. And to me that makes them even more perfect. That baby. You. The family that we're going to be.'

He turned then, back to face me, clinging to me. I felt him crying and hugged him. It was a good cry as my mother would say so I let him go and didn't try to fix it.

After a moment I kissed the top of his head. 'There's only one thing that bothers me.' I took his hand and tugged him toward the bedroom after bending to bite his collar bone through his T-shirt. It turned him on, the biting, and I wanted him to know my intent.

'What's that?' he asked, voice high and breathy and ready.

'I can't wait to get that cast off you. It fucks every thing up.'

He froze, his eyes going wide. 'Why?'

'Because I can't tie you up proper,' I growled and tugged him again. 'Come on. I'll prove it to you.'